THE
FLOWER
GIRLS

THE
FLOWER
GIRLS

ALICE CLARK-PLATTS

RAVEN BOOKS
LONDON • OXFORD • NEW YORK • NEW DELHI • SYDNEY

RAVEN BOOKS
Bloomsbury Publishing Plc
50 Bedford Square, London, WC1B 3DP, UK

BLOOMSBURY, RAVEN BOOKS and the Raven Books logo are trademarks of
Bloomsbury Publishing Plc

First published in Great Britain 2019

A catalogue record for this book is available from the British Library

ISBN: HB: 978-1-5266-0214-5; TPB: 978-1-5266-0215-2; eBook: 978-1-5266-0212-1

2 4 6 8 10 9 7 5 3 1

Typeset by Integra Software Services Pvt. Ltd
Printed and bound in Great Britain by CPI Group (UK) Ltd, Croydon CR0 4YY

To f   loomsbury.com

For Tom, Constance and India

PART ONE

CHAPTER ONE

1997

Rosie was aware of nothing apart from her sister's shadow. It spiked, jagged and black, across the stippled, sunburnt grass. She skipped inside its edges, her white leather sandals dipping into the cool before springing out, feeling once again the blister of sunlight.

She hopped in and out of Laurel's shadow like a sprite, seeing only the ground as she danced, watching the grass change to asphalt beneath her. They flitted past the unoiled swings where children squeaked, throwing their flying silhouettes onto the grey concrete of the playground, then past the colossal oak tree that shaded the white-and-red awning of the trailer café where a circle of mothers clustered, holding Styrofoam cups of coffee. Then they turned left, in the direction of the old metal rocking horse that creaked back and forth, its seats worn shiny and pale.

Jumping over the cracks in the concrete, Rosie skidded to a halt at the platform alongside the horse. Still gazing down at the ground, she could see her sister's feet below the horse's mouth, her scuffed red trainers, one on top of the other, the laces split short and untied. Above the trainers, attached to legs astride the horse, she could see the flowery buckled shoes of a toddler, her podgy toes bunched up beneath a strap, her ankles fat like coddled cream.

Rosie lifted her head. Her eyeline reached that of the blank-faced horse. Metal rolls of hair curled down the mane to where the toddler's fingers clung tightly to the strands of frayed rope that served as reins.

'Where's your mother?' Laurel asked the little girl.

Rosie moved her gaze to her sister. The leaves of the oak tree swayed quietly above them; a breeze kissed their foreheads damp with sweat.

'Do you like sweeties?' Laurel said. 'I've got some if you like.'

Rosie felt the top of her lip prickle. She said nothing, though. Just waited.

The toddler shifted on the seat at the front of the horse. She wore a yellow T-shirt with a daisy on it. Light blue shorts. She had a clip in her hair, pink and shimmery. Rosie raised her hand to touch it. It was beautiful. Like the toddler's golden hair.

The little girl turned her head to where her mother stood, coffee cup in hand. Her mouth opened in a soft little 'oh'.

'Sssshhh . . .' whispered Laurel and the toddler hesitated. 'Do you know where the fairies live?' she asked. 'They live in a little dell, just down there.' And she flung her hand out, pointing over the playground fence, to where the grass dipped down and the land stretched out beyond where they could see. 'Just there. They live in tiny houses. Under buttercups and snowdrops. It's beautiful,' she said.

Rosie watched as the toddler's gaze followed the line of her sister's hand. As her eyelashes widened at the beautiful and incomprehensible names her sister gave the fairies: *Titania*; *Cobweb*; *Mustardseed*.

Rosie began to dance and spring again, in and out of the shadow of her sister as it moved once more across the playground. She whispered the names to herself: *Lily* and *Bluebell* and, her favourite, *Rosebud*.

They skipped over the rough ground, the grey of the paving stones, through the gate and back onto the sun-stained grass, its coarse, unmowed tufts grazing their calves, flattening dock leaves as they passed. And then down the slope they went, down into the cool and the shade of the line of oak trees that stood guard, wise and silent, running the whole length of the old canal path.

That was where they went.

Down to the grass-filled gully as the trees whispered above them, watching them and waiting.

For what was yet to come.

CHAPTER TWO

It is on Hazel Archer's twenty-fifth birthday that the second girl goes missing.

The child is only five years old, with hair like Snow-White's and a rosebud mouth all puckered and soft in a never-ending pout. She was last seen as the light fell away from the land and the Devon coastline became a swathe of rough, black shadows. Night has drawn in quickly around the hotel, which perches high on a promontory over the English Channel, dark folds of rock stretching down to where the sea pounds on the wintry shore, gravelly waters pulling in and out like monstrous pistons.

Hazel is at her dressing table in the hotel room when the alarm is sounded. Jonny hums to himself, shaving at the bathroom mirror. Evie is next door in her own room, undoubtedly plugged into her headphones, eyes half-closed, long painted fingernails tapping along to the tinny beats in her ears.

The rapping on the bedroom doors begins along the corridor. At first, Hazel assumes it is room service, delivering aperitifs before the New Year celebrations start in earnest. But the knocking is too quick and moves on too swiftly for that. There is no cheerful clank of a bottle on glass, no surprised laughter or thank yous. Instead, there is a swift and sudden change of mood. A sea mist seems to swirl frantically down the corridors, chasing ahead, while searchlights beam on each and every room.

Jonny opens the door. A towel is around his waist, soap still clinging to his cheeks, his cropped, dark hair damp from the steam in the bathroom. Mr Lamb, the manager of Balcombe Court, stands outside in the corridor. Across the way, another staff member is knocking on doors opposite. Inside their bedroom, all is soft-furnished and -hued: a four-poster bed, winged velveteen-covered armchairs, mahogany bow-legged tables. Outside, it is a different country: the air is fraught with panic.

'Is everything all right?' Jonny enquires.

Mr Lamb is short and compact. He bounces uneasily on the balls of his feet, his breathing pinched and held tight. 'A little girl's gone missing,' he says. 'Her name's Georgie. Over an hour ago – nearly two.' He skewers Jonny with a stare before shifting his gaze beyond the line of his shoulder, over to where Hazel sits. 'Have you seen her, either of you?'

Jonny turns back to Hazel and they look at each other. After the merest second, they shake their heads almost in unison, mouths drawn closed, perceptibly nonplussed.

'No,' Jonny says. 'We've been in here for an hour, I'd say. Wouldn't you, Hazel? I haven't seen any little girl.' He frowns. 'Maybe at lunch? I think I saw her in the dining room earlier. She's the small dark-haired one, with the baby brother?'

Hazel's eyes are wide, her skin shiny with moisturiser. Her hands are gathered in her lap. 'Where was she last seen?' she asks.

Mr Lamb shakes his head impatiently, keen to be off looking for the girl. 'She's five years old,' he says, as if that is an answer. 'Her mother is distraught. If you see her ...'

Jonny nods again.

'Of course,' Hazel replies. 'Let us know if we can help.'

'We can join in a search,' Jonny adds.

'Yes, yes,' Mr Lamb answers. He lifts his eyes to the ceiling, as if praying to the gods. 'There's a storm coming, you see. If she's outside …'

Hazel glances out of the mullioned window. The sky is pitch black beyond the glass. Balcombe Court is isolated, balanced as if on the air atop the sea. If Georgie is lost out there, she could fall down over the headland. She could be badly injured.

'You could ask Evie,' Hazel suggests. 'Jonny's daughter is in the room next door,' she explains. 'Jonny, go with Mr Lamb to check.'

'Hang on, let me get some clothes,' he says, retreating to the bathroom. He emerges a few seconds later, tousled in jeans and T-shirt, and he and Mr Lamb hurry along the corridor. Hazel stands as she hears a short rap on a door, the sound of Evie's voice as she opens it, the murmurings explaining why they are there. Hazel moves to the window and looks out to where the yellow lights of the hotel seep onto the snowy ground.

She scrutinises her reflection in the dark glass. From downstairs, the aroma of roast meat, caramelised vegetables and garlic, of fruit punch and red wine, creeps into the room and she feels a similar sense of nausea as she had done once as a child, lying upstairs with a fever while her mother fried onions down below. She leans her forehead against a diamond of cold, damp glass framed by lead and history.

'Happy birthday, Hazel,' she whispers. 'Happy birthday, precious girl.'

CHAPTER THREE

The cries of Georgie Greenstreet's mother are tearing through the hotel like violent jags of rainwater.

Hazel is clothed now, her red dress on, her high-heeled shoes ready by the door. Jonny is in his suit and they stand facing each other, their faces strained.

'They'll cancel the dinner, I expect,' he says.

Hazel presses her lips together, a bite of irritation stabbing within her at his acceptance of the status quo. They have been stuck in this room for an hour since the manager's visit, despite Hazel trying to persuade Jonny to go downstairs and see what's going on, what's happening with the other guests. But he has been firm, telling her they should wait for further instructions from Mr Lamb.

'They don't need us bothering them now,' he says. 'They've got enough on their plates.'

Hazel tries to ignore the feeling she has been having lately – only in the last few weeks, since they have been planning this trip, in fact, and cajoling Evie to come with them – that Jonny's concern with not bothering other people is a trait which, later down the line in their relationship, will cause Hazel to resent him, to lash out in frustration, pound a figurative wall with her fists, that he is so laid-back.

At the same time, she looks at him standing there in his crisp white shirt and his dove-grey tie and feels wrapped in a strength that shields her from everything in the past, and what might happen in the future. Even when he is dressed, she can imagine the weight of him, the feel of his muscular arms around her. Is this what marriage is like? she wonders. A constant balancing act between infatuation and impatience. Not that they are actually married yet, but it seems probable, and Jonny has never caused her to worry that it won't be the case. He is an ally, she knows this. He has taken on burdens with her that no other man would shoulder. Even with Evie, his daughter from his previous marriage – even then – he has introduced Hazel with such eagerness, such pride to have her in his life.

But despite all of this, surely he must see the danger of the situation? With the girl missing? She turns back to the mirror, searching her perfectly made-up face, trying to imagine what others will think when they see it. How she will be judged. Her heart roils inside her chest, caught between the childish sense that what is happening is unjust, and fearful anticipation of what is yet to come. Whatever Jonny says, they should be downstairs, figuring out what to do, finding out what the hotel management are planning.

'Will they call the police?' Hazel asks him, her eyes febrile and bright.

'Coastguard first, I would think,' he answers, hands in his pockets, leaning back against the door. 'If Lamb's right, and the weather's turning bad, they'll want to search the beach before it kicks in. Storms are epic around here. You wouldn't want to be anywhere near the sea in one.' Jonny stops talking and takes a breath as if a thought has just occurred to him. Again, Hazel feels that bite of irritation, that feeling of being ten steps ahead. He comes over to her and cradles her face between his palms. 'Oh, sweetheart, are you worried? About the police coming?'

With an effort, Hazel swallows her frustration. Her hands tremble as she places them on his shoulders. 'Of course I am. What do you think?' She closes her eyes briefly. 'A five year old going missing. It's . . .' She shakes her head, unable to finish.

'It's going to be fine,' Jonny says. 'I promise. You've got nothing to worry about. I'm here, aren't I?'

Hazel leans her head against his chest, breathing in the scent of him, feeling that solid frame, strong as oak, which props her up. It's only when she straightens that she sees, with the force of a whiplash, electric-blue swirls chasing rapidly across the walls. Then she realises that her fears have materialised, and her head begins to spin along with the lights that circle the room from outside.

Turning together to the window, they see the harsh, unremitting lights burning from the two police cars that have drawn quietly up in the snow.

CHAPTER FOUR

The jaunty Christmas trees by the hotel entrance twinkle persistently under the barrage of freezing water that has begun to fall like nails from the sky. Detective Constable Lorna Hillier pulls up as close to the front door as she can, her car skidding slightly as she brakes.

She has a checklist running through her brain at high speed. Close off entrances and exits; check CCTV (if any); confirm timings of guests; search all hidey-holes; PNC checks on everyone in the hotel for sex-register entries; liaise with the coastguard regarding search parameters; consider the necessity of a child rescue alert. Words like *murder* and *kidnap* leap around her head. Her eyes flit from wall to window, ears pricked as the weather changes shape outside.

'Could do without this storm,' she says to Mr Lamb, who greets her in the hotel lobby. They stand in front of the fireplace, their shadows dancing around the mahogany panelling. Behind them seven-foot-tall Christmas tree dominates the area in front of the desk, where an eavesdropping receptionist leans forward. 'It's going to make the search near-on impossible.' Hillier glances at the ceiling. 'Are the parents upstairs?'

'Yes – with the baby. They're not in a good way.'

'That's understandable,' Hillier replies. 'How many guests are staying here?' she says, assessing the two corridors leading off from reception. There will be other exits, she thinks, other nooks and crannies where a child could hide or be hidden. 'How many staff?'

'I'll get you a full list from the register,' the hotel manager answers, shifting in his tweed suit, rising up onto his toes. He is barely an inch taller than Hillier and this is bothering him, she observes. 'Would you like to see the parents now?'

Hillier glances at him, noting his glum expression. 'Yes, and then I'll want to talk to the guests. Perhaps you can gather them in the lounge? And . . . the chef?' She looks at her small spiral-bound notebook. 'In your call, you said he saw Georgie at around three p.m.?'

'She came to see the kittens,' Mr Lamb says. 'We found them in a box down on the beach earlier. Someone obviously wanted to dump them. Marek – the sous-chef – brought them here. He put them in the pantry, just out the back of the kitchen.' Mr Lamb nods in the direction of the wall behind Hillier. 'Marek says that Georgie came in earlier, wanting to see them, and he showed her and they gave them some milk together. Then she went away.' He exhales mournfully.

'Went where?'

Mr Lamb hesitates. 'I don't know – we don't know,' he says at last.

'How long has Marek . . . Surname?'

'Kaczka.'

'How long has he worked at Balcombe Court?'

'Eighteen months. He's a good lad. And why would he say he'd seen her if he'd . . . ?' Lamb's sentence peters out.

Hillier says nothing, making another note on her pad. She looks up as the constable first on the scene, Tom Ellis, comes into the hotel from outside, shaking droplets of water from his jacket.

'Nothing,' he says in answer to her unspoken question. 'The boys are searching everywhere. Checking all the guest rooms, the places you told us about.' He jerks his chin at the hotel manager.

'OK', Hillier says, raising her voice above the steady gun-fire sound of the rain drumming on the windows. 'Mr Lamb, think carefully, please. Are there any other places you know of that Georgie might have crawled into? If she was exploring, could she have found a secret hiding place? The hotel's so old, surely it has crawl spaces that might be attractive to a five year old?'

'I've racked my brains,' he says, his voice edging towards contained hysteria. 'I've told you everywhere I can think of. The coal hole, I told you about. The outbuildings.' He shakes his head, eyebrows pulled down deep together. 'I'm sorry. I can't think of anywhere else.'

Hillier nods and squares her shoulders. 'Right then,' she says. 'Let's go and see Mr and Mrs Greenstreet.' She turns to leave, pulling Ellis to one side. 'In the meantime, run checks on all the staff's and guests' timings. Especially the sous-chef, Marek Kaczka. He's the last person to have spoken to Georgie. And then I want to see all the hotel guests for a chat.'

CHAPTER FIVE

The rain continues its arrhythmic drumming as the police search the hotel. They bring the bitter wind inside with them, which mingles impudently with the warmth of the reception and the smell of pine needles. The piano ballad playing softly through the speakers is drowned out by their damp hustling. It is as if the legs of Balcombe Court have been shoved out from beneath it and now it lies flat on its back, struggling to right itself in the eye of the storm.

Max Saunders watches the police from his observation point in an alcove a little way down the hall from the reception desk. He sits there with a whisky and ginger and a copy of *The Times*, studying the activity over the rims of his glasses.

He looks on as the hotel staff usher the police through, under the medieval stone archways of the reception hall, into the lounge where velvet curtains hide the ice clouds outside, poised and waiting, thick and furred and cold.

Balcombe Court.

First a Saxon hall then a nest of the Bubonic plague, later a coaching inn then jewel of the English Riviera. And soon-to-be location of *The Buccaneer's Daughter*. What was it his agent had called it? Historical fiction with a twist. Everything has to have a bloody twist these days, Max thinks, folding his paper and getting to his feet. Why, in

God's name, can't he just write a good old-fashioned story and be thanked for it?

He heads in the opposite direction from the police, into the billiards room where low lights do nothing to assuage the force of the Devon dark. He wraps his arms around himself, feeling the shape of his mobile phone in his shirt pocket. He should call home, speak to Alison. Wish them all a Happy New Year. It feels wrong though somehow, with the child missing. He looks at his watch. She's been gone for three hours now. He feels sick at the thought of it.

He paces around the billiards table, his glass dangling in his hand. Where are you, Georgie? Max thinks. Are you still alive, or are you floating somewhere in the deep cold waters of the Devon coastline, reaching down to the ghosts of pirates who lie on the bottom of the sea?

He's seen the little girl only a couple of times. She's a spritely thing, always jumping around, never still. She has a younger brother, a chubby blond baby who always seems to be sucking on a piece of soggy toast. But Georgie is dark-haired with eyes like black almonds and a mouth like a red bow tied on top of a present. Her parents are nice enough, with the ubiquitous purple shadows under their eyes of those with very young children. They've got that anxious quality about them, Max has observed. Forever second-guessing which ornament Georgie might crash into or which tablecloth the baby might make a grab for. Parenthood seems to Max to be a constant attempt to corral the wind. He and Alison had been through it with Polly and Grace, but now the girls are teenagers and as condescending as alms-giving courtiers (them) to peasants (he and Alison).

He shivers although the room isn't cold and moves to the window for some reason, searching beyond his reflection into the cold of the night. He holds his hands up, fingers touching the glass, tracing the rain as it gushes down in an endless stream. He feels the warmth of his breath, the sound of his exhaling ominously calm. It is as if time has stopped for a millisecond. There is a fraction of silence in the midst of the rattling on the glass. It seems as though the downpour might have eased, that the weather has exhausted itself, turned in and gone back home. Then the sky is ripped from corner to corner, with a blistering light and a tearing sound.

Now he understands.

The ice comes slowly at first. Deliberate, with pointed teeth. It strikes the ground like spears. Max's breathing catches as he watches it fall indiscriminately, shattering through the dark like crystal shards. He presses his fingers against the glass as if he's reaching for outside, feeling for the cliff top where the coastguards search with their sweeping beams. He shuts his eyes briefly, flashes of his own daughters' faces shooting through his mind, realising how desperate the situation is. Because if that little girl isn't found soon, she will be dead.

Trapped under frozen rain in the ice storm.

CHAPTER SIX

There is a faint bellow of foghorns on the wind. Then the sound of ships tussling with the waves, doing battle with the ice falling from the sky in sheets. The noise engenders a terrible sense of claustrophobia in Hazel and pinpricks of fear pinch at her as she and Jonny make their way down the staircase to the hotel lounge.

Outside, a world of white that has transfigured the garden. Ice debris covers everything in sight. A water barrel resembles the bottom half of a snowman, and intricate webs of snow and remnants of hail are strung together like diamond necklaces between the bare branches of the apple trees.

The tension in the air crackles like cellophane. But despite this the lounge clings bravely on to the mellifluous calm of a cosy room on New Year's Eve. Hazel's hand is clamped in Jonny's. If she could shut her ears and ignore the sound of the storm, try and swallow down the fearful bile that burns in her throat, she might be able to pretend that this is all just as they'd planned, Jonny and she: a trip to Devon for her birthday, to the hotel where he'd come as a boy. Bringing Evie with them, hoping that the holiday would draw them closer together, because the fact that Hazel is only eleven years older than Jonny's daughter is an itch everyone acknowledges but no one dares to scratch.

Evie has followed them into the room, fully made up, tottering on heels that only a fourteen year old would wear for an interrogation by the police. Hazel and Jonny sit quietly on a love seat underneath one of the ice-battered windows. Balcombe Court is fully booked for New Year's Eve. Forty guests have gathered, sombre and grave-faced. Before them stands Mr Lamb, hands linked behind his back, swaying to and fro on his feet, waiting for them and the staff to settle like birds onto branches at sundown.

Max has wandered into the lounge from the billiards room. He fingers a packet of cigarettes in his trouser pocket and leans on a wall at the back, his eyes moving from staff member to guest, observing their muted anxiety, their nervous chatter. He is the first to notice DC Hillier when she enters, her notebook tucked away, her eyes bright and keen. She is in her late-forties, he surmises, with curly brown hair scraped back into a tight knot. Energy buzzes from her as she surveys the gathering, gazing at each of them as acutely as Max has done.

'It is our view,' she begins, 'that Georgie Greenstreet is no longer in the hotel.' She waits a second to let that sink in. 'We've searched the building thoroughly but I'm afraid to say she still hasn't been found.' Hillier lifts her head towards the window as a crack of thunder splits the sky above. 'As you can see – and hear – the weather is abominable. I've been told by the coastguard that the search will have to be abandoned until morning.'

A wave of concern breaks through the room at this. A spark flies from the fire and lands on the rug by Hillier's foot. She grinds it into the carpet with her black lace-up shoe, eyes never leaving her audience. 'I know that you are eager to help in any way you can,' she continues. 'At present, however, there isn't much that can be done until daylight returns and the storm dies down. Right now, all we need is for you to provide myself and PC Ellis with your details and an approximation of your movements this afternoon and evening. Then all we can do is wait.'

'How is Mrs Greenstreet?' an elderly lady asks from a corner of the lounge. 'The poor woman . . .'

A sympathetic murmuring breaks out among the guests and Hazel grips Jonny's hand, her thumb rubbing his in a compulsive pattern.

'She is very grateful for your concern,' Hillier answers. 'And doing OK under the circumstances.'

'Officer,' a man in a colour-blocked rugby shirt cuts in. 'Look, I'm ex-TA. The weather's fierce, sure, but this is a little girl we're talking about. You can't call off the search. If she's out there in this . . .'

Hillier holds up her hands, palms facing out, to stop him talking. She looks calm but Hazel can see a gleam in her eyes. It's an expression she recognises. A drive deep within, with tentacles so fierce and probing that they will reach into dark places, secret places that once were thought well hidden. It makes Hazel catch her breath, this look. At once she feels unutterably exhausted, beaten to the quick. She drops Jonny's hand, feels him glance at her uneasily but cannot meet his eyes. It's all she can do to remain upright and still, and try to keep invisible.

'As I say,' Hillier goes on, 'we do appreciate your concern but we would ask that you do as we advise. We don't want any more people outside, getting lost in this storm. It's treacherous. Please leave the searching to the professionals. We would also request that no one departs from the hotel at present.'

'What do you mean?' the man in the rugby shirt interrupts again. 'Are you saying we can't leave?'

Hillier smiles at him. 'The weather wouldn't permit it in any event, sir. But I would ask that if you need to check out of the hotel tomorrow, you do so only after you have been questioned and provided us with full contact details.'

Hazel's hand searches again for Jonny's and clutches it tightly.

Hillier looks around the room, taking in their faces one by one. 'Right then,' she says brightly. 'PC Ellis and I will call you in one at a time. Thank you.'

As she spins round and leaves, Max is reminded of a soldier and wonders briefly if Hillier is ex-military. He studies the guests as they sink back into random disquiet. The man in the rugby shirt is gesturing to his wife, a disgusted look on his face. A group of older women sitting together in a huddle seem close to tears. The couple on the window seat are motionless and silent. Their teenage daughter appears bored by the whole occasion, chewing gum and studying her fingernails.

Something about the woman by the window seems familiar although Max can't place what. It niggles at him like a prickle on his skin. There is an almost childlike quality about her, the way she clings to the man beside her. She's pretty but with the kind of delicate, petite appearance that he has never found wholly attractive. She's got a freckled, snub nose and dark brown hair cut like a boy's. But her eyes are those of a Cinecittà heroine and her lips have the warm, pendulous pout of an Ingrid Bergman. She seems sweet, a slight person; the type Alison would immediately pin down as *a girly girl*.

Alison is very much the opposite of a girly girl, with her Scandinavian genes and her strong-boned looks of a milk-maid. She'll be at the farm in Coventry now. He looks at his watch. They'll be sitting down to dinner, Alison raising her eyebrows if she sees his number light up on the screen of her phone. She'd probably show it to Rachael, and her sister would give her a sad look, rub her arm and pour her more wine. His name will be mud there tonight.

He's said sorry a thousand times. Explained that if he doesn't meet his deadline, he won't get his money. And then they'll be late on the school fees and that will incur a penalty. And, no, he can't write at Alison's parents' farmhouse because it will be filled to the rafters with a horde of family members, yelling and arguing at all hours of the day and night, and he unable to hear himself think. Despite the (tax-deductible) expense, he has to come to Balcombe to write here, where *The Buccaneer's Daughter* is set. It was all obvious to him, but unfortunately not to Alison, who sets family above all other concerns, including, it appears, keeping a roof over said family's head.

And so, on the day after Boxing Day, Max packed his case and hoisted his laptop bag over his shoulder and took the three trains required to travel from the terraced house he and Alison live in just outside Birmingham to this remote edge of Devon. Now he sighs, abandoning the pointless rehashing of it all. He feels for his cigarettes again and decides to brave the freezing cold for a smoke.

Hazel barely notices him go; she sees nobody else in the room, so immersed is she in her thoughts. She stares down intently at her thumb circling Jonny's, over and over again.

That look.

That look the policewoman had given her right before she left. It's a look that takes Hazel straight back to the old canal path.

And, at once, it is as if a chasm has opened up beneath her, and all the castles in the air she has built over the years – with Jonny, with her job, her colleagues – are minutes away from being dashed to smithereens. Like the pirate vessels on the rocks down from the headland where the hotel sits, her treasures will be discarded, tossed out, picked over . . . and then the vilification will begin.

And Jonny. Is he brave enough for this? Can he see it as she can, what's to come? She stays small and tight, curled up like cigarette paper, her heart warm and beating, but damaged. She comes to this place tonight with all of that inside her. But Jonny? He can't understand what it's like. How can he? Can he really know that he will stay, when everything is out in the open, trickling down, carving its mark in the rocks forevermore?

That look.

Down in the gully behind the garden.

By the willow trees above the bank, spouting leaves onto the ground like a lime-green fountain. The far-off laughter of children running in the playground, the sun on their faces, wind in their hair.

That's the look that started it all. The look that meant everything from then on must be hidden. Tucked away in secret.

Her secret.

Her past.

CHAPTER SEVEN

The guests file one by one into the room where Hillier and Ellis sit behind a stack of paper and two cooling cups of coffee. They sit down. Some are nervous, some brash. Most of them have inexplicable guilt washed over their complexions, a desperate need to convince Hillier that they are not the ones responsible, that they have not taken the child.

Hillier recognises this misplaced reaction from the fifteen years she has spent on the force and the seven years before that serving as a lawyer in the Royal Navy Court Martial. She knows it well: that foreign and dirty beast that comes unwarranted to the entirely innocent because – and this is the bit she has never completely understood – it actually represents the thoughts these people are beyond relieved never to have acted on themselves. Hillier is certain that criminal impulses lurk unbidden in everyone. But it is only the people who act on those impulses that guilt can claim as its victims. The rest of us feel it but shake it off, thankful to God, or whatever it is that guides our moral compass, that we are able to control it.

Thus Hillier is confident that most of the guilty-looking guests who come before her and Ellis have no knowledge of what has happened to Georgie Greenstreet.

Most of them.

There are two, however, who interest her.

The first is the sous-chef, Marek Kaczka. It is now nearly midnight, and the witching hour, compounded by the fact that it is New Year's Eve, means normal response time at Brixham police station is slower than usual with a skeletal overtime budget meaning a skeleton staff. The rest of her colleagues will be tied up dealing with the drunken fights and skirmishes that dominate proceedings this time of year. Instinctively, Hillier feels that Kaczka will have a record, some kind of infraction in his past, but she is not going to be able to trace that tonight. So she bides her time and leaves him to sweat a bit. She interviews him cursorily, suspecting that anything he says will be tainted with untruths in any event.

Her second point of interest is the petite, pretty woman who comes into the room with her partner and can't look Hillier in the eye.

Hazel Archer.

Something in her face is familiar to Hillier. It buzzes at her, exasperatingly out of reach, like a troublesome fly. The woman has an unusual quality about her. Hillier can't tell what it is. Either she is entirely cold, or she has buttoned up her feelings and is in fact completely paralysed by fear. She and her partner, Jonny Newell, claim to have been together all afternoon, either as a couple or with his fourteen-year-old daughter, Evie. They arrived at the hotel yesterday morning and today is Hazel's birthday. They have come here to celebrate that, and the New Year, and they are terribly, awfully worried about Georgie and where she could be.

But something in all that they say rings hollow for Hillier. A glimmer in Hazel Archer's eyes sparks a feeling in her. It's an instinct born of hundreds of nights spent dealing with drunks and tramps and burglars, sifting through them to find those people who are truly worthy of her attention: the real criminals. Hillier has refused any promotion up the ranks, has deliberately remained as Detective Constable for the majority of her career. And the reason for that decision is because *this* exact moment, that dances around her now, is what thrills her, rare as it is. She can leave management evaluations to her superiors, along with budget concerns and staffing problems. As DC, her chief responsibility is to get to a crime scene first and this is the moment she relishes. That flash in time when a hunter trains her rifle sights on an animal quivering in the bush. When she faces the mask of innocence and knows, right down to the marrow in her bones, that it is a lie. Whether Hazel Archer is guilty of the disappearance of Georgie Greenstreet is yet to be determined. But Hillier can feel that Archer is, without a doubt, guilty of something.

The policewoman sniffs and dismisses her for now, stashing her papers away, her mind still whirring with what she has gleaned from the interviews tonight.

One by one the lights are switched off, first downstairs and then above, as the guests all go to bed with tired eyes open, staring into the dark, wondering about the missing little girl and where she might be.

Ellis puts snow chains on the car and he and Hillier drive off into the Devon countryside. She doesn't look back, as the pale outline of the hotel fades into the ghostly snow-filled night.

She will return first thing in the morning.

CHAPTER EIGHT

New Year's Day in South London is slow. Coffee and more coffee and a shower turned blistering hot and then freezing cold. Joanna Denton bites her lip, shutting her eyes to the physical sensation, welcoming the pain and discomfort. This is what will make the hangover dissipate. Caffeine and agony.

Last night in the club she'd drunk tequila shot after tequila shot, trying to reach that place in her head where she could forget everything – as 'Auld Lang Syne' so aptly suggests. But the buzz had eluded her as she'd stood on the periphery of the club where her friends were jumping like jacks to House of Pain and she'd thought, *Yeah, that sums it up.*

So she'd left the club. Walked alone on the Embankment in shoes soaked with booze, breathed in the frosty London air and watched the lights of the city burn. As she'd left the river, she'd had the usual thoughts. The fear that her life was meagre in contrast to that of her friends. Where their lives gush with invitations – to parties and dinners; gallery openings; children's birthdays; beach holidays – Joanna merely subsists. Day after day, rousing herself to do battle with better-paid lawyers in nicer offices with, unlike her, a supportive partner at home who listens sympathetically to tales of their day whilst pouring endless amounts of red wine.

Where was the joy for her? she'd asked herself for the millionth time, her feet sore and cold from the walk. For a brief moment, glancing up at a broken street light, she had felt like crying. Where was the sense that her life had meaning? That it fed something inside her, apart from the anger she had clad in armour for all these years?

She had wiped a hand across her cheeks crossly. What was the point of crying? She can't forget her job. Can't go and do something painless, something mindless, because always the loop returns to the fact that she can't let it go. She can't ever stop thinking about those people who leave so much pain in their wake, so much chaos. Those criminals who, in their selfishness – or their madness – reach inside another human being and rearrange the configuration of their spirit. Change them indelibly so that they are never the same soul as they were before *it* happened.

At last Joanna had arrived at her flat, wanting desperately to sleep but unable to block out thoughts of the stack of paperwork she could envisage waiting on her desk at the office or the memory of what drives her every day.

The image of two-year-old Kirstie Swann.

Her niece.

Brutally murdered in the gully of a long-disused canal. Beaten to death and then left to rot while her killer went home for dinner.

Joanna's always thinking about her.

Kirstie's killer.

And how she will never be allowed to leave prison while Joanna Denton has anything to do with it.

She dresses quickly, pulling on jeans and flat boots; an old university hoodie over a plain white T-shirt. Her only concession to vanity is to brush her long brown hair and tie it up in a bun, but then she is out of the door and striding for the Northern line back up towards Borough, where the Bang to Rights office is situated. As it is New Year's Day, everything is shut up and quiet. The café where she normally buys her daily croissant is closed and the Tube is empty, seats stretching beside her filled with nothing more than the ghosts of the usual thousands of commuters.

Joanna reaches the office after she's found an open Pret A Manger at Borough Tube and bought another coffee and an apple. She can't stomach anything more. The tequila from last night still churns inside her, making her feel as though she could throw up at any moment.

She doesn't expect Will to be there, but he is. The door is unlocked and his bike is blocking the tiny corridor of the small space they rent. Joanna and Will met at Manchester University over twenty years ago in their first contract law tutorial. In the Union bar they had become friends, drinking pints of beer and planning their future. They would both leave their childhood homes in the North and come to seek their fortunes in London. Will would work for a City law firm, learning how to merge and acquire, and – as Joanna would point out – survive on minimum sleep while making money for a bunch of men in suits who would barely know his name. She, on the other hand, would train at a high-street firm that specialised in immigration and criminal law, earning approximately a quarter of what Will would be paid.

Joanna would tease him that he would become a sell-out, wasting his life lining the pockets of people who didn't deserve to benefit from his brain cells.

'And what about you?' he'd ask, fixing her with a stare. 'How are you going to change the world, stuck out in Shepherd's Bush helping a bunch of crims?'

Joanna wouldn't answer this but sat silently instead, curled up on the ratty leather sofa, a cigarette dangling over the edge of one arm, ash lengthening until it dropped into the ashtray on the floor.

Then, just before they graduated, she had received the telephone call that had changed her plans forever. As intended, she had moved down to London to work.

But Joanna did not become a lawyer.

Throughout the entire trial of the killer of her niece, Joanna had sat holding her sister's hand, making sure she ate enough; helping her to stand and leave the courtroom when it all got too much. And after that, she had begun working for Bang to Rights.

It was a tiny organisation that lobbied the government on behalf of victims. BTR liaised with Victim Support, it mediated between victims and the police, and it campaigned tirelessly for longer sentences proportionate to the crimes committed. Eventually, Joanna's old boss had retired and she had taken on the running of the lobbying group herself. In that time, Will had married and, upon the birth of his daughter, resigned from his City law firm and come to work with Joanna. It meant that he took home far less money, but he insisted that he would at least be able to see more of his family and do so with a clear conscience.

Old habits die hard, though, and a workaholic nature is hard to tame.

'But I'm not here for long,' he says as he hears Joanna jogging up the stairs to the minuscule office they share. 'Lucy's at her parents' house today with Jemima so I thought I'd put in an hour or two before heading there for lunch.'

'I would have got you a coffee if I'd known,' Joanna replies. 'Thanks, Will. There's so much to do,' she continues, looking round at the piles of paper on every available surface. 'We really need a secretary.'

'Fat chance on our budget. How was last night?'

'Oh, all right. Too much booze.' She grimaces and puts her coffee to her lips. 'There isn't enough caffeine in the world today, frankly.'

'Why didn't you stay in bed then?' Will asks, knowing what the answer will be. 'One day isn't going to hurt.'

Joanna sits down at her desk and reaches across to turn on her computer. 'Yes, it will,' she says. 'Remember Mo Farah, William. Let us always remember Mo.'

Will grins, turning back to his own screen. Joanna had once read that the Olympian Mo Farah always trained on Christmas Day because, he said, other athletes would take it as a holiday, meaning he would be one day ahead of them in training.

'Anyway, I've got that radio show today. Remember? The New Year's debate on justice and sentencing?'

Joanna takes a gulp of coffee before clicking on to the BBC website and then exclaims, sucking in a breath. 'I don't believe it,' she says in a voice like lead. She swings the computer screen around so that Will can see. It's the third headline on the site, after the announcement of the Queen's New Year's Honours list and a bus crash in Wolverhampton. Joanna's eyes scan Will's face as he reads what's before him.

'Fuck,' he says at last.

'Yep,' she answers, rubbing her palms over her face before staring up at the ceiling. 'My thoughts exactly.'

31

CHAPTER NINE

'I think we should leave,' Hazel says. Their bedroom is glaring white from the fresh snow that covers the ground outside. 'There's a poem,' she says, running her hands over her face. 'I can't remember who wrote it, but it's stuck with me. It says the snow is winter folding her linen. But it's not, is it, Jonny? It may as well be a pit of writhing snakes. Where we are. Now, I mean.' She turns round to look at him, propped up in bed, bare-chested, sleep-tousled. 'We're stuck here and the snakes are coiling round our ankles. It just seems crazy to stay when they're going to say it's me, pin it on me. Say that I'm involved at least. And . . .' She looks at him, panic shadowing her face. 'I want to go. Get out of here.'

'We can't,' he answers, his eyes fixed on hers.

The early morning is quiet, the winter sun just above the horizon. The sounds of the hotel are muffled: the occasional clang of cutlery on glass, the aroma of coffee percolating up through the floor. The air has that stillness, an atonal hum of peace, which lengthens languidly before it is overtaken by the clamour of industry and the brio of a day that is gathering momentum.

'If we leave,' Jonny says, 'we look guilty. It's obvious. We have to stay and see what happens. See if the girl is found.'

Hazel extends her arms to him, splays her palms as if presenting him with the room. 'But all of this, Jonny – all of this will be gone. You don't understand. You haven't been there. I have. Once people know . . . all of this – all of my life as I know it now – will be taken away from me.'

Jonny breathes in deeply, pushes back the covers and gets out of bed. He pulls Hazel towards him. Her arms drop down by her sides, limp as a doll's.

'You can't hide forever,' he says into her hair.

'But this,' she says again, pushing him away, 'isn't the way. With a girl missing it's too similar. To before. They'll attack me – attack us. They'll say it was me.'

'But we know it isn't.'

Hazel looks at him. 'It doesn't matter. Once the press come – and they will – they'll be like a pack of dogs.' Her voice begins to rise. 'You don't know what it was like. For my parents. For all of us. They won't let it go.'

'They will.' Jonny's voice is firm. 'They'll have to. There's nothing to link you to this girl, to what's happened here. It's just . . .' He grabs a handful of his hair in frustration. 'I do accept that it's appalling timing. I'm sorry.'

Hazel manages a small smile for him. It's all she can do as she realises that Jonny is on a different path from her. He is hoping that this is an aberration, something that will pass in the night like a fever. He doesn't see that nothing will be the same for them ever again. 'Oh God, Jonny,' she says and turns her back on him, looking once more out onto the snow. 'God help us now.'

Max is up too, sitting at the desk in his room, eyes glazed as he faces his laptop. He slept badly last night, staring up at the dark ceiling, thinking about Alison and his girls.

And Georgie.

Is she out there? he kept wondering. Huddled near the rocks, trying to get warm. Or is she being held somewhere against her will? Little Georgie, crying for her mother, not understanding why she's been taken away from her. Eventually he had got up and paced his room. Memories of Polly and Grace as babies, as toddlers, chubby, built like tanks, scattered through his mind. That utter dependence, no concept of fear, of any insecurity. He remembers them waddling around, big-eyed and messy-haired. Their smell of Johnson's baby powder, dried milk, lavender shampoo.

Now it is light and the night before seems like a dream. The New Year has come in less like a lamb than a phantom, a reckoning over a line drawn in the deep snow banked outside. Max can hear the sound of shovels as staff clear a path from the front door down the driveway. They are trying to lead the hotel back to reality, exorcising the spectres that floated above its medieval walls last night.

Balcombe Court is already filled with ghosts. Max has done his research. Headless coachmen; gluttonous gargoyles feasting on the entrails of maidens; lost loves of dead sailors; hung, drawn and quartered pirates. It has them all.

And now it has the spirit of Georgie Greenstreet. A half-spirit as yet, calling to them from wherever she is, alive or dead or somewhere in between. Max rubs his face and takes a long gulp of instant coffee made from the tiny kettle in his room before swigging from a bottle of Gaviscon, trying to quell the constant heartburn he has felt for weeks now. He has to work. He has fifteen hundred words to write today, missing child or not. His deadline looms just the same as it did yesterday and if he wants to make it back to Alison and his girls by the middle of January, he has to finish this book.

He opens up the document and stares at the last paragraph he typed yesterday lunchtime. He had shut down the computer and then gone to the dining room to stretch his legs and order a sandwich. He had seen Georgie, sitting with her parents attacking a plate of spaghetti bolognese. The dining room was fairly empty. The only others in there were the people he had seen again last night, huddled together on the window seat. The pretty woman he now thinks of as Ingrid Bergman, and her partner and the teenage girl.

Max frowns and then closes his eyes. Where has he seen that woman before? Maybe in London when he was working there a few years ago for a literary magazine? A friend of a friend? He prods his fingers into his forehead, straining to remember, before sighing and giving up. Reminding himself that memory never works to order, he turns his thoughts back to *The Buccaneer's Daughter* and the scene he was struggling with the day before, where Constance Mandeville discovers that she is bound in marriage to Jago D'Aubert despite her love for Santo Perowne.

Max begins typing, his lips moving as he does, writing the scene again from the beginning, changing the location to the top of the cliffs where Santo climbs down to his ship, abandoning Constance after hearing of her betrothal. As he climbs, Constance – in her grief and despair – tosses a flower down after him. She chooses a primrose, the county flower of Devon.

Primrose.

Max's hands hover above the keyboard, his whole body frozen as the memory ricochets back to mind at last.

Minimising his manuscript, he brings up the internet and does a rapid search.

Of Primrose.

And murder.

CHAPTER TEN

Hillier and her team arrive in a cacophony of slamming car doors and the crunch of boots on snow. She is the first into the hotel, removing her heavy black jacket and gloves as she steps into the fug of the reception hall.

The panelled walls of Balcombe are oppressive today, the lights on the Christmas tree glitter in the gloom, but Hillier doesn't register any of this. She heads straight upstairs to where she will find Georgie Greenstreet's parents, calling to the receptionist to let Mr Lamb know the police have arrived.

The hotel is doing its best to maintain an air of normality. Breakfast has been served as usual and guests are permitted to move around freely, although the severity of the weather restricts what they are able to do outside.

'People are asking to leave.' Mr Lamb appears, looking harried, calling after Hillier, scurrying behind her as she makes her way along one of the upstairs corridors. 'What should I tell them?'

Hillier stops and turns on her heel. 'They can't check out yet,' she replies. 'Let me talk to Jane Greenstreet, fill her in on what's happened overnight. Not that much *has*,' she concedes. 'But there are a couple of people I want to talk to again and I don't want them leaving before I do. So just hold fire, OK?'

He nods and backs away. 'Do tell Mrs Greenstreet that she is welcome to order anything from the menu. On the house of course.'

A moment later Hillier is knocking on the Greenstreets' door, opening it slowly as Declan Greenstreet calls for her to enter. His wife is sitting on the four-poster bed, her knees curled up to her chest. The curtains are half-drawn and Hillier can just make out the shape of the couple's youngest child asleep in his cot.

Seeing the door open, Jane Greenstreet swings her legs off the bed in Hillier's direction. Her face is wild and tear-stained, her hair coming loose from a raggedy knot at her neck.

'Have you found her?' she blurts hoarsely.

'Sssshhhh,' Declan says, gesturing to the cot, but Jane doesn't listen, crossing the room to where Hillier stands.

'Have you?'

Hillier tilts her head. 'I'm sorry. The coastguard sent the helicopters up at first light. You can probably hear them. The boats are out too and we've got search parties down on the beach. We're doing everything we can, I promise, Mrs Greenstreet.'

'It's been too long. She'll be cold and hungry and fright-ened . . .' Jane's voice rises, her fingers clawing at her face. 'I can't bear it. I can't think of her like that. I just can't . . .'

Hillier glances at Declan, who stands pale and immobile, apparently unable to approach his wife and comfort her. 'You've seen a doctor?' she asks him quietly.

He nods, rousing himself from his trance and moving over to Jane to lead her back to the bed. 'One of the other guests came up. They've given her some pills.'

'I know it's hard,' Hillier says, glancing over at the cot. 'But you need to look after yourselves and Charlie. Try and rest. We are doing everything we can,' she repeats firmly. 'Please trust us. We know what we're about.'

'What about one of those child rescue alert things?' Declan asks in a low voice. 'Have you done one of those?'

Hillier shakes her head. 'Georgie's disappearance doesn't meet the criteria for an alert. At least not at the present time,' she answers. 'Realistically, someone from outside the hotel would have struggled to get up to Balcombe last night, let alone remove a child in that weather.' She looks at Declan's expression. 'I'm not ruling anything out,' she says. 'But a child rescue alert is only used in specific circumstances where the public can help us find a missing child. We haven't established that Georgie has left the perimeter of the hotel as yet. We need to rule out the beach and the surrounding land which the coastguard is doing right now. The relevant public are the guests here, the staff, not anyone in a wider vicinity. Please trust me,' she says again. 'We know what we're doing.'

Jane Greenstreet pushes her hair out of her face and looks searchingly at her. 'You promise?' she asks desperately.

'I swear,' Hillier says, before turning and leaving the room.

Upstairs, from her bedroom window, Hazel has watched Hillier and the other policemen and women arrive. She sits winding her arms around herself and shivering. Jonny and Evie have gone down to breakfast but she can't stomach a thing. Seeing the police has brought back the fear, visceral and hot. She feels panic rise in her, tries to swallow it down but can't. Her eyes are fixed on the horizon, at the place where the cliff edge meets the sky, the white of the snow almost indiscernible from the pale grey above. Down there, past the snow-covered heather, is the marled sea, bottle-green and angry. Is that where Georgie is? she thinks.

Oh, Georgie, come home, she pleads. *Come back and then all of this will be over. Where are you, Georgie? Where are you?*

Tears begin to fall from Hazel's eyes and she whirls round, her open suitcase the first item she sees. She hefts it onto the bed, and starts to throw things in. Some hers, some Jonny's, it doesn't matter. If she can just get out of here, she can work this out. She can drive away, back into civilisation where there is noise and the snow has melted and gone and she can think about what to do. She's got everything now, she estimates, and slams the case shut, drags it onto the floor. And then she's opening the door and is out in the corridor. She's boiling, sweating underneath her jumper and jeans, the case running along awkwardly behind her on its wheels. She'll call Jonny later, tell him where she's gone. Some travel inn on the motorway where no one can find her, where no one will know who she is.

The case bumps along the carpet until she reaches the top of the stairs that lead directly to reception. Hazel pauses, breathing hard, straining to hear whether anyone is down there. She has the car keys in her other hand and their car is parked five spaces away from the front door. For some reason, she counted them when they arrived the day before yesterday. It's as if she knew she would have to escape at some point. That nowhere is ever safe for her, that eventually she will have to resume running.

But now she just has to make it to the car and then pray that they've cleared the driveway of snow so that she can get out. They must have, it occurs to her sharply, otherwise how would the police have got up here? Once she's beyond the hotel grounds, she can make it.

Hazel begins to pull the case down behind her as she descends. Why has she brought it? she thinks. So stupid. She doesn't need clothes. She just needs her purse and the car keys. Too late now. She carries on, trying to make as little noise as possible. She rounds the bend on the small landing in the middle of the stairs, and halts as sounds emerge from below. She waits until she sees a guest leave the reception desk. She can hear the receptionist tapping on her computer. Does that matter? Will the girl stop her? Ask where she's going with her case? So idiotic to bring it, she tells herself again. Should she just leave it here on the stairs? Walk down casually without it, and out of the door to freedom?

'Hello there,' a voice says softly in her ear.

Hazel freezes.

'Checking out early, are you?'

Hazel is too terrified to turn around; to see what she imagines – *what she knows* – is a policeman, standing behind her. What will she say? How can she get herself out of this nightmare? She swallows, tears springing once again to her eyes.

'I wouldn't leave if I were you,' the voice continues. 'It wouldn't look good and you know it ...

'. . . Rosie.'

CHAPTER ELEVEN

1997

The baby has stopped crying for the moment. Her face, which for the last hour had been scrunched up and covered in snot, has flattened, exhausted by her yelling. Her little chest still heaves, though, as she hiccups in oxygen, her eyes wide as she stares at Laurel and Rosie.

The girls gather the baby like hens rustling a chick to one side, pushing her into the bushes, squashing themselves into the space only they know, where only they have been before. The movement makes the baby cry again, but Laurel and Rosie wear exhilarated expressions, their hearts big in their chests, thumping from the heat and the repeated realisation that the baby is with them.

It was never said out loud, the game of taking the baby. It was just there one day in that unspoken way they have between the two of them. A charm or a spell that, once it had been cast, was as binding as the bell at break-time or their repeated refusal of broccoli. Skipping in their garden, opening the gate and dancing towards the playground on their toes, Laurel and Rosie had known in their bones that soon a baby would come, a round, chunky baby with a delicious smile and open hands. The baby would want to play with them, that was also certain. And they would go to their secret place, down into the gully scored through the grass where the canal used to run under the willow tree. There, the earth was dark and dank and the leaves made a bower perfect for hiding in.

The game was usually 'schools', or sometimes Laurel wanted to play 'Saturday Night', which Rosie didn't really understand but pretended to. This involved a sequence where Laurel feigned putting on make-up and then got upset with 'Dad' (who was Rosie) and stormed off, hips waggling, declaring that she would 'never be back, not even if the baby is crying until morning'. That was what they'd started to play this afternoon. Except the baby wouldn't cry. So Laurel had pinched her hard on the arm, just above her elbow. And then the crying wouldn't stop.

Soon, though, Rosie felt hungry and a bit bored and began to look around for something else to do. Laurel was busy looking in the 'mirror' on the tree trunk and applying 'mascara'. The baby was still sobbing and a smell came from her that reminded Rosie of the school toilets. The sun dipped fractionally and something had changed. It felt as if the energy of the afternoon had been whisked away, along with the excitement, the pleasure of just being there in the dappled light under the trees without any adults.

'Let's go home,' Rosie said.

But Laurel ignored her, murmuring, her hands enacting all manner of things known only to herself.

'Let's go home,' Rosie insisted. 'I'm bored.'

The baby was sucking its fingers now, soothing herself, her eyes still big and wet. She began rocking back and forth, her legs stuck out in front of her.

'The baby's boring,' Rosie said. 'I want to go home.' She stamped her foot, grabbing a low branch and pulling it down to the ground, letting it ping back up with a loud thwacking sound so that the baby stopped moving for a moment and stared upward, her mouth open in surprise.

Laurel turned to Rosie then, her face dark with a sulk. 'You always spoil everything,' she said. 'I want to play.'

'No,' Rosie retorted.

Laurel got to her feet, her chin low. 'I want to play,' she repeated.

'I want to go home,' her sister replied.

And then the baby began to cry again. Rasping, heavy sobs that seemed to scratch the very soul of their special place. She was ruining it for them.

It was a sickening, desperate sound that, in the end, had to be stopped.

CHAPTER TWELVE

It had taken place in 1997, in the drowsy, innocent summer before Princess Diana was killed. That's what always placed it in the public's mind. The widespread disbelief and shock that had been felt after the murder. And then, six weeks later, after a car accident in Paris, when the grief of the nation was compounded as life became tinged with unreality and everything that was accepted before seemed to disintegrate, leaving people floundering, not knowing what to believe in any more.

Kirstie was the only daughter of Debbie and Robert Swann. They lived in Grassington in North Yorkshire, in a terraced house on the edge of the Dales. On 15 July, a five-months-pregnant Debbie took Kirstie to the local playground, a short walk from their home. There, she met her friend Christine and the two women chatted by the trailer café beside the play area. Debbie had watched while Kirstie busied herself in a tiny maze just inside the playground fence. She had ordered a coffee and turned away to pay when it had arrived. When she circled back to look at the play area, Kirstie was gone.

Debbie had been at the park for less than half an hour.

At first, she thought she was panicking unduly. She checked the maze and walked quickly over to the other side of the playground where the mouth of the old canal had been, looking underneath benches, the see-saw, the roundabout, calling Kirstie's name. When the toddler failed to appear, Debbie began to cry. She raced out of the playground and down to the line of oak trees, shouting for her daughter, desperately searching for a flash of her blonde hair. Christine had run the other way to look, behind the café, and soon all the other mothers had joined in the search, Styrofoam cups dropped, abandoned on the asphalt.

Then the police arrived and fanned out across the grasslands bordering the park. Kirstie's father, Robert Swann, was contacted, haring to the playground to kneel before his wife, breathless and pale in the face. Paramedics were called for Debbie, to force her to sit and rest, for fear her distress would endanger her unborn child.

The search continued for two days. The sound of Kirstie's name echoed through the village as people shouted for her while they searched. Journalists descended on the community. For the first twenty-four hours, Debbie refused to leave the playground, sitting huddled on an aluminium chair beside the café, willing her daughter to appear, making bargain after bargain with a god she had never believed in, promising anything just to be able to see her little girl again. In the end, she agreed to move after the paramedics told her flatly that the heart-rate of the baby inside her was weakening and, if she didn't allow herself to be hydrated, he could die.

Rigid with grief, Debbie was driven by ambulance to the local hospital whilst Rob stayed, walking endless miles over the wine-coloured heather of the Dales. Scores of policemen and women accompanied by hundreds of volunteers from the village inched forward in sombre lines, looking for any evidence of the missing toddler. As daylight faded, a soft and unrelenting rain began to fall.

On the second day of the hunt, they found Kirstie's body. She had been covered by a sodden mound of branches and leaves in a grass-covered gully half a mile from the playground. She had died from blunt trauma to the head. She had hundreds of tiny scratches all the way up her arms and down her legs. Half of her left earlobe was missing and her left arm was broken. Police detectives gave a statement to the press, stating in shocked and disbelieving tones that in their view Kirstie had been tortured for several hours before she was murdered. Torture that involved deliberately slicing her arms and legs and biting off part of her ear.

The following day ten-year-old Laurel Bowman was arrested for the toddler's kidnap and murder.

Laurel and her six-year-old sister Primrose – known as Rosie – had been seen by numerous people at the playground. After the investigating officers had interviewed all those present, it became horrifyingly apparent, from several eye-witness reports, that they had led Kirstie away. The story screamed from every front page. *The Flower Girls* the tabloids called them, fair-haired Laurel and dark-haired Rosie.

The sisters came from what police described to the press as a 'normal' family. Their mother was a dental receptionist; their father the manager of a small travel agency. They weren't rich but lived in a respectable household and nothing in their lives would have led anyone to predict that their child would commit such a heinous crime.

St Michael's Primary School, which the girls both attended, issued a statement saying they were not considered troublesome in class, that they had friends. They were just ordinary children. Much was made of the fact that Laurel had squeezed her pet hamster to death some months before Kirstie's murder. Amy Bowman, her mother, had shakily explained to the police that this was not, in fact, the case. The animal had escaped its cage, crawled underneath Laurel's pillow one night and she had slept on it, unintentionally suffocating the creature. But by that stage, nobody was interested in the truth. Laurel was the personification of wickedness and she must pay for her crime.

The girl insisted she was innocent, saying to the police and the social workers that they had just wanted to play with Kirstie, taking her from the playground and down to the old dried-out canal. But that wasn't wrong, was it? Their mother often left them to play down there. Laurel said she had liked 'the baby', as she described Kirstie. She wouldn't have wanted to hurt her. But, as they'd trundled down the bank, the little girl had stumbled and fallen and hit her head. Laurel and Rosie were frightened then, scared of the trouble they would be in, and so they abandoned her there and ran home, going upstairs to play until Amy called them down to the kitchen for their tea. Laurel didn't know how the marks on Kirstie's arms and legs had got there, or what had happened to her ear. Maybe it was animals, she had suggested. Or a man who came along later to hurt her.

When the police questioned Rosie, she wouldn't speak. One of the officers present, who was interviewed years later for a book on the case, described her state as catatonic, her eyes 'big as saucers' while she sat on a chair with her legs dangling, not yet long enough to reach the ground. During the interview she merely shook her head repeatedly, her mouth pinched tight. Only after an hour of cajoling by the social workers and her mother, who was allowed to sit in with her, did Rosie reveal that she remembered nothing. She could recall going to the park with Laurel, but after that, the whole afternoon was a complete blank.

At the time, Laurel was ten years old and thus considered fit to stand trial for Kirstie's murder. Rosie, on the other hand, was not. At six, she was below the legal age of criminal responsibility. One year and four days after the body of Kirstie Swann was discovered, Laurel Bowman was found guilty of her abduction and murder and sentenced to detention at Her Majesty's pleasure, with a recommendation made by the trial judge that she should be eligible for parole only when she turned eighteen. Rosie and her parents were given new identities and moved out of Yorkshire to a secret location kept hidden from the press and all who had known them before.

Joanna has lived with the impact of this crime ever since. It stretches like a conduit from Kirstie, through her sister Debbie, and into her work. Even once Laurel was imprisoned, the girl's punishment has never felt weighty enough, not in comparison with the devastation her crime has wrought. In 2005, when she was eighteen, Laurel came before the parole board for the first time. Joanna didn't sleep during the campaign she mounted to keep her niece's killer behind bars. She was interviewed with Debbie and Rob on national television; on radio; in every newspaper, arguing that Laurel should never be allowed to leave prison.

The final decision was covered worldwide. In light of the nature of the torture that Kirstie had suffered; Laurel's continued denial of any culpability; and the public outcry to the possibility of her being freed after serving only seven years, parole was denied. Laurel was moved from the young offenders' institute where she had been detained to date, to an adult women's prison.

Bang to Rights were tireless in their lobbying. In 2000, when the European Court of Human Rights denied the then Home Secretary the right to fix tariffs for public interest prisoners, they instead petitioned the Attorney General to keep Laurel incarcerated. When she was found to have been granted permission to study for a BTEC in Childcare Development inside prison, they ensured that this was plastered all over the tabloids, which meant Laurel was quickly reassigned to a less contentious study programme. BTR continued to campaign against her release, and in 2010 she was denied parole for the second time.

Debbie had given birth to her son Ben four months after Kirstie was killed. He was now nineteen and as committed as his parents and aunt were to the campaign to ensure Laurel Bowman would never be allowed to leave prison. Every anniversary of Kirstie's death saw Joanna and BTR and at least one parent on morning television or giving a press interview, describing how the life they had known previously had ended on the day that Kirstie was murdered. If Laurel were allowed to leave prison before serving a minimum term of at least thirty-five years – the normal tariff for a violent child murder – it would be as if she had got off scot-free, they argued. Where was the justice for Kirstie – for all of them – in that?

Now Joanna stares over the desk at Will, while chewing her fingernail down to the quick. 'We'll argue it's unreasonable,' she says after a long pause. 'I'll get on to the Attorney General's team right now.'

'Yep,' he answers, turning his eyes back to the BBC website on the screen. 'But . . .'

Joanna leaps to her feet and marches to the window where she looks down on the narrow street below. Normally there is a fruit and vegetable market bustling beneath them, the smell of fried okra floating in the air. On New Year's Day, though, the street is bare and disturbed only by a pigeon waddling down the centre of the road. She watches it move, thinking back to those first days after Kirstie's body was found. How it was all she could do to keep Debbie breathing and calm, contain her hysteria for the sake of her unborn child.

'But what?' says Joanna, turning back to face Will. 'I mean, she can't apply for permission to review the decision of the parole board again. We've been through this. Time and time again, right?' She eyeballs her friend, who has leaned back in his chair, his expression pained.

'I just think we might need to steel ourselves for the worst this time,' he says at last. He holds up his hands as Joanna starts to speak. 'I know,' he says. 'But eighteen years is a decent stretch. She was a child when she went in. She's nearly thirty now. I'm worried that you're not taking on board the fact that some people might consider it enough. They might think she's paid her dues.'

'She beat Kirstie to death,' Joanna spits. 'She cut her arms and legs so badly that my niece would have died from blood loss if she hadn't been beaten to death first. She *bit off her earlobe*. She's never shown any remorse, never admitted her guilt. Is this really someone you want loose on our streets?

Wandering into school playgrounds? Where's any evidence of her rehabilitation? She can't even say sorry for what she's done, because she isn't sorry.' Her tone is scathing. 'She couldn't care less. And meanwhile Debbie and Rob have to live with what she's done – *every single day*. The parole board are competent. *More* than competent. We say they are capable of deciding whether prisoners should be released on licence. And they have said that Laurel *isn't safe*. But that's not good enough apparently. Because she's got more time on her hands than . . . I don't know what. She can sit around the livelong day, bringing legal challenges against their decisions!'

Joanna hurls her paper cup into the waste bin and snatches up her backpack. 'I need to call my sister,' she says. 'I just hope she hasn't seen the news before I speak to her.'

CHAPTER THIRTEEN

'Primrose . . . Rosie,' Max says softly, staring into Hazel's eyes. 'That's who you are.'

They are standing at opposite ends of Max's room, he by the window, which overlooks the back of the hotel, the small delivery bay and the snowy fields stretching away from the sea. Hazel is positioned with her back to the door, ready to flee if necessary, keeping a wary distance between them. She feels a line of perspiration drip down her chest as she stares at Max. His face is eager, like a bloodhound's. Hazel's expression by contrast is taut, carefully controlled, apart from the feverish eyes that glitter at him, like a fox's at the start of the hunt.

'Please,' he says levelly, 'I don't want to upset or frighten you. That's not what this is about. I'm here doing research for my novel. That's who I am – an author. I'm down here writing my book because it's about here. It's set here in Devon,' he explains, aware of the clumsiness of his words. He's so wired, they feel like party balloons popping. He needs to rein them in, keep her calm. Keep her here, in his room.

'I was writing a scene,' Max continues, forcing himself to ignore her obvious distress, 'about a primrose.' He waves his hands as if that's irrelevant. 'Anyway – the thing is – it reminded me. I *knew* I'd seen you somewhere before. Couldn't place you, though, you know? But I'm good with

53

faces. Always have been. And then it came to me!' He snaps his fingers. 'Primrose Bowman. Laurel Bowman's sister. You were the Flower Girls.' He looks at her, rubbing his chest. 'I googled it. Found your photograph from when you were little. With your sister. The one they used in all the papers. You were both so famous then, everyone knew your faces.' He shakes his head. 'I can't believe I didn't get it straight away, but . . . well, you're older now, aren't you? Taller. But you still look the same. Your features . . .' He stares at her. 'I'm right, aren't I? You're Primrose Bowman.'

Hazel watches him, silent and pale. After a moment, she nods slowly.

'I knew it!' he exclaims and rocks back on his heels, almost triumphant. They look at each other in the aftermath and Max coughs awkwardly. Now he's got his answer he's nonplussed, not sure what to do with the weight of his satisfaction. The quiet lengthens and stretches its legs inside the room. Hazel lets the silence settle. Her brain is noisy and fast, but she tells it to calm down, to be still. There is a grain of hope here. Somewhere in this hotel, she still has some power.

'So . . .' she begins. 'What are you going to do?'

Max looks confused. 'Do?' he asks. 'About what?'

Again, Hazel feels that familiar buzz of irritation, that people can be so dense. Surely he knows what he has here?

'About Georgie,' she says. 'The police. What are you going to tell them, now that you know?'

A bird squawks hoarsely outside. There is the faint sound of a car engine. Max rubs his hand across the back of his neck, his expression changing from anxious to blank and reverting to worried in a matter of seconds.

Is he getting it now? wonders Hazel. *Is he seeing what he has on his hands?*

'Oh,' Max says, taking a step forward but moving back again swiftly when he sees her turn rigid. 'Oh, God. It wasn't you, was it? With the girl?' A thin layer of sweat shines on his forehead. 'You didn't . . .'

'No!' Hazel cries. 'I didn't mean that! I wouldn't. I haven't. I swear. I don't know where she is. I haven't touched her, I promise you.' She closes her eyes and gathers her thoughts. 'I'm not the guilty one. It wasn't me then and it isn't me now.'

Max's expression is suddenly miserable. 'I haven't thought this through,' he mutters, staring down at the carpet.

'I haven't touched that girl,' Hazel says again, her voice a little firmer. 'But, listen . . . Max, is it? If the police find out who I am . . . God, if the *press* do, if they come here . . .' Her eyes fill with tears as she holds her hands out to him, her smallness, her cropped hair, emphasising how vulnerable she is.

How little she was, back then, thinks Max.

'I'm trapped,' she whispers.

Something in his face changes. 'But you were going to run,' he says as the thought occurs to him. 'You had your suitcase. You wanted to leave.'

'Wouldn't you?' Hazel's voice cracks, a tear rolling down her cheek. 'That policewoman. Hillier. I know she recognises me from somewhere. I just know it. She'll have me arrested before you can even blink. I've seen it before, Max.' And now it's she who steps forward. 'Trial by media. By the public. They've decided you're guilty before you've even said a word. They wanted to bring back the death penalty for us. For me and Laurel.' She swallows, draws her hands together in a prayer. 'I swear to you – on my mother's grave – I haven't harmed that girl. I tried to leave because I'm scared.' She shuts her eyes again. 'You must see that.'

Max is looking at her, trying to take it in, trying to discern what is true.

Hazel takes another step forward. 'I was never tried,' she says. 'I was six years old. Can you imagine? I was only just older than Georgie is now.'

After a small thrust of his neck, Max shakes his head. 'No, I can't,' he answers, his voice cracks a little.

Hazel nods. 'Everything was . . . God, when I think about it. Because of my sister and what she did, we were all so tainted. So damaged by it.' Her voice is rising, emotion catching in her throat. 'We were finished that day. Kirstie was dead,' a sob breaks through, 'and so was I . . . Rosie Bowman. My old life was dead to me.' She takes a jagged breath, pulling herself to her centre before fixing Max with an anguished look. 'Don't make me go through it again, Max. Please. I'm begging you.'

He is silent, thinking. His fingertips tingle at his sides. To be faced by this woman. This *pariah*. At one moment in time, after Princess Diana and Laurel Bowman, she was the third most famous person in the world. He remembers the photographs, the interviews, the screaming crowds outside the courtroom, the desperate tears of Kirstie Swann's parents, the mother with her pregnant belly, staring into the camera with such vacant despair. He thinks about his own beautiful daughters and the girl who is missing. About her mother, weeping upstairs. And the press that will soon descend on the hotel like vultures. The policewoman, Hillier. He thinks of it all as he studies Hazel Archer's face, her beautiful eyes pleading with him, asking him to make her safe.

'It's time to go downstairs,' he says, at last. 'I'm sorry. But we need to tell the police who you are.'

Hazel shakes her head, expelling a long, slow breath. 'Then I'll die,' she says simply.

'Of course you won't,' he answers, firmer now. 'We'll just clear it up, remove the suspicion, and then you can go home. It'll be all right, you'll see. But you must be upfront with the police. It'll only cause you more trouble if you try and leave.'

Hazel isn't answering. Tears are streaming down her cheeks.

'Come on,' Max says, stilted and uncomfortable now that he has brought a woman into his bedroom and made her cry. 'I promise I'll help you. I'm sure that everything will be fine.'

'No, it won't.' Her voice catches, her breathing ragged. 'You don't know what you're doing.'

'I do,' he says resolutely. 'This is the right thing. I'm sure of it.'

'But you don't know about . . . oh, what's the point?' Hazel trails off, exhausted and limp. She sags a little at her knees, as if she might fall to the floor.

'About what?' he asks, moving towards her, suddenly aware of a different kind of fear in her face. 'What is it you're afraid of? Not the press or the police?'

'No, not them.' Hazel's voice trembles. 'It's the other one. The person I don't know . . .'

Max shakes his head, confused. 'What other person?'

Hazel crouches and reaches into her handbag, rummaging until she finds her phone and looks at it for a few seconds, before jerking it towards him. 'I haven't told anyone about this,' she says. 'I didn't know what to do.'

Max takes the phone and stares down at the screen. Then he lifts his eyes to meet Hazel's. 'Who sent this to you?' he asks.

She moves her head from side to side, her face wild and tear-streaked. 'I don't know,' she says. 'I just don't know.'

CHAPTER FOURTEEN

Hillier examines Marek Kaczka as he sits in front of her, his knees pressed tightly together, a lock of dark hair falling into his eyes, the rest of it tied back in a stumpy ponytail. He's in his early twenties, she surmises. He looks at her distrustfully. There is stubble across his cheeks; he has deep brown eyes that undoubtedly some women would consider attractive.

Hillier was given Kaczka's full record this morning and it set her teeth on edge. Two years ago he was brought in for an alleged sexual assault on a minor. He'd become involved with a local girl from Brixham, claiming when reported by her school that he'd believed she was above the age of consent.

In reality, she was only fifteen.

Despite the school's complaint, her parents had done nothing to support it. Three days after her sixteenth birthday the CPS had abandoned the charge for lack of evidence. But infractions such as these are generally only the tip of the iceberg. Hillier has seen the picture of the girl in her school uniform. Kaczka clearly likes young girls.

Just how young remains to be seen.

Hillier is on a ticking clock. It's New Year's Day and Georgie has now been missing for over twelve hours. The Major Investigation Unit and their associated forensic teams will be here within the hour, hampered by the weather and their longer journey from Torquay. But until they arrive, this remains Hillier's case. And she wants it, it's hers. She wants to find Georgie before the case is snatched away from her. She's just hoping that a body isn't going to propel things out of her remit before she can establish a definite suspect.

Marek is nervous, that much is apparent to her, although he is trying to disguise this with an unattractive braggadocio, his shoulders squared and his jaw dropped, mouth open a little.

'Talk me through yesterday afternoon,' she says, pen poised over her notebook. 'You've said you came on shift at one p.m.?'

Marek nods. 'It was going to be a late night with the New Year's party so I was on the afternoon stint.'

'What did you do when you got here?' Hillier barks questions, keeping the momentum up. She wants him uncomfortable, ill at ease.

Marek pushes his hair back from his face and swallows hard. 'I went straight to the kitchen, started peeling the carrots. Karen – the waitress? – she'd been down on the beach earlier and seen a box by the rocks just leading up to the headland. She runs there every day.'

Something in his tone makes Hillier suspect that there is a romantic connection between Marek and this Karen. It nudges him out of focus for a second as a potential paedophile. Just a nudge, but there all the same.

'Inside the box were the kittens. Three of them. They were tied together with string and someone had put rocks in the box. Karen was upset. She, you know, thought someone had been trying to drown them. Then maybe they changed

their mind? Left them there on the beach to starve instead?'
Marek crosses one leg over the other, his nerves dwindling
now that he's talking.

He's voluble, Hillier thinks. Likes the sound of his own
voice. Good. Keep him talking.

'So she brought them up to the hotel,' he continues.
'When I got here and saw them, I knew Chef wouldn't like
it. You can't have animals in a kitchen and she'd put them
right where the cold box is for the veggies. So we decided to
hide the kittens in the storage room where we keep the dry
ingredients, the flour and beans, what have you. I gave them
some milk, untied them, kept them warm.'

'You're a big bloke,' Hillier observes.

'So?'

'So, you don't strike me as a guy who'd go out of his way
to save some cute fluffy animals.'

Marek allows a smile. 'Well, Karen liked them so . . .'

'And you like Karen?'

He shrugs again. 'Yeah. I mean, why not? She's cute. We
get on.'

Hillier nods. 'And then?' she prompts.

'Karen must have told the guests. Or some of them. In
the dining room at lunchtime before she went home and I
got there. Or after, I don't know. She wasn't working that
night.' He sighs. 'I didn't really think about it. I was just
working, getting everything ready for evening prep.'

'Peeling the carrots?'

'That's right, yeah. And then I heard something by the
door. And I turned round, and there she was just standing
there. Georgie.'

'Where was everyone else?'

61

'They were around,' he says. 'It was busy, right? Everyone was running all over the place so they didn't notice her. But I was standing by the swing door where she came in. And I knew immediately I clocked her, I knew why she was there. Chef was down the other end, where the fridges are, and I didn't want him to see her or find out about the cats, so I put my fingers to my lips like this.' And he makes the action.

Something about his finger on his moist, full lips engenders an internal shudder in Hillier.

'And then I pointed to the storage cupboard and beckoned her over. She's sweet, right? She looks like my niece, Alicia.' His eyes dart down to Hillier's chest as if comparing the image of a child with that of a grown woman. His mouth curls.

'So she came into the cupboard and knelt down and started stroking the kittens, playing with them.'

'What time was this?'

'I don't know. Three o'clock, maybe?'

'And how long was she in there?'

'I don't know,' he says again. 'I left her there. Went back to my station. And then, time went on. I finished the carrots. Then I had to do the potatoes for the gratin. So . . . you know, I really don't know how long she was in there for.'

'You must have seen her leave, though?' Hillier asks.

Marek shakes his head and clears his throat. 'I didn't. By the time I got around to thinking about her, it was dark outside. I went to the cupboard to tell her she'd better leave but she was already gone.'

'And you didn't see her go? Didn't notice what the time was then?'

'No. Look, I'm sorry. I was busy. I wasn't watching the clock.'

Can that be true? Hillier thinks. Isn't clock watching a necessary part of working in a kitchen? Planning the service, timing things to perfection? Her instinct is not to believe this.

'And did you see her again?'

'No,' he answers, lowering his eyes, his long eyelashes almost touching his cheeks. 'The poor kid. I don't know where she went after that.'

'You've got form in this area, though, haven't you?'

Marek narrows his eyes. 'What do you mean?'

'You know what I mean, Marek. You like them young, don't you? Girls, I mean.'

'That was totally innocent,' he says, straightening in his chair, anger flashing across his face. Hillier notices his fists, flexing on his thighs. He's strong. 'She told me she was seventeen. She looked like she was in her twenties.'

'Really? Doesn't mention that on the file. She looks positively pre-teen in her school uniform.'

'I never saw her in her uniform,' he snaps. 'And I was never charged. It was a mistake. It's got nothing to do with this. I'm not a fucking paedo.'

Hillier raises her eyebrows.

'I'm not!'

'Maybe,' she says. 'Have you got a girlfriend?'

'Not at the moment, no. Not that it's any of your business.'

Hillier begins shuffling her papers, giving the signal that the interview is over.

'And the kittens?' she says as she gets to her feet.

Marek looks confused. 'The kittens?'

'Where are they now?' Hillier asks, looking down at him. 'Are they still in the cupboard?'

'I don't know,' he answers, bewildered by the sudden turn in the conversation.

'You haven't checked on them since you prepped the dinner service last night?'

'Yes. I mean, no.' His eyebrows are drawn together, as if he's flummoxed by this detail. 'I don't think so. I'm sure Karen has . . . Or somebody else?'

'Karen went home, remember?' Hillier says. 'You told us. And you hid them in the cupboard to keep them a secret. So if you haven't been feeding them since Georgie went to see them,' Hillier's stare is beady now, zoning in on the faint line of sweat dotted along Marek's brow, 'they're going to be pretty hungry, I'd think. Shall we check?' she says brightly, gesturing for him to follow her as she sweeps quickly out of the room.

CHAPTER FIFTEEN

The first email had arrived two months or so before Hazel and Jonny had gone to Balcombe Court. It was a Wednesday morning and Hazel had, as usual, checked her iPhone on the way to work. She'd been walking over Waterloo Bridge, the wind in her face, a bright hazy sun in the sky. Black cabs and red buses lumbered past her, the usually rambunctious *Big Issue* seller on the corner more subdued this morning.

She'd fished her phone out of her handbag as she passed the homeless man, guiltily aware of her salary, her good fortune to be working as a legal secretary in a warm and comfortable office. She'd clicked on her emails, wanting an excuse to look elsewhere.

And then her heart had stopped.

She pulled up immediately on the pavement, causing a commuter behind her to slam into her back, almost sending the phone skittering out of her hand and onto the ground.

'Watch it,' the person had growled before pushing past, tutting at her as they moved away. Hazel barely acknowledged the exchange, her eyes fixed on the screen.

The sender's email address was primrose.bowman@gmail.com.

Her name. Her old name. The sight of those letters, forming those words, the old her, who she used to be . . . it lodged inside her like a knife rammed up to the hilt.

Barely thinking, she opened the email.

I know who you are, Flower Girl.

Hazel's vision swam and she moved over to the parapet of the bridge, taking in big gulps of air, her eyes fixed desperately on the shimmering river.

Who had sent this to her?

Nobody knew she was a so-called Flower Girl. Other than her parents – and her mother was now dead – nobody else knew. No one.

The Bowmans had left Yorkshire the year Laurel had been sentenced. Even before then, they had been living in various hotels under assumed names. When Laurel was arrested, their house had been covered with graffiti, faeces smeared through their letterbox. When she was found guilty, a glass bottle filled with petrol had been smashed against their front door, alight and explosive. Before and during the trial, they had been bombarded with letters and posters. Email was in its infancy and so they were spared aggression online. But after the trial had concluded, the police had advised that it would be better for them to move away and that, just like the reviled Maxine Carr, or James Bulger's murderers, for their own safety, they would be given new identities.

The Houses of Parliament had even approved this with a vote. The Home Office had provided them with a small budget to finance the move and arranged their new identification documents because everyone involved with their case had known that, if they were discovered by the public, they would be harmed.

Laurel had been moved to a secure unit in an undisclosed location immediately after the conclusion of the trial. At first, the Bowmans considered moving down south to be near their daughter. But then Hazel's father had suffered a massive heart attack while packing up their things. His wife Amy had found him an hour later, the radio playing while he lay unconscious on the floor. He had endured a triple bypass and valve replacement, after which time the three of them hadn't seen Laurel for over six weeks.

By the time the identity change was organised and put into place, Amy – stuffed to the gills with antidepressant medication – hadn't visited her eldest daughter for nearly four months. They chose a town between Newcastle and Berwick to be their new home. Far away from London and Yorkshire and all the places where people might remember their faces, remember the crime that had made the family pariahs, they called themselves the Archers. Amy became Louise. Gregor became Duncan.

And Rosie became Hazel.

Provided with the cover of a new job for Gregor, the Archers slowly settled in to their new pace of life. They became members of their little community. They were accepted.

One evening, as she left her room to sit on the stairs, unable to sleep, Hazel had overheard her parents speaking together. She could see them through the half-open door, in front of the sitting-room fire, a television programme playing that neither of them was watching.

'I miss her,' Gregor said softly. 'Amy?' He had turned to look at his wife but she only stared at a patch on the wall. 'Look at me,' he'd persisted. 'She's down there, sleeping God knows where. Locked up all by herself. At the trial – and right after it – I was so caught up in everything. I couldn't believe it. I was angry with her. My girl . . .' He had broken off then, shifting in his chair. 'Now, though, time has passed and . . . I think we need to arrange a visit. Go and see her. We could write to her too. Now things are more settled. Amy?'

'Rosie . . . I mean . . .' Amy jerked her head at the mistake. '*Hazel*, I mean. Hazel's only seven.' Her eyes darted quickly to Gregor. 'She's got a chance to live a normal life. Nobody here need know what happened. Ever.'

Her husband had frowned then, pushing himself forward in his armchair. The flickering firelight revealed his careful expression. 'But what about Laurel?' he asked. 'Won't Hazel want to see her sister?'

'She hasn't mentioned her. Not to me. Has she to you?'

Gregor didn't answer.

'Not once since we came here,' his wife persisted. 'I think . . . I think she's traumatised by it all.'

'So, are you saying that we shouldn't see Laurel again?'

'Not forever.' Amy swallowed with difficulty, as if the words were stones in her mouth. 'Just until Hazel is older. When we've put this behind us a bit more.' She closed her eyes. 'Laurel's got Toby,' she said.

Gregor frowned at the mention of his solicitor brother, who had tried to help Laurel. And who had said things to him in the course of the trial that Gregor would never forget. Or forgive. Things he hadn't told his wife.

'I can't bear to lose you,' she had continued. 'You or her. We've lost so much already. Too much. I can't take any more.' She pressed her lips together, eyes fixed on the fire. 'We need some time to recover. We must feel safe again, Gregor.' She rested her hand on the arm of her chair and Hazel could see from her perch on the stairs that her mother's knuckles were white.

As the fire burnt itself out into embers, Gregor looked at his wife. He wanted to go to her and hold her. Feel her close to him again. Then he wanted to scream at her that this conclusion made his newly patched-up heart break again into a thousand pieces. That his Laurel – whatever the press and the courts and the police had said about her – was his little girl and he loved her with his whole being and that the idea of not seeing her every day, or every week at least, was as soul-destroying to him as the idea that she had taken the life of that baby, Kirstie Swann.

But Amy wasn't close to him any more. She had been far away for a while now. And the truth was, his daughter Laurel too had become something foreign to him, a ghost of her former self, with a vacant space where he had thought he'd known her wholly. That void had been filled in with other ideas, terrible thoughts and images, and, if he were truly honest with himself, he didn't know what was real about his Laurel any more.

And so he had said nothing more to his wife about visiting her, but waited for the fire to burn down and eventually the ashes turned cold and they went up to bed.

And they never saw Laurel again.

They didn't mean it to be the case. But they were so far away from London and their letters were often returned to them unopened. As time went on, the gaps between the impulses to write, to make contact, became longer and longer, until it was a month between them, and then a year. And then it was as though Laurel had died. The town they lived in became insular, comforting to them, it became their world. A world they didn't want to leave; one they were frightened to disturb.

Hazel went to secondary school, then on to college in Edinburgh. She trained as a legal secretary and eventually she moved to London, starting work at the property law firm Peller and Gerrard where she had now been employed for eight years. And in all this time, she had told no one of her past, of who she really is.

Her mother had died three years ago. Hazel couldn't talk about it, didn't want to think about it. Her mother's death had been so searing, it felt as if a layer of skin had been removed. Since then, her father had diminished. He had his few new friends in his new home and that was all he needed. Hazel spoke to him once a week. But she was essentially alone, with no one to confide in, no one she could trust.

Until Jonny had come into her life.

What happened in the past – with Kirstie and with Laurel – remains alive inside Hazel all the time. It never leaves her, like the daemons she's read about, those shadows that follow people, sit on their shoulders, ever-present. But she blocks it, tries not to think about it, because to unpeel the layers of onion skin she has carefully pasted over the past would lead to more than tears. Kirstie's face was carved from Medusa's image and Hazel has already turned to stone. To gaze directly upon what happened to the toddler on that day might fracture that shell, it might cause feelings to leak through her like blood warming in her veins. And, deep down, she is frightened by that thought.

She has got used to it now, over the nineteen years it's been with her. She bears it like a disability, something she is always aware of, but can live with. She just needs to be careful of it, protect it from public consumption.

She forces out thoughts about Laurel too. She can't think about her sister. She is something like a shadow on a negative. She exists but she has no substance. She flits through Hazel's head intermittently: on a cold walk home, after a few glasses of wine, when she pictures a little girl with her hair in bunches on a beach or on the carpet in their tiny pink bedroom.

But Laurel Bowman is gone. She has been erased from Hazel's life like the deleting of a film, along with all those images of that day, down by the disused canal. It is as if she and the younger Rosie never existed.

Except that someone else knew that Hazel was Laurel's sister.

Someone else knew that Hazel was one of the Flower Girls.

CHAPTER SIXTEEN

'I need to see Jonny,' Hazel says to Max. 'I don't know where he is. He must be with Evie somewhere . . .' She stares around the bedroom as if he might materialise in front of her.

'Does he know?' Max asks. 'Does he know who you really are?'

Hazel nods, looking down at the photo on the phone she is clutching in her hand. It's a shot of her and Jonny taken on Waterloo Bridge at sunset, the Houses of Parliament in the background. They'd taken the selfie on their six-month anniversary after dinner at the Oxo Tower. They'd had scallops and steak and gallons of red wine, and on the walk over the bridge, back to Hazel's flat, Jonny had made them stop. They'd leaned over the parapet, looking down into the water, a late-evening water taxi passing under the bridge. And, for the first time, he'd said he loved her.

'He's known for a while. Since not long after we got together,' she murmurs. 'But not Evie. It never seemed the right time to say anything. It's hard enough for me getting to know her without . . . that.'

Max bites his lip. 'It must be difficult,' he says, crinkling his brow at the scale of the understatement.

Hazel closes her eyes, thinking back to when she had first met Jonny in a bar next to Waterloo station. At that stage she would never have dreamt of telling him. Even later, when they'd been seeing each other for a few months, had slept together, knew each other's favourite films, had had their first argument. Even then, she hadn't told him.

But that night on the bridge, when he'd said those three words, which were a game changer, a world turner – because she felt the same way – then she knew she had to tell him. She hadn't planned it, had never considered it would be possible to tell anyone, ever. How could she even begin to put into words something she had never dared speak of to anyone before? To reveal that Hazel Archer was, in fact, Rosie Bowman. One of those names in the public psyche that is never forgotten. Like Dennis Nilsen. Fred West. Myra Hindley.

But staring down at the water flowing beneath the bridge, she knew that she had to do it. That, without her sharing the truth with Jonny, they would have no future together. They would have nothing.

She suggested moving on to a bar and they went to some tiny, intimate place. Jonny was still buzzing from his declaration; Hazel was quiet, withdrawn. They sat at a small table with a candle stuck in a wine bottle, wax dripping over the neck. It was so dark they could barely see anyone else. There was no reception so Jonny, for once, could resist the urge to look at his iPhone. He wasn't an idiot. He knew something was up with Hazel and she knew that he was worrying that she had closed off because of what he'd said, that he'd been too forward, scared her away.

She'd taken his hands over the table, their glasses full and both of them more than a little drunk. He'd looked at her and she'd felt the muscles in her face contract as if she couldn't keep her desire for him hidden.

'I have something to tell you,' she'd said. 'Something difficult. And, well, something I've never told anyone before.'

He'd smiled uncertainly at her then, wanting to be reassured. 'What is it?'

Hazel shook her head and looked down at her hands on top of the table. At the pink nails she had so carefully polished before she had come out that night. Her heart thumped inside her chest. Was she really going to do this?

'Do you remember the Flower Girls?' she asked him at last.

He nodded, confused.

'The older one, Laurel Bowman,' she had said. 'She went to prison. Still is in prison, in fact. Do you remember what happened?'

'She killed a toddler, didn't she? Years ago. Down by some canal up north. With her sister. Although,' he frowned, stopping his glass in mid-air, halfway to his mouth, 'the younger one didn't get done for it, I seem to remember.'

'No. She was too young. She was six, which is under the legal age of criminal responsibility,' Hazel said then. 'And, also, she was innocent. She hadn't hurt the little girl. It was her sister who did.'

Jonny drank from his glass. 'All right. And? What about it?'

Hazel scored a line in the wood grain with her index fingernail. 'The older girl – Laurel,' she said. 'She's my sister.'

Jonny looked at her. 'What?'

'Laurel Bowman is my sister.'

He frowned. 'Your sister? But . . . but that would mean . . . ?'

'Yes,' Hazel had said, forcing herself to meet his gaze. 'I am Primrose. Rosie Bowman. I was the six year old. I was the other Flower Girl.'

She stared into his eyes and suddenly he seemed far away, as if he had retreated somewhere very cold and impossible to reach.

'But I was innocent,' she made herself continue, although now it was hard to speak for the lump forming in her throat. She carried on digging her nail into the wood until a splinter pierced her skin. 'I'm not who they said I was in the papers. I didn't do anything to hurt that child. I've lived for years with the secret. Alone. But I'm a good person. I haven't done anything wrong. It's just that . . . you told me you loved me tonight. And if you do – if you really do – then you have to know this about me. We can't have any secrets. Nothing can come between us. Nothing. So I'm telling you.' She wiped away the tears that had spilled from her eyes. 'And I just hope that you can accept it. And believe me when I tell you that I'm good. I'm a good person. I really am.'

He had looked at her for a long time, after she'd said all of this. He'd looked at her and then he'd got up from their table and walked off, into the dark of the bar, where she couldn't see him. She waited there for five, ten, fifteen minutes but he didn't come back. She couldn't think clearly. Every coherent thought she'd ever had seemed to be beyond her, out of reach. She watched her tears fall onto the table and, eventually, she had picked the splinter out from her finger. Taking a deep, shaky breath, she got up and went to the toilets, calling Jonny's name into the Gents. There was no reply. That's it, she had thought. He's gone. She returned to the bar and paid their bill and made her way up the stairs where she found him outside on the pavement, smoking a cigarette, although, as far as Hazel knew, he hadn't smoked in fifteen years.

'I'm so sorry,' she had said. 'I completely understand if you want to go. If you never want to see me again.'

Jonny had looked at her, the cigarette dangling from his fingers, his breath frozen in the cold night air. He said nothing for a while and then threw the cigarette onto the ground, mashing it out with his foot.

'You know, I always thought I'd recognised you. You seemed so familiar to me. But,' he gave a bitter laugh, 'I put it down to how I felt about you. That we were meant to be together.' He pushed a hand through his hair, thinking. 'Was it you?' he asked at last. He looked at her intently, stuffed his hands into his pockets.

'Did I kill her, do you mean?' Hazel answered, her voice soft. This was the nub of it. Their relationship stood or fell by this question.

Jonny nodded, his eyes filled with something she couldn't quite identify. She could see the pulse jumping in his neck, imagine the banging of his chest where his heart thumped beneath.

'Would it matter if I had?' she had asked. 'Because I was there. So . . .' Her tone was shaded with the weary acknowledgement of someone who has conducted this conversation many, many times before in their head. When she had dreamt of meeting someone she actually wanted to spend her life with – and who wanted to be with her, even though she knew they could never accept everything that she was. 'I wasn't legally able to stand trial. I was only six. Besides, I've never been able to remember what happened that day.'

They were silent for a moment and for once London was quiet. The cars and the cabs and the buses seemed a universe away from them. The sounds they made were oddly distant, on another planet. There were just the two of them, looking at each other, wondering what the truth of all this was.

'I need you to say it because it does matter,' he said. 'In so many ways, it matters.'

Hazel had nodded in a long moment of realisation and relief. It felt like the buzz of drinking chilled wine on a summer's evening. She smiled at Jonny and held out her hands. 'If you can believe me,' she had said, 'then I can tell you, right here and now, that I didn't do it.'

He looked at her, his pupils filled with what seemed to be a kind of longing.

'I didn't,' Hazel went on. 'I was a child. I followed my big sister and I was led by her. When things turned out . . . the way they did, I didn't know what was going on. I was so affected by it that I blocked it out. I still don't remember anything about that afternoon. But I do know this.' And here she grabbed his hands tight, pulling him to her. 'I know,' she said with perfect conviction, as if delivering a speech, 'I *know* that I did not hurt that baby. I wouldn't, I couldn't. I would not have been able to sleep since then if I had done such a thing. Of course, the public believe differently and that's why I've lived the life I have, why I've got a different name. And no one knows about this. Apart from you.' She stared up at him. 'Nobody. I haven't told anyone else this, ever. But when you said what you did tonight, it was amazing.' Hazel's eyes shone. 'And I feel the same way, Jonny. So I thought it was right that you should know.'

She stopped talking then, searching his face for some kind of sign that he was hearing her, that he understood.

'But I'll understand – really I will – if you want to end it.' She had waited, every muscle taut, breathless.

And then a cab pulled up, its yellow light shining in the gloom.

'Take the cab,' she'd said, absorbing the hit. *That's it. He's gone,* she thought again. *He can't be with me after this.* What she had always expected had come to pass. She would be left alone. Maybe that was OK. She would go home on her own in another cab. Listen to music. Drink some more wine. And tomorrow she'd wake up, free from hope at least. Because to hope is to expect. And she couldn't live like that any more.

And that was when he took her hand. They climbed into the back of the cab together and Jonny put his arm around her, and Hazel had never felt so safe and loved as she did at that moment.

'Shall we get him then?' asks Max in the hotel room, where they remain on opposite sides of it. 'Your husband Jonny?'

'He's not my husband,' Hazel answers. 'He was at breakfast with Evie. I don't know where he is now.' She closes her eyes and runs her hand through her hair. 'This is a nightmare.'

'Let's go downstairs and find him,' Max says, moving towards the door where Hazel is standing. 'It's not a nightmare.' He stops in front of her. 'We just need to sort it out.'

'But what about the emails?' she asks, stepping sideways to allow him to approach the door. 'You've seen them now. Emails from someone – maybe more than one person? – pretending to be Rosie Bowman. They've sent me dead flowers. Unsigned cards. They know where I live. I don't know who is watching me, following me, or what they want. It's terrifying.'

'Well . . .' He stops with one hand on the door handle. 'I don't know about that. My feeling is that it's separate from what's going on here. But I think if we just sit down with the police, and tell them who you are, you'll be much more at ease. It all needs to come out in the open. Listen, Hazel.' Max reaches out for her and she shrinks back. 'Sorry – I'm sorry. But hiding yourself away like this isn't going to help. Anonymous people emailing you from an account called Primrose Bowman is horrific. It needs to stop. We need to bring in the authorities. I really mean it. Then you might get some peace.'

He's looking at her so earnestly that she can't help herself. She feels a spasm of optimism that, somehow, everything might still be all right.

'Do you really think so?' she asks.

'I do,' he says, and turns the handle, opening the door onto the bright lights of the corridor, trying to ignore the hammering in his head, the adrenaline coursing through him, the terrible, delicious thought that has only just occurred to him.

That now he is going to be famous.

CHAPTER SEVENTEEN

Hillier and Marek stand in the doorway and look at the empty box in the pantry. She has forbidden them to enter, not wanting to disturb any forensic evidence that may be present. Nevertheless, they can see the entirety of the space. The walls are stacked with packets and cans; long rows of silver canisters are labelled things like *Molasses*, *Mustard Powder* and *Bicarbonate of Soda*. The smell is pungent, a mix of spices and dust and paper gone soft and curled with age. Level with Hillier's shoulder, a weevil moves lethargically along a metal shelf. Underlying the converging aromas is the distinctive reek of urine.

'They must have escaped.' Marek gestures to where the door is propped open and the kitchen beyond. 'Run out of here, gone outside somewhere.'

'It certainly seems that way,' Hillier says, folding her arms. She's known the kittens aren't here since the search of the hotel last night. But she'd wanted to study Kaczka's reaction to what could, in all probability, be the scene of a murder. She is already envisaging the forensics team, who will be here soon, swabbing for DNA, using their ultra-violet lights to detect blood spatter. Now she shifts her gaze from the abandoned box to the narrow corridor that runs between the counters and work surfaces in the kitchen.

'Where's the door to the outside?' she asks.

Marek backs out from the doorway immediately, relieved to escape the sight and aroma of the cramped pantry, the proximity to Hillier. 'There.' He points away from the cupboard, to the other end of the gleaming stainless-steel range of kitchen equipment, to a door with an exit sign displayed on it. Above it is a large clock with Roman numerals. Hiller looks at the time and then down at her own wristwatch, noticing that the kitchen clock is slow by about half an hour.

'And the only other way out is . . . ?' she goes on without mentioning the clock.

'Through into the restaurant,' he answers, gesturing behind her to the pass, a brightly lit counter, beyond which she can see the white tablecloths of the hotel dining room.

'When Georgie left the pantry, she would have had either to walk through the kitchen – where presumably there were a lot of you preparing for dinner – or, more likely, leave by this route,' Hillier points to the pass, 'and then out through the restaurant.'

She walks that way herself, her lips moving as she does, as if she's describing the movements of the five year old. She leaves the kitchen for the cool empty space of the dining room, recently vacated after breakfast. There are two doors here: one into the hotel's interior; the other leading outside, where diners not resident in the hotel have to access the restaurant.

Marek shuffles nervously beside her, reflexively lifting his index and middle fingers to his lips in a way that makes Hillier understand he is in need of a cigarette. She can smell his body odour, the bitter aroma of adrenaline. Outside, there is the distinctive buzz of a helicopter moving

81

above them as the search for Georgie continues along the coast. Hillier's phone pings loudly and she frowns at the message.

'Can I go now, please?' Marek says, his face sulky like a child's. 'I'm dying for a fag.'

As Hillier considers this, there is a knock at the restaurant doorway, a timid sliding of knuckles on wood. She looks up sharply to see Max Saunders – the writer, as she remembers it – and Hazel Archer standing in the gloom.

'Excuse me,' Max says. 'We don't want to disturb —'

'Yes?' Hillier replies as Marek edges away from her, back towards the kitchen.

'We wondered if we could have a quick word?' Max asks. He is dressed comfortably, in cords and a fawn-coloured woollen jumper. Hazel's face is drawn, very tight and still, Hillier observes. Her hair is brushed neatly away from her face. She wears no make-up and her dark eyes are wary, unable to meet Hillier's for long. She reminds the policewoman of a woodland animal, seconds away from darting into the trees. And still that strange sense of familiarity niggles at Hillier.

What are they doing together? she wonders. *What am I about to hear?*

'Off you go then, Mr Kaczka,' she says to the already disappearing Marek. 'Don't go anywhere too hard to find.' She looks back at the odd couple in the doorway and beckons them in, turning to sit at one of the tables in the middle of the dining room. The room feels cold, the whiteness of the tables emphasising the lack of heat in the dark inglenook fireplace. Thin glass vases on the tables are empty and the impression is one of vacancy, of absence.

'Have a seat,' Hillier says, her voice cutting through the blankness as she moves the silver cutlery away from under her elbows. 'What can I do for you?'

They approach quietly and Max pulls a chair out for Hazel before sitting down himself. He looks across at her but she says nothing, staring down into her lap. 'Hazel?' he says at last. 'Tell DC Hillier what you told me.' He speaks as if to a child, his tone kind but firm.

Hillier feels her heart begin to thump in her chest. She places her fingertips carefully on the linen tablecloth. She looks at Hazel, who still is unable to meet her gaze. 'What is it?' Hillier asks softly. 'What is it you want to say?'

Hazel's hands are tangled together in front of her on the table. She lifts her eyes. And then she begins to speak.

CHAPTER EIGHTEEN

'It isn't me,' Hazel blurts, her cheeks flaming under Hillier's gaze. 'I don't know what happened to the little girl but it wasn't anything to do with me, I swear it. You have to believe me.'

Max is nodding next to her, his breathing calm and unhurried. Unconsciously, Hillier adopts the same rhythm for her own breath – in and out – keeping it steady, keeping everything wrapped up tightly, under control. A helicopter still cleaves through the sky above them, its juddering sound weaving around the room, growing louder, then quieter, as it pitches nearer then heads out again to sea. In the back of her mind, Hillier hopes that, as agreed, Ellis is down on the beach liaising with the coastguard. She knows that uniformed police are standing outside the hotel, forming a barrier against the few cars that have managed to get themselves up the snow-covered roads, cars packed with the sharp eyes and eager cameras of local and tabloid journalists.

She can sense Hazel's fear. Her checks on the woman's name on the Police National Computer this morning yielded no results, but still, thoughts of Hazel and Marek circle inside her head like basking sharks. She is certain that one or other of them is connected in some way with the missing girl's disappearance.

'Hazel,' she says smoothly. 'Why are you telling me that you have nothing to do with what has happened to Georgie? Why would you think that you are suspected of being involved?'

Hazel hesitates as the chasm of the words she is about to speak yawns before her feet. She swallows and steps over the edge. 'My name is Hazel Archer,' she says. 'But when I was a child ... when I was six years old ...' She pauses and briefly closes her eyes. 'My name was Primrose Bowman. Rosie Bowman.' She opens her eyes and finally meets Hillier's stare.

Hillier can't help herself. She recoils.

Primrose Bowman. The Flower Girls.

Looking at Hazel is like staring into the eyes of a person you have thought and talked about for months of your life, without ever really knowing them. But she feels now as if she does, considers that she understands everything about her. For so long she has debated this woman with her colleagues on the force, with her family; analysed the case on criminology courses she's taken. She shed tears for Kirstie Swann when her body was discovered, eventually scooped up from the damp ground, abused beyond anything that any living person would ever want to imagine happening to such a small and innocent being.

Primrose and Laurel. Laurel and Primrose.

Those names. So beautiful and yet so vile. So steeped in the evil that had made them who they were. They looked so normal. They had come from such a nice family, their parents as shocked as the rest of the world at the depravity bubbling up from their gene pool.

Evil.

Hillier had used that word only once or twice in her career. Of Hindley and Brady perhaps. Levi Bellfield. And the Flower Girls. Laurel and Rosie Bowman. She had used the word evil about them, and she had meant it.

Hillier rouses herself, conscious that she has said nothing since Hazel's admission, aware that her mouth is open a little, her lips dry with disbelief.

But there it is.

This is why Hazel's face provoked a sense of déjà vu. Because she *has* seen her before. The photographs of the Flower Girls were pasted all over newspapers both national and international when the body of Kirstie Swann was found. They were the most famous faces in Britain, and across the world. Laurel, with her direct stare into the camera, forthright, unashamed, defiant. And Rosie, her eyes dipped downwards, her lips pursed, her brown hair capped tight around her face. Both of them looked tiny, so incongruously small and vulnerable in the midst of such horror. Those faces, put in the mix with words like *murder* and *abuse* and *torture*. Hillier remembers feeling it at the time; the very core of it all was so wrong, it didn't make any sense.

'I see,' she says eventually. She looks down briefly at her hands on the tablecloth, at her mother's antique ring on her engagement finger. She clears her throat, her mind buzzing. Wonders how on earth to play this, because nothing in her experience has given her any clue as to how to handle such a situation. She looks over at Max, reaching out for something to prop her up for a moment. 'And you, sir. Mr Saunders, is it?'

Max nods again, his presence oddly reassuring in this cold room. His bulk seems warm, his pallor pink and comforting next to Hazel's icy sheen.

'Do you know Ms Archer?'

'Well, I knew I recognised her from *somewhere*. She's older, though. Obviously. And unless you have the association in your mind, it doesn't immediately ring a bell . . . But then, it came to me suddenly, after breakfast. I found the old photographs online, looked at all the articles again. And, of course, there's also been all that fuss recently in the papers about Laurel Bowman's upcoming parole application. Faces change but . . .' He gestures towards Hazel. 'Once you realise, you can see.'

Hillier glances again at Hazel and knows he is right. The image of that six-year-old girl morphs over Hazel's face and Hillier sees her as the child she was. There had only ever been one photograph of Rosie Bowman and then, because of her age and the fact that she would not be standing trial, the courts had banned any further identification of her. All the world really knew of the two sisters were the court sketches of Laurel, along with her mug shot, and the one photograph of Rosie they'd been given of her in school uniform.

'I went to find her,' Max continues, 'and she was terribly upset. Worried, as I'm sure you can imagine, DC Hillier, that she will be considered the prime suspect in the situation we find ourselves in here.' Max's voice is rich with rationale, with logic and compassion.

Hillier puts her head on one side, considering this. 'You have proof of your real identity, I suppose?' she asks Hazel, the thought coming to her that she'd better check she's not just dealing with an utter loon, an attention-seeking crazy.

'Yes,' Hazel answers, her tone meek. 'And Jonny . . .' She stares around the room as if she can magic him here.

'My partner. I don't know where he is. But you can ask him. He knows.' A tear rolls slowly down her left cheek. 'He's the only one who does. Apart from my father.' She lifts her head at that, an appalled expression on her face. 'We won't have to involve him, will we? Please, no. He's old now. He's been through so much. I don't want him to know about any of this . . .'

Hillier rubs her nose with her hand. 'Let's take this one step at a time, shall we?' She glances over at the window, at the clear white light outside where a cloud of steam is escaping from pipes snaking out from the kitchen. 'So, from what you said yesterday, you were with your partner all evening, at the time Georgie went missing. With the girl – Evie? She's your . . . partner's daughter?'

'Yes. We all went down to the beach in the afternoon. Jonny used to come here as a kid for his summer holidays. He wanted to show me the coast. Then we hiked back up to the hotel and Evie went to her room while we had tea in the bar. It was cold, we were wet through from the rain. Afterwards we went upstairs to change for dinner. It was my birthday yesterday.' She bites her lip. 'It was supposed to be a celebration.'

Hazel looks over at Max as she speaks and Hillier is suddenly reminded that he is still in the room.

'Mr Saunders, thank you so much for instigating this meeting,' she says, getting to her feet. 'But perhaps you could leave us to it now?'

Max reluctantly rises, desperate to hear more but realising that his time on the frontline, at least for the moment, is up. He leaves after touching Hazel gently on the shoulder and giving her a weak smile, which she barely returns.

'It's just not fair. Any of this,' Hazel says bitterly after he has left the room. 'I'm not that child any more, if I ever was. I'm an adult. I've lived a life since then. I'm not my sister, Detective. I'm not her.'

Hillier trains her mind back to 1997, when the Flower Girls were arrested. Laurel, certainly, was charged and tried. But why wasn't Rosie? She frowns, trying to remember. Something about her age. That the younger sister couldn't legally be held responsible. She studies Hazel who has sunk into her seat, concave with despair. A seagull squawks outside one of the restaurant windows and it brings Hillier back to the present.

'But you were there, weren't you?' she says. 'Even if you weren't put on trial. You were there when Kirstie Swann was brutally murdered.' Hillier leans back in her chair and considers the woman before her, wilted, soft, as if you could put your hand right through her, into her, and you wouldn't feel a thing.

'So you tell me, Hazel,' she says. 'Tell me why I shouldn't think you're the most likely person to be involved with the disappearance of Georgie Greenstreet?'

CHAPTER NINETEEN

'Welcome back to *The Daily Talk Show* with Jeremy Williams. Today we're having our annual – and, traditionally, rather contentious – New Year's debate. This time we're talking about justice, about sentencing, and about the application by notorious Flower Girl Laurel Bowman to challenge the recent decision of the parole board to keep her incarcerated. This is, I believe, the third application of hers to be released, which has – like the two previous – been denied.

'She has never explained her actions at the time of Kirstie Swann's murder. She has always remained silent as to what actually happened on that day. Nothing about this application will be of any comfort to Kirstie's parents, Debbie and Rob, I'm sure. But what it *does* do is raise the possibility that – perhaps – Laurel Bowman has served her time and should be set free.

'With me in the studio is Joanna Denton from the non-governmental organisation Bang to Rights and full-time campaigner for *Justice for Kirstie*. As Debbie Swann's sister, Joanna was also, tragically, the aunt of little Kirstie.

'Joanna, firstly, I must ask how you and the family have coped over the years with the impact of this terrible crime? How does your sister Debbie carry on, day after day? And particularly given all of the media interest in Laurel Bowman and the Flower Girls.'

'Thanks, Jeremy. And thank you for having me on the show. I want to say that Debbie is an incredibly strong woman. She's had to be. Everyone in our family – including and especially her – has learnt that the only way we will get justice for Kirstie is – not to forget our emotions, we could never do that – but to put them to one side, so that we can fight for our daughter and niece and ensure that Laurel Bowman can never prey on anyone else.'

'I see. And so what is your view on this argument on Laurel Bowman's behalf that the parole board are wrong to deny her release and an eighteen-year prison term is more than enough to have served? Particularly given that Laurel was only ten years old when she was first sent to prison. Isn't that enough?'

'No.' Joanna is adamant. 'It's not. Laurel Bowman is a murderer, and a person who takes the life of another human being should have to live out the rest of her days in prison. If you consider other child murderers with the same profile – Ian Brady, Ian Huntley, Myra Hindley – these individuals were all given life sentences that actually meant *life*. Why should Laurel Bowman be any different just because she was a child when she was convicted? Debbie and Rob are the ones who are serving the true life sentence. They have to live every day for the rest of their lives with the fact that their daughter was taken from them in the most horrific and brutal way. *That's* a life sentence. If Laurel Bowman is released now, it would be a joke.'

'I see your point,' Jeremy counters into the microphone. 'But some would say that when the crime was committed, Laurel's life effectively ended at that point. She's had her freedom curtailed for eighteen years. Isn't it preferable for society that she now contributes to it? That she's rehabilitated and joins us as a better person, rather than draining our taxes. What purpose does it serve, locking her up for the rest of her life?'

'She's not rehabilitated,' Joanna points out sharply. 'She's been refused parole on her last three applications. She gets into fights, she's aggressive. She's beyond the pale, Jeremy. She's never apologised, much less admitted what she's done. And, frankly, I don't want a person like that walking down my local high street. I'd rather keep her where I know she can't hurt innocent people, in a place where she can be controlled.'

'OK, some strong points there. Thanks, Joanna. Obviously a tough issue. So, we're going to open this up to the phone lines. And I've got Derek from Sanderstead on the phone. Derek, what's your view on all of this?'

'Hi, Jeremy. Well, I think she should have been hung from the start.'

Jeremy raises his eyebrows at Joanna, who remains impassive. 'You'd have had Laurel Bowman hanged at ten years old?' he says.

'No,' Derek says. 'I'd have had her in prison and then hanged when she was old enough to understand properly what she'd done.'

'Thanks, Derek. Joanna, do you agree with that? Is the death penalty the only appropriate punishment for crimes of this kind?'

'I'm not going to discuss that here, Jeremy. A debate on the death penalty is a matter for a different forum. I'm here to talk specifically about Laurel Bowman and whether the time she serves in prison can ever make up for the terrible murder she committed.'

'OK. But it's obviously an emotive subject. Crimes involving children tug at our very heartstrings. Do you think that that should necessarily affect our attitudes to punishment and the rational way in which we deal with criminals and their crimes?'

'Again, Jeremy, I'm not here to discuss crime and punishment in general. It is my view, and that of many, *many* other people, that Laurel Bowman has not been adequately punished for her culpability in Kirstie's *brutal* murder. My niece was two years old. Kirstie didn't get to live her life because of Laurel. She was horribly abused by her. She suffered beyond anything we can imagine. To put the perpetrator of that horror in a comfortable environment where she is cosseted, given a television, an iPad, an education, a swimming pool . . . All of those opportunities were denied to Kirstie. She is dead. Taken from all of us before she could live her life.'

'So what *would* be the appropriate punishment then? Let's move back to the phones. And I've got Carol from Leeds on the line. Carol, what's your view on what Joanna is saying? Do you agree that Laurel Bowman has been punished adequately?'

'No, I don't, Jeremy. I lived in Grassington when poor little Kirstie was killed and I can tell you that we will never forget it. We were there, Joanna. I don't know if you remember us? But I was so sorry for you all. We will never forget that poor lass or Debbie and Rob. We pray for them every day.

'The Bowman girl is evil. She is wicked and vile and she should never be allowed to leave prison. What she did to that poor little child . . . I can't even bear to think about it. We hunted for Kirstie when she went missing, the whole town did. We were out until midnight that night. It was heart-breaking. And to think that Laurel Bowman will be out and allowed to go and live amongst us makes my heart grow cold, it really does. I don't care what some stupid people say about it. She is wicked through and through and I agree with your last caller. She should have been hanged.'

'Thanks, Carol. Obviously you feel very passionately about this. So you were there when Kirstie went missing? What was that like? It must have been dreadful.'

'Oh, it was, Jeremy. At first, we just thought she'd wandered off, you know. Maybe tripped over. Fallen asleep and woken up in the dark and couldn't find her way home. But then time went on and you started to think, well, it doesn't look good. It's probably some paedo or weirdo. I couldn't bear to think about it too much myself. But then . . .'

'Joanna, you're nodding at this. Do you want to jump in?'

'Yes . . . hello, Carol. The reason we all feel so strongly about this is that Kirstie wasn't taken by a weirdo, as you put it. She wasn't taken by a sad old man. She was taken by a child. A *child*.' Joanna pauses briefly. 'And what makes a child do that? Lure a toddler away from her mother, lead her away, keep her hidden for hours and then subject her to systematic beating . . . lacerations . . . torture. The pathologist had to use Kirstie's dental records to identify her, she had been beaten so badly. What does it take for a ten year old to do that? What does it take?'

'Evil,' Carol says. 'Pure evil.'

CHAPTER TWENTY

The red bricks of the prison always make Toby Bowman think of a 1980s office block. He parks a few streets away and approaches it through a light drizzle, the January weather doing nothing to dispel the month's miserable reputation.

The reception area is always uncomfortably hot and, knowing this from experience, Toby removes his jacket to sit and wait in shirtsleeves with a stack of the files he invariably brings to read, using the time he will sit in this room waiting for Laurel as usefully as he can.

On New Year's Day the wait is unusually quick. Normally Toby wouldn't be given permission to visit on a public holiday but he has been granted special dispensation due to his client's upcoming court hearing. The air is stultified, thick with resentment, but the waiting area is unnaturally calm. Usually the room is packed with scowling inhabitants, slumping in their chairs, bulging plastic bags at their feet. Today, though, the grinding of the vending machine's organs slams loudly into the quiet, normally filled with the low hum of chatter, of noses being blown, of children whingeing that they are bored.

Toby tries to concentrate on the papers he has received from Laurel Bowman's barrister concerning her recent challenge to the parole board. He reads rapidly, the papers resting on his – as he would admit – rounded stomach. He has dark half-moons of sweat under his armpits and his pate is shiny with moisture. His stomach rumbles but he refuses to buy a chocolate bar, forcing his brain to focus on the legal arguments in front of him, knowing that he has to lose two stone before his prostate can be operated on. So successful is his mindfulness that the guard has to call his name twice before he lifts his head.

Quickly he gathers his papers, stuffing them into his satchel, and moves to the other side of the room where the security barrier stands like castle gates. He leaves his bag and jacket in a locker, placing his watch in a plastic tray, walking through the scanner without issue. The guard is sour-faced, ushering him through without recognition, despite the fact that Toby has come here pretty much every month for the last ten years. Then again, once people know he represents Laurel, he is generally given a cold shoulder, if not outright abuse. Toby proceeds through three sets of doors and into a musty white corridor, which seems to stretch to eternity. Halfway down is a framed poster of a sunset over water with the words *Believe you can and you're halfway there*. Every time he visits, Toby wonders why the powers that be believe a motivational quote from Theodore Roosevelt will have any influence on the prisoners. He doubts they have ever heard of him and, even if they have, the fatuousness of the statement always drains a little more hope from Toby's well.

He waits for a buzzer to sound before the gunmetal-coloured door in front of him clicks open. He walks into a long narrow room filled with lines of small tables, a single chair to either side. Laurel is already at a table, waiting with her legs apart, her tattooed arms folded across her chest. As he walks over to her, a smile fixed on his face, he wonders, once again, whether she has the strength to survive what she is about to go through with this application.

Laurel looks ghostly, dark shadows under her chocolate-brown eyes. Her blonde hair is scraped back into a tight knot on the top of her head. There are nicotine stains on her fingers, her eyes like a rifle trained on her lawyer.

'All right, Toby?' she says, leaning back in her chair, a grim smile on her face. She plays with an unlit cigarette in her fingers. Smoking is only allowed in the cells and the exercise yards. 'Shit, isn't it?' Laurel says, looking down at the fag. 'This is just when I want one the most. When I'm talking to you. Could pretend we were in a pub or something then,' she snorts. ''Bout as close as I'll ever get to one, of course.'

Toby nods, settling himself into his seat. He doesn't mention that smoking was outlawed in pubs ten years into Laurel's sentence. 'Happy New Year. How are you, L?'

'Yeah, Happy New Year. Good one.' She looks up at him from underneath her eyebrows. 'I'm all right. Missing my four-poster bed as always.'

'I came last month, did they tell you? For Christmas. But you were denied privileges, they said. What happened?'

Laurel shrugs. 'New girl on the block racked me up so they put me on basic.'

'But they told me you were segregated?' Toby says. 'Not just confined to your cell.'

Laurel looks down at the cigarette and twirls it between her third and fourth fingers. She is thin – too thin – Toby thinks, and he has a dull sensation that he knows what she is not telling him. He bites his lip and leans forward.

'L, look,' he says. But she doesn't, her gaze is fixed downwards. 'You've got to start helping yourself. If you keep getting into fights, it gets harder and harder for me to help you. Every time we make representations to the parole board, they just point to a long list of infractions and tell me that you're still violent, you're aggressive, you remain a risk.'

'Well, maybe I am,' Laurel says, her mouth a stubborn line.

'You're not,' Toby sighs. 'And it's no use to anyone if you act like a sulky child. Is it, Lulu?'

Laurel's lips twitch at that.

'You're a bright young girl with a great deal to give,' he says. 'And I want to help you. It's not right that you're here. Stuck in this place.' He scratches the back of his neck, aware of his body odour, his hunger and increasing frustration. God, he hates prison. 'Have you started up the GCSE course again?'

Laurel nods. 'I'm a couple of weeks out because of . . . you know, the basic. But I'll make it up. I'm sorry, Uncle Toby.' She looks at him and her eyes soften, losing the brittle glare that normally shields her from friendship, from any attempt to bring her on side.

'I want the world to see what I see, Lulu,' Toby says. 'I really do. We are appealing the parole board's decision, as you know. And I think, this time, we've got good grounds for gaining permission for judicial review. It's not just a shot in the dark. But a lot of people are still angry about the past.' He shakes his head. 'You should have heard Debbie Swann's sister – that Joanna Denton from Bang to Rights – on the radio this morning. The woman is sadly deranged . . . But, look. You've got to work with me.

Everything we're trying to do will mean nothing if you're acting up the whole time.

'We've got to think about the next few weeks. The application for review. If the court grants us permission, we'll have an oral hearing. We can bring in evidence then that proves you're not such a risk as everyone keeps making out. You want that, don't you?'

Laurel sighs, putting the unlit cigarette in her mouth. 'What's the point? No one's going to believe me anyway. They want me in here forever.'

'I could lie. I could say no, but you know the truth as well as I do.' He leans back. 'But it's worth the fight, isn't it, L? Worth fighting for your freedom?'

Laurel looks at him for a long moment. 'Depends whether you think I deserve it or not, doesn't it?'

CHAPTER TWENTY-ONE

Wailing pierces the quiet of the hotel restaurant where Hillier and Hazel remain sitting opposite each other. A primeval sound that seems so animalistic it can only have originated from the snowy woodland outside. But the noise draws nearer as Hazel stiffens in her seat. The door, which had been so delicately closed by Max, is thrown wide open, banging against the wall and rattling the sepia photographs of the Devon coastline in times past.

'Where is she?' Jane Greenstreet roars at Hazel, eyes wild, sucking in oxygen in deep rasping breaths as she advances. 'What have you done with her, you evil bitch?' She pulls up then, noticing Hillier. 'And you! You let this monster come here, to this place. Knowing who she is. What she's done. You let her come here and take away my baby . . .' Jane is sobbing now. She rubs one hand across her face, her eyes screwed up in pain. 'How could you? How could you?'

Hazel and Hillier are dumbstruck. Behind Jane stands Max, open-mouthed and appalled. Next to him, Declan Greenstreet flexes his hands at his thighs, as if he wants to reach out to Jane but can't. As if some invisible shield surrounds his wife, her grief armoured against intervention. Ellis is visible behind him, a look on his face that Hillier doesn't like. He isn't trying to stop Jane, he's letting her vent her fury.

'Mrs Greenstreet.' Hillier gets up, but it is too little, too late. Jane leaps for Hazel, flailing hands grabbing at her hair, pulling her down onto the floor. She lies on top of her, pummelling her in the chest, digging her fingers into Hazel's face, screaming at her: 'Where is she? Where is she? Tell me, you bitch!'

It takes a millisecond for Hillier and Ellis to react then they both dive to pull Jane off Hazel. Georgie's mother is hysterical, her words incomprehensible, batting at the air with clenched fists. Hazel lies on her back, her arms wrapped over her head. She is breathing heavily but she says nothing. When Ellis finally manages to get his arms around Jane's waist and hefts her away to the other side of the dining room, Hillier kneels down at Hazel's shoulder.

'Are you all right?' she asks. 'Here, let me help you up.'

Hazel lifts herself into a seated position then and removes her hands from her face, revealing the three long and bloody scratches that Jane Greenstreet has gouged on her forehead and cheeks.

'What the hell were you playing at? Letting Mrs Greenstreet come anywhere near me while I was interviewing Hazel?' Hillier asks Ellis.

'How was I to know?' he responds sulkily. 'You didn't tell me we had the sister of one of the world's most infamous murderers staying at Balcombe Court.'

'Less of the backchat, Ellis,' Hillier snaps. 'I've got about twenty years' experience on you, so a little respect if you don't mind.' She sighs, sinking down into yet another empty seat at a table in the deserted restaurant. Jane and Declan have retreated to their room upstairs and Hazel is behind reception having first aid applied to the cuts on her face. Jonny had appeared at the end of the brawl, scooping her up and away from the Greenstreets.

'How did Jane find out that Hazel is Rosie Bowman?' Hillier asks in a tired voice.

Ellis's mouth turns down.

'Ah, let me guess. Marek Kaczka?'

The policeman nods.

'Yeah, makes sense. Thought he'd take the heat off himself, didn't he? Must have been listening to us from the kitchen. Fucking *hell*!' Hillier bangs the table with the heel of her hand. 'What an absolute mess.'

'Forensics and DS Gordon should be here any minute,' Ellis says, referring to Hillier's direct superior. 'The roads are finally clear from Torquay.'

'I don't need Mum and Dad to come and sort things out,' Hillier snaps at him. 'We should be able to handle this ourselves. You should have stopped her coming in here. You must have known she'd want to beat the crap out of Hazel Archer.'

'In all fairness, I didn't. She said she wanted a coffee and was coming downstairs. She must have met Kaczka in the hallway and then come storming in here. We chased after her but it was too late. And anyway . . .'

'What?'

'Well, I don't blame her, frankly. If it was my kid that'd been hurt, I'd want to kill the person who did it. Stands to reason.'

'No, it doesn't, Ellis.' Hillier gets to her feet and pulls her jacket straight. 'At the moment, we have no evidence that Hazel Archer has anything to do with what's happened to Georgie. For all we know, Kaczka could be telling all and sundry about Hazel's true identity in order to take the heat off himself.'

'With her background, though.' Ellis shrugs. 'It makes a lot of sense.'

'Facts and evidence leading to logical deduction, Ellis.' Hillier walks past him to reach the doorway. 'That's what policing is, not some gutter-press version of events.' She pauses as she hears something, her head on one side. 'That's a car engine.'

'Looks like Mum and Dad have arrived,' he says.

CHAPTER TWENTY-TWO

1997

They trip along the line of the grass- and daisy-filled canal, the sun dipping ahead of them, pushing its light through the leaves above. Night is far from fallen but there is a low moon in the sky, hanging there as a warning that soon it will be dark.

They hold hands, teetering on tiptoes, swinging on their own weight away from each other. Their feet trace the narrow meander of the canal, one after the other, one after the other. It is quiet now. Leaves brush against each other in furtive whispers. There is the occasional rattle and high-pitched call of a starling, but otherwise the air is soft and kind, and the girls say nothing as they walk along hand in hand.

They reach the part of the path where the willow tree weeps over their fence, then they stop and turn like ballerinas on a child's wind-up jewellery box until they are facing the gate at the bottom of their garden and they know it is time to go inside.

Once inside the parameters of the fence, it is as if the magic has gone. The spell washes clean off their clothes as they cross over the boundary from the wild, untended land outside and step onto the neat, trimmed grass of the postage-stamp-sized lawn that their father mows religiously every Sunday. The calm on their faces fades as they push the gate open, falls from them like dress-up clothes, and they run across the garden like two happy playful girls, over to where their mother waits.

The gate swings behind them, slamming back against the fence in the breeze. Beyond it lies the canal, all-knowing and all-seeing, silent guardian of the secrets slithering on their bellies along its length.

As the sun sets and the windows pop with light in the house where the girls eat their tea and watch television, night eventually comes, lush and perfumed, the gate still banging in the breeze.

CHAPTER TWENTY-THREE

'Can I have a word, mate?' the man says, his breath frosting in the air as he moves off from where he has been leaning against his car. It is a beaten-up navy blue Volkswagen and the man is tall, big around his middle, wearing a fur cap with flaps that dangle over his ears.

Max has retreated outside the hotel for a cigarette, trying to calm down after the drama of the attack on Hazel in the hotel restaurant. His heart is thumping painfully in his chest as he replays the scene and there is a lump in his throat as he acknowledges his own culpability in the matter. They should have been much more discreet. He should have spoken to DC Hillier by himself first and then she could have interviewed Hazel privately in her bedroom, instead of publicly where anyone could overhear and stir up trouble. Everything that Hazel feared has come to pass and, ultimately, this is a huge distraction from the bigger issue of where little Georgie is. The search is continuing, down on the beach and on the cliff tops. Above him, the coastguard's helicopter circles, peering down through the clouds like a telescopic eye. The hotel guests remain trapped inside the grounds on police instruction, waiting for the news that they can either get on with their holiday or go home.

Max exhales smoke and grinds out the butt in the snow at his feet. He can't help but admire the beauty of the landscape in front of him. The ice storm has frozen the countryside in time. Mini mountains of snow are dotted around the car park, covering the vehicles parked there overnight. Handlebars from a bicycle poke up from one mound. The trees look like crystalline scarecrows, reaching up to the white and heavy sky.

Now Max studies the stranger suspiciously as he approaches and first impressions are not good. The man has a squashed red nose, broken veins in his cheeks, and his eyes are beady, rich with greed. 'Yes, what is it?' Max asks in a neutral tone.

'Are you a guest here at Balcombe?'

Max shoves his hands in his pockets and sets his mouth.

The other man shoots him a brief smile. 'Let's assume you are,' he says. 'Look, pal. I don't want to cause any trouble. But there's a few of us up here now.'

Max looks over and sees the distant huddle of grey shapes, indistinct in the frosty air. *Journalist vultures,* he thinks with disdain, knowing from experience that they will have heard about the search for Georgie from scanning police radios. Then his pulse quickens as he realises it's imperative to keep the fact of Hazel being here completely hidden from the press. What he holds in his hand isn't so much carrion as dynamite and if the descending hordes discover that one of the Flower Girls is staying in the hotel where another young girl has gone missing, he'll lose this story. And it's his.

Hazel is his.

'We just want to help, is all. Get the information out there so that people can pitch in, provide information. That's all.' The man splays his gloved hands as if to reassure Max. 'If we get the story out by close of play today, the communication lines will be up and running. We can start asking the public what they know.'

'And what can they know?' Max asks. 'I mean, what is someone in, let's say, Hull, going to know about what's taken place here in the hotel over the last twenty-four hours?'

The journalist shrugs. 'People might recognise a guest. They might know about their backgrounds. You know . . . have something to contribute in that sense.'

'Label someone a risk, you mean?' Max tries to level his voice, to look normal.

'Well, maybe.' The man exhales a long glacial breath into the air. 'Look, pal. Where a child is concerned, you'll do anything, right? Isn't it better that we know about the guests here? Work out if anyone *is* a risk? Someone who might potentially have a reason for harming the poor child? If we find out who they are, we can start putting pressure on them to say where she is. What they've done with her.'

'What about me?' Max asks.

The other man looks confused. 'What about you?'

'Well, couldn't I be the person you're concerned about? Why are you so sure that I'm not the sinister paedophile you're referring to?'

The journalist frowns. 'You don't look the type, mate.'

'What does the type look like?'

'Point taken,' the man sighs. He looks over at the hotel entrance, longing in his eyes. 'I see that you're wasting my time.'

'No,' Max says as he turns to leave. 'You're wasting mine.'

He walks briskly away, his heart still hammering, but now he doesn't know if that's from the adrenaline of the fight inside the hotel, the visceral fear that someone else will work out Hazel's identity before he has a chance to do anything about it, or his anger with the so-called journalist. *Bloody predators,* he thinks. *How dare they?*

He walks back into the warmth of the hotel, shutting the door behind him with relief. Through an archway, he can see Hillier talking intently to two men in suits. In the reception area are huddles of suitcases and weekend bags. People must be asking to leave, he thinks. To be released by the police and allowed to go back to their homes. Even though there is no Georgie. Dead or alive.

Max turns the other way and heads to the lounge, glancing at his watch and wondering if it's too early for a whisky. *Sod it,* he thinks. *It is New Year's Day.* He orders one at the bar and sinks into a chair by the fire in the blessedly empty lounge, resting his head on the cushion behind him. Heartburn rears its acidic head up his gullet but he tries to ignore it. The hotel still has the feeling of a party halted before it began. Tension hangs in every room, thick as the ice clouds outside. There is an ever-present hum of sound, tight, clipped voices issuing instructions, trying to quell the panic which creeps along underneath it all.

That poor woman, Max thinks, sipping at his drink. He isn't sure if he means Jane Greenstreet or Hazel Archer. Both of them, down there in the dining room, had seemed so bewildered, so at sea. Their faces were pale and exhausted, from fear and from trying to control a situation that was rapidly slipping away from them. He inhales deeply, the smell of woodsmoke from the fire and recently polished furniture incongruous against the awful thoughts that converge in his head.

Rosie Bowman.

How *can* she be here? Max thinks. Of all places when such a terrible thing has occurred. But not since he first realised who Hazel Archer really was, has he considered that she might be responsible for Georgie's disappearance. Aside from the fact that Max can't comprehend why anyone would want to take and harm a child, it seems such an outlandish act for a woman to undertake, on New Year's Eve, with her boyfriend and his daughter in tow – on her *birthday*, for Christ's sake. Regardless of any of this, it would also be beyond stupid as the whole episode has served only to bring her to the attention of the police and potentially the press. The last thing she must have wanted. And look how terrified she is about those emails she's been receiving. Max is confident in his assessment that Hazel is innocent of any wrongdoing towards Georgie.

But this doesn't explain what has happened to the child. As time ticks on, it seems the likely solution is that she wandered off into the night and fell down the cliffs and has been swept out to sea. It is the logical conclusion and one Max is fairly sure will be reached soon.

He stares into the flames, glancing at his now empty glass, thinking about Hazel. The whisky sits hot in his chest, burning through him, fuelling the sharp indignation he also feels. That the poor woman should never be able to escape her past is appalling; that she should be tried by the media for a crime she has had absolutely nothing to do with is equally so. That she is getting these emails from someone who wants to torment her, try and make her insane with worry; that these so-called journalists are leeching information from the hotel like blood-sucking vampires.

He leaps up, galvanised, and exits the lounge abruptly, leaving his empty glass behind him, determined to do something to help Hazel. He will go and find her and Jonny, talk to them about a strategy to protect them from the press. That idiot outside – all of those blood-suckers – would give their eye teeth to be where he is right now.

But as he climbs the stairs, an earlier, guilty thought resurfaces. It keeps returning, like a barrel bobbing on the waves, refusing to sink.

This story will make his career.

This story will change his life.

CHAPTER TWENTY-FOUR

It is only just past lunchtime but already the day is darkening again. The waves continue to crash onto the shore in angry bursts, the sound a constant rebuke to the coastguard that what they are doing isn't enough. Twice now, they have had to call off the search by lifeboat, the foam-crested waves too high for them to be out there safely. Sea spray hampers visibility to impossible levels on the beach and in the water. Conditions are not yet as treacherous as they were yesterday, but the gale is once more heightening to a storm and the coastguard's helicopter is grounded yet again.

Hillier has been standing on the cliff top, looking down at the shapes on the beach scuttling forward and back, battered by the wind. Her feet are like ice in the boots she has put on to come outside and she can no longer feel the tip of her nose. Her boss, DS Gordon, has arrived and declared himself Senior Investigating Officer. Having updated him, she has retreated outside to think, breathe in the landscape, and wonder again where Georgie has gone.

Once Gordon heard about Hazel Archer's identity, he was convinced she was behind the little girl's disappearance. But, Hillier thinks, even if that's true, there's every chance Georgie is still alive. It is still less than twenty-four hours since she went missing. Looking down at the sea, Hillier doesn't believe that the girl is in those gritty, frightening towers of water. Some instinct in her feels certain the child is huddling somewhere out of view, cold and terrified.

But alive.

Something at the edge of her vision catches her eye and she spins round. Marek Kaczka is standing outside the kitchen door at the back of the hotel, exhaling smoke into the slowly bruising sky. Meeting her eyes, his lips flicker in a smile before he casually drops his cigarette where it fizzes out in the snow.

Filled with disgust at the insouciance of the chef, and frustration that the investigation is now out of her control, Hillier spins round and strides towards the beach. What are the coastguard doing, for God's sake? She will look for Georgie herself, and she will find her. The feeling grows in her gut, propelling her down to where the waves crash like toppling skyscrapers onto the shingle. The wind is dogged in her face and she bends her head against its strength. The pathway is bracken- and briar-filled and the ice underfoot causes her to slip several times. She can make out the full curve of the beach by now, a scythe of melancholy, bending away from her in the wintry light. The ochre sandstone of the cliffs appears almost bleached in amidst all of the snow. She peers out, searching the white-blanketed terrain before her, for any nooks or holes where a small child might be cowering.

Or lying unconscious.

She carries on for a little while, running over the events of the last twenty-four hours in her mind. She thinks about Hazel and Kaczka. About how Georgie could slip away from her parents and the timings of it all. It gets dark at four p.m. at this time of year. It would have been easy for the child to have become disorientated outside as the ice and the rain descended.

Hillier stops to catch her breath. She looks ahead of her and then behind, chest heaving, her anger dissipating. Snow again is falling from the sky and, reluctantly, she decides to return to the hotel and succumb to Gordon's control of the situation. As she turns, just along the coastline, about a metre down from the top of the cliff, she spies what looks like nothing more than a dark shadow. But something about it makes her heart-rate spike.

She leans forward, trying to make out its edges, discern its shape. Tilting herself too far, she overbalances and stumbles. With sheer effort, she digs in her heels so that she lands on her rump and not face-first, sliding into a frozen bramble bush. She is now perched on a ledge, boots hanging into the void. Breathing hard, she pulls herself back up onto the flat cliff top. Mumbling swear words, she fixes her sights again on the dark shape below. Is it a cavern in the cliffs? Or is it a tiny figure?

She bites her lip, fumbling for her radio, relaying her sighting to the coastguard, trying to describe the exact location of the shape.

'It might not be anything,' she says with urgency. 'But you need to check.'

She hauls herself round, onto her knees, trying to get a purchase on the icy bracken. Getting to her feet, a particularly violent gust of wind buffets her and she wobbles precariously. The weather is vicious, howling around her, biting into her cheeks, causing her eyes to water. As she carries on towards the shape, she begins to doubt herself. Maybe it was just a hollow in the side of the cliff? Maybe, in her desperate need to find Georgie, she has fabricated a place where the girl might be hidden. Can it be possible

114

that she alone has seen what a trained search team has failed to spot? But then again, the force of the storm has meant they have been combing the beach from the bottom. They wouldn't have reached the cliff edge last night. They wouldn't have had the same perspective.

Hillier mutters to herself as she struggles on, hot and out of breath. She has now nearly reached the curve in the cliff top that would be above where she saw the dark hollowed-out shape. She trudges across the hardening snow through the sea mist, stopping for a moment to catch her breath. And that is when she sees it. The dark spot she had noticed is moving. Hillier's eyes narrow, her stare trained on the approaching figure. She shakes her head like a dog worrying a rabbit, trying to see past the spray shooting up from the beach and the rocks. The shape is shimmering in the white but as it gets closer, she can see its arms tucked round its body, its shape hunched into itself, a tiny, tramping figure. She violently pushes back her hood and starts to run, pounding over the snow in her boots, tripping over herself, arms flailing.

'Georgie!' she yells, sprinting until her lungs are fit to burst. 'Georgie Greenstreet! Is that you?'

She reaches the frozen creature. Its eyes are large as planets, red-rimmed and filled with water. She rips off her jacket and kneels down, wraps it around the child. At the same time, she removes the frozen lifeless bodies of the kittens from Georgie's arms and lays them gently on the ground. She pulls the child in against her chest and rubs her fragile limbs as if coaxing the very life back into her. 'It's OK, Georgie,' she says, her voice a grateful whisper. 'You're all right. You're going to be all right.'

CHAPTER TWENTY-FIVE

'You have to tell your side of the story,' Max says, sitting down on the window seat next to Hazel. He is turned sideways, his focus solely on her. In front of them, Jonny stands with legs apart, thumbs thrust through the belt loops on his jeans.

The window behind them is white from the glare of the snow. Despite the apparent calm, the hustle of the search for Georgie is still tangible. It colours the conversation with a distracting rattle of anxiety, a sense of distant, breathless momentum. Max is desperate for more booze, something to quell the adrenaline that sears through him like mercury. But he restrains the desire. He has to keep his head clear, his motives exact.

The scratches on Hazel's face are still raw and swollen, a brutal reminder of the hatred shown towards her by Georgie's mother. 'And that's exactly why,' Max says, pointing to the marks, his words running away from him as he tries to slow down, to gather his thoughts. 'That's why you've got to tell your version of events.' He swallows, bringing his palms together, taking a steadying breath. 'Nobody has ever heard it, have they? You were so little and then ... well, then you were given your identity for witness protection. And because of that, everyone just lumped you in with your sister – *the Flower Girls* – there's been no distinction made between the two of you, has there? It's not fair, frankly.

'But now you've got the chance to set things straight. Say what really happened, how it wasn't you. That you were an innocent bystander, that you weren't involved.'

Hazel gazes at Max, a hard knot in her throat as she considers his eagerness, his confidence that what he's saying is right. She glances up at Jonny, at his broad stance. As always, Jonny's solid masculinity is reassuring, it comforts her.

'I don't know,' he says into the resulting silence. 'If we put this out in the papers, our lives will become a nightmare. We'll have press everywhere. I've got to think about my job. About Evie. What's she going to go through, with her friends at school?' He turns to Hazel. 'I mean, are you even allowed to say who you are? Tell everyone your real name? Won't you get into trouble for revealing it?'

'No, I don't think so,' she replies in a tiny voice. 'There was never a court order. They did the identity change for us out of kindness.' Her tone borders on sarcastic. 'It's only for criminals when they're released that it causes a problem, I think. And I'm not a criminal. Am I?'

'Well, I hate to say it, but unfortunately the Greenstreets know who you are now.' Max smiles ruefully. 'And there are journalists outside the hotel doors, itching to get inside. The story of a little girl going missing is huge. The Greenstreets will talk. They want their daughter found and they think you're responsible. Nothing's reached the press right now, but it will do very soon. You don't want it happening in an uncontrolled way when all hell will break loose, frankly,' Max says. 'Your only hope of putting this all to rest, once and for all, is to – very calmly and rationally – tell your side of the story. Explain that you're just a normal woman, living a normal life with a job and a family. That you wouldn't dream of hurting a child. Not Kirstie Swann, and not Georgie Greenstreet.'

Hazel goes to speak but Jonny cuts in, one leg jiggling inside his jeans. 'Well, all right, I can see that. But how would it work?'

'I'll write a proposal and look to get us representation. Then,' Max says carefully, 'we can think about an interview. Or even . . . a book.'

'Do you have a background in this stuff? Have you written anything like this before?' Jonny asks, shooting a look at Hazel to check she's noticed this pertinent questioning.

'I worked in print journalism for fourteen years before I turned to fiction,' Max says. 'I've done freelance work at the *Mail*, the *Evening Standard*. Since then I've had two novels published under my own name and I've also ghostwritten a biography. I've got the experience and contacts and, believe me,' he looks directly at Hazel here, 'it won't be hard to sell this story.'

'Right,' Jonny says, placated.

Hazel has yet to say a word, watching Max and Jonny, considering what she hears. She wants to speak, to cry until she is wrung out. But she can't hear properly over the banging of her heart in her chest, like a moth trapped in a lampshade, getting ever closer to the white heat of the bulb. The scratches gouged on her face are smarting and she can't rid herself of the image of Jane Greenstreet's expression as she hurtled across the dining room to attack her. It was so filled with loathing. The effort to keep rising sobs within her is making it hard for Hazel to swallow or speak. So she concentrates on the men, their plan-making. Jonny will know what's best. Max seems to be completely on her side too. She doesn't understand why he is, but she is deeply grateful for it.

'What do you think, darling?' Jonny asks her, his voice soft. 'Can you see yourself doing this? Do you think it might help? I mean, I can see Max's point. I can see the advantage in putting across what you know about what happened back then. You've never said, have you? What do you think?'

Hazel shakes her head and touches her face gingerly. 'They hate me,' she says. 'All of them. Hate me.'

'But maybe this is a way to turn things around?' Max suggests. 'Maybe if you explained things, said what really happened, people would think differently about you. You know,' he says, leaning forward, warming to his task, 'people judge when they don't know any different, when they're only given one story they can latch on to. Tell them a different story and then you've got an opening, a way of letting them make up their own mind. There will always be people who close their eyes to certain ideas. But in this case, there isn't another version for anyone to think about. All everyone thinks is that Laurel' – he doesn't notice Hazel flinch at her sister's name – 'was responsible for the death of that child.

'At the moment – I mean, you must have heard about this – your sister's challenging the courts for her release, she'll want to flood the media with her side of events. But if you give them another story – a better one – make them see you as a human being, not a monster . . . then,' Max sits back in his chair, unconsciously rubbing at the pain in his chest, 'you might win your own freedom. Imagine that. You might be able to live a normal life again.'

119

'I've never had a normal life, Max,' Hazel says. 'I've never had my freedom. I've lived a lie since I was six years old. For nineteen years, I've lived like this. I don't think I know any other way to live.'

'OK, but what about Jonny?' Max replies. 'Wouldn't you like to be together out in the open? Not always worried that someone will find out who you are? Able to tell Evie about your past? Not to lie to your future step daughter?' He chooses the words deliberately.

Hazel looks down at her lap as Jonny reaches over to grip her hand tight. 'Yes,' she answers in a small voice. 'I would.'

'Then why don't we try?' Max continues. 'We could do an interview and I could write the book proposal. And then you could just read it and see what you think. You can make any changes to it that you like. If you hate it, or you get cold feet at that stage, you can withdraw it, take it back. You'll have my word that I'll destroy it. I promise . . .'

'Hang on, mate,' Jonny interrupts, his tone suddenly urgent and panicked. 'What's that? Can you see outside behind you?'

He pushes forward, his chest almost flat against Hazel's face as he leans up close to the window. 'Over there. Can you see it?'

Hazel twists round uncomfortably so that she can look outside and Max does the same next to her.

'It's the policewoman, isn't it?' Max says. 'Hillier?'

'She's carrying something,' Jonny says, his voice shaking, his knuckles white as he grips Hazel's shoulder. 'She's carrying something in her arms.'

CHAPTER TWENTY-SIX

Hillier lifts Georgie up and over her shoulder, turning back to where the lights of the hotel are amber now in the burgeoning dusk. She trudges slowly under the weight of the five year old, hearing only the sound of her own breathing, hoarse and laboured, as she eventually reaches the hotel entrance.

She kicks it open with her foot and the heavy oak door swings back to reveal the newly arrived DS Gordon standing at the reception desk, fairy lights twinkling beyond his shoulder on the Christmas tree. He turns to face her as Hillier stumbles in, flutters of snow shooting in behind her, white slush trailing in from her feet. The air is cold and sharp and Gordon's shock at the sensation, at the sight of his colleague carrying the missing Georgie, delays his reaction for a few seconds and, when it comes, it's words rather than actions.

'What the . . .' he blurts.

'It's her,' Hillier gasps. 'It's Georgie. She came up over the cliff outside. She's hypothermic. Paramedics . . .' she manages to say before collapsing into one of the chairs to one side of reception, Georgie still clinging to her, her eyes closed, her lips the colour of marble.

Gordon reaches for his radio at the same time as the woman behind reception gasps and makes a grab for the phone.

'Don't bother,' he barks at her. 'I'll be quicker. Get blankets. Foil from the kitchen. And get her parents down here *now*.'

Hillier leans her soaking head back against the chair, shutting her eyes to the scene, putting her icy fingers on Georgie's wrist, feeling that faint pulse still beating. She whispers a prayer, thanking the heavens for this moment, the feeling of this wet, cold body against hers.

'You're all right, Georgie,' she murmurs. 'You're all right.'

Within moments, an industrial-sized sheath of aluminium foil is found and Georgie is carefully removed from Hillier's lap. The girl's wet cardigan is taken off, along with the T-shirt that sticks to her chest and back like a second skin. Georgie's red and mottled skin is dried before the foil is gently put around her and then two woollen blankets; another towel is rolled and put around her neck. Then her skirt and tights are removed and she is tucked into the roll of blankets, her head just visible at the top.

'Keep talking to her,' Gordon says. 'Georgie, can you hear me, sweetie? Hello there. You're safe now. Mummy's coming.'

Georgie's eyes are still closed, her breathing shallow.

'Come on, Georgie, that's it.' Gordon's voice is loud, persistent. 'Wake up, Georgie. Come on, girl. Stay with me here.'

Hillier watches, hardly daring to breathe as someone removes her own clothes. She is barely aware as her jumper and shirt are lifted over her head, a blanket wrapped over her bra. She is shivering uncontrollably.

'That's good,' Gordon says, noticing her trembling. 'Shivering is good.' He glances back at Georgie who is motionless. 'Where is that ambulance?' he barks.

'The roads . . .' Mr Lamb interjects. A small crowd has gathered, looking on silently at the two cold bodies trussed in blankets by the Christmas tree. 'It could take some time. Can you turn off that racket, Lucinda?' he snaps at the receptionist. A minute later and the lull of panpiped classical music is replaced by the sound of rapid breathing, of the concentration involved in watching and waiting.

The uneasy silence is broken by the cries of Jane Greenstreet, who comes flying down the staircase and throws herself at Georgie.

'Hold up!' Gordon says, putting out a hand. 'Be careful with her. She's in the recovery position, Mrs Greenstreet. Just watch yourself. Talk to her, though, keep with her. The ambulance will be here soon.'

'Oh, thank God, thank God,' Jane cries, tears streaming down her face. 'My baby. Where have you been?' She kneels at Georgie's head, stroking the black hair that just pokes out from the towels and blankets. 'Georgie . . . Georgina. It's Mummy. Look at me, sweetheart. Why won't she open her eyes?' She stares up desperately into Gordon's face. 'Why won't she look at me?'

'She's hypothermic,' he says, his expression dark. 'We need that ambulance.'

'Oh, God, no . . . Not now we've found her. Please! Declan, someone, help us.'

The cries of her mother reach something in Georgie and she opens her eyes suddenly, bright stars of cool and gelid ice. Her mouth opens a little, lips devoid of colour, death seeping over her skin like a glass filling with noxious liquid.

'She's arresting,' Gordon says, bending down rapidly. 'Please, Mrs Greenstreet, out of the way.' He unwraps the blankets one after another, exposing Georgie's tiny bare chest to the room. He lifts her waxy chin and blows into her mouth, once so rosy and red. Then he begins compressions. As he counts, pushing on her chest, Hillier hears the faint crack of a rib. Jane rocks back on her heels, her hands to her mouth, dry sobs racking her body as she watches.

'Someone take over, please,' Gordon gasps, and another member of the Crime Squad edges over on his knees to carry on the compression as Gordon breathes intermittently into Georgie's mouth.

'Is she breathing?' Hillier asks, unable to stop herself. 'Is she?'

Gordon doesn't answer, his knuckles flexed on the carpet.

Hillier can see a tiny shake of his head as they swap again. It's been too long, she thinks. Georgie's little heart is too tired. Her blood is too cold. She sends up another plea to the skies. She will never complain again about her work, her life, her mother, her anything. She will do it all with a happy, warm heart, if only God will let this little girl live. She has drawn blood from her lip where she has been biting it, still shivering continuously, but she only tastes it, only notices it, when she hears the sirens, the swish of tyres on ice, and a chip of hope returns once the paramedics are on the scene.

That now perhaps Georgie will live.

PART TWO

CHAPTER TWENTY-SEVEN

1997

It was after nine p.m. and the sky was only just turning inky, the night reaching its dark tentacles over the houses, pulling them into blackness.

The pavement was filled with bodies, cameras round their necks, cigarette butts and empty coffee cups filling the gutter. The house they clustered around was in darkness, empty and cold. Outside, though, the air was hot with bursts of chatter like machine-gun fire. Either side of the house, people stood in their front gardens, staring at it, pointing and shaking their heads. A flock of birds flew over them as the sun finally set and the air began to cool.

An unmarked car slowed down, idled at the kerb for a minute before pulling off again and away down the street. As it did so, the crowd moved as one, sending their blinding flashes of light to chase it as it drove away.

'Mrs Bowman! Mr Bowman! Have the girls been arrested? Have they been charged with Kirstie's murder? Mrs Bowman, how do you feel as a mother? Just one statement for our readers!'

Feet slapped on concrete as journalists ran after the car, flailing their arms to gather speed, their breath raw in their nicotine-filled lungs.

Inside the car, all was very quiet. Rosie's head lay in her mother's lap, her eyes closed fast as Amy hid her face behind the collar of the shirt she had put on that morning when all was normal and fine. Her throat was parched and her eyes felt grit-smeared. She touched a lock of Rosie's hair as it curled on her knee, then drew her hand back involuntarily. All she could see when she closed her eyes was Laurel's face as they had left the police station. Something in her expression had frightened Amy. There was a coldness to it, as if she could see right through her mother.

Gregor had said he would stay overnight with Laurel before they questioned her again in the morning. And so Amy had stiffly got to her feet and pulled her handbag to her chest, holding out her free hand to Rosie, as she had done a million times in the ten years since she had had her girls. Rosie had taken it and they had been led to the car outside. Before she left, Amy had looked back and seen her eldest child standing framed in the doorway of the interview room.

Amy had left hurriedly then, dragging Rosie behind her, trying to force down that image of Laurel, somewhere it would be suffocated. Rosie had said nothing in the police station. They had interviewed her in what must have been a family waiting room with a mural of inappropriately jaunty cartoon characters peeling off sporadically around the walls. She had failed to answer a single question from the officers there. She seemed to sink lower and lower into the chair they had put her on until the social worker had said it was too late to continue, that Rosie should be allowed to go.

Social Services had arranged for them to stay in a cheap hotel nearby. One of the other police officers had picked them up some nightclothes and toothbrushes. Their own house was dangerous, they had been told. Their safety was compromised there. Amy hadn't quite believed it, though. She'd wanted to see her home for herself. Now she realised, as the social worker's car sped away, that what they had been told was true. They could not return to this place.

Since leaving the station, Rosie had maintained her silence, only nodding when she was offered a Ribena. Then, as they sat huddled in their seats in the car, waiting for the social worker to buy it in a petrol station, Rosie had turned to face her mother.

'Will Laurel be OK?' she had whispered, her pallor sickly under the harsh yellow lights.

'Yes, of course she will,' Amy had replied. 'She's going to be absolutely fine, Rose-Red. Don't you worry about anything. Mummy's here.'

Rosie had lowered her chin and tears had spilled onto the pale pink of her unicorn T-shirt. Fifteen minutes later, they were outside their hotel room with the social worker briskly telling them that she would pick them up at eight a.m. sharp and they should try and get some sleep.

Sleep, Amy thought as she stared up at the lights from the dual carriageway outside traversing the ceiling, the hum of traffic still constant even this late at night. She turned and looked at her daughter, lying next to her peacefully, her eyelashes dark on her cheeks. Sleep was very far away from Amy as she lay thinking about her girls. One so close to her, and one a thousand light years distant in the way she had always been.

Oh, precious girl, Amy thought, anger flaring and battling for purchase against the tears that threatened to fall.

Oh, silly, silly girl. What have you done, my precious girl?

CHAPTER TWENTY-EIGHT

'How on earth have they managed to stay together?' Will asks as he stands in the queue at the crowded deli with Joanna.

'Hmm?' she murmurs, running her eyes over the blackboard in front of them which soars above their heads to ceiling height. 'Who on earth would ever want tuna and banana in a sandwich?' she asks nobody in particular, a look of disgust on her face as she moves over to the drinks fridge next to them in the cramped space.

'Your sister and Rob,' Will answers, taking the two bottles of San Pellegrino that Joanna passes him. He shuffles forward in the line behind two suited men, heads bent to their iPhones. 'I've always wondered. Because I mean,' he says, his voice low to prevent anyone overhearing, 'it's a common phenomenon. Couples breaking up after the death of a child. Particularly after a murder.' He glances at Joanna to check she's OK with this line of questioning. Sometimes she can be robust about Kirstie's death but often she will clamp down and not want to discuss anything about more personal details relating to her family. 'It's much rarer for them to stay together.'

Joanna shrugs, taking one of the waters and rooting through her handbag for her purse. 'Debbie was pregnant with Ben at the time. So they had to stay together to look after him. And,' she moves to the counter, putting her bottle on top, 'they do just *love* each other. I don't know what Deb would do without Rob. Tuna mayo and sweetcorn on a baguette, please,' she directs to the woman wearing a hairnet behind the counter. 'Really, I think they were just lucky. It brought them together rather than pulling them apart.'

'I sometimes wonder about the Bowmans, though,' Will says. 'Ham and cheese on brown, thanks.'

Joanna gives him a sharp look. 'What do you mean?'

'Well, did *they* manage to stay together? They were put under so much stress themselves.'

'Nothing by comparison to Rob and Debbie's suffering,' Joanna retorts.

'No, of course,' Will says, handing a twenty-pound note over the counter. 'But imagine dealing with it nonetheless. Your own child responsible for one of the most horrific crimes the country has ever seen. Having to live another life, in secret.' He grabs the white paper bags containing the sandwiches along with his change, not noticing the wide eyes of the woman behind the counter. Joanna gives her a quick reassuring smile, raising her eyebrows as if to say: *What's he on about, eh?*

'How do you ever get past that? How can you live your life knowing that someday, somewhere, someone could turn around and point a finger and say – "I recognise you. You're the parents of that murderer."'

They exit the shop into a clear and cold January day. 'Seriously, Will? I have absolutely no pity for them *whatsoever*,' Joanna says as they walk together along the pavement, edging past a woman with a double buggy. 'They raised Laurel Bowman. They have to be held responsible.'

'Really? Is that what you think?' He looks surprised. 'Ah, look, never mind. We probably shouldn't talk about this.'

'It's fine,' Joanna says. 'It's nothing I haven't thought about before. Been asked about by the liberal media . . .' She smiles at him.

'Well, OK,' Will goes on tentatively. 'So, there was never any evidence of abuse or bad treatment of Laurel, was there? She did well at school. She had piano lessons, for God's sake,' he snorts. 'They were so bloody middle-class. It's hardly the stereotype the *Daily Mail* would have us believe. Under-privileged, abandoned, angry little match girl.'

'That would be the *Guardian*'s view,' Joanna corrects him. 'The *Daily Mail* would just say that she's wicked. And they're not wrong. I mean,' she halts outside the door to the Bang to Rights office, putting her key into the lock, 'like you say, she had no reason to do it. None. One day, she just wakes up and decides to kidnap a toddler. Kirstie, as it turns out.' Her voice is bitter. 'Do people – kids – do that unless they've been primed for it, unless something in their background has led them to that point? Meaning they've watched it on films, played video games – like the Bulger murderers, Thompson and Venables. Normal kids don't just think one day: *Oh, I know! I'll go and torture and abuse a baby girl.* Either they're nurtured into it or they're just born evil.'

'Thompson and Venables didn't play video games. That's apocryphal. Presumably the judge mentioned it in his sentencing to give some – any – kind of rationale for a crime he considered incomprehensible. But there's no evidence they were playing violent games,' Will says, following her up the stairs. 'Anyway, what you're saying is that Laurel Bowman must have been genetically wired to be wicked.'

'Yep. And that explains the parents too,' Joanna says, sinking down into the chair at her desk and pulling open the sandwich bag. 'It lets them off the hook to a certain extent. Which,' she points her baguette in Will's direction, 'I know negates my earlier point.' She looks down, thinking. 'I just don't feel any pity for Amy and Gregor Bowman. I can't. Because whatever they're suffering now, or have suffered in the past, is nothing – *nothing* – to what Debbie and Rob have been through. There's no comparison,' she repeats. 'And even though they are still together, they were destroyed by it. *Destroyed.* We all were to a certain extent.' Joanna puts her sandwich down, her appetite gone. 'That day, all those years ago, it changed everyone's lives. None of us will ever forget it.'

'And what about if you don't believe in evil?' Will asks. 'What's the answer then?'

Joanna is silent, contemplating this. She picks up her barely touched sandwich and flicks it into the bin. 'Then you've got a problem,' she says.

CHAPTER TWENTY-NINE

Toby sits in the hospital waiting room, his hands still cold after the walk from the Tube. A huge cast-iron radiator clanks in one corner, water gurgling inside, a negligible heat emanating. The room is filled with chairs occupied by wan-faced patients, sitting obediently with crossed legs, newspapers aloft. They are all men of a certain age, a certain portly stature. Toby looks round the room and feels like a clone of a middle-aged man, a man on the cusp of old age, a man with a prostate bulging uncomfortably inside him.

He sighs and folds his newspaper, placing it across his knee. He looks up at the ceiling and shuts his eyes. Six pounds lost since his diagnosis, with twenty-two more to go if he is indeed to be operated on. Life is a slog at the moment, a trawling through treacle with a monkey on his back. And he can't even eat the treacle.

He had once considered his job the most noble of all professions. A criminal defence solicitor. A paragon of non-judgement. A man who would counsel and provide fair and just legal advice, whatever the crime, whatever the type of defendant. He wouldn't be one of those lawyers who would gradually get worn down, mired in the sinewy fats of their own cynicism. This would never happen to him, for the simple reason that he believed in the system so absolutely that any variation in his thinking could only indicate the most abject turnabout in his personal philosophy. And, of course, as a twenty-one-year-old law graduate, beginning his legal Articles with stars in his eyes, his philosophy was as grounded in him as his love for his parents or the memory of his home address.

Thirty years later, though, while he can remember the address of his first flat out of law school, he can't remember the details of its rooms any more. They blur into dashes of brief memories, spasms of recollection when faced with a particular smell, or a song playing on the radio.

And as for the love he had for his parents: well, there was a narrative that ended with his representation of Laurel. His brother Gregor had decided to break all contact with him because of his continued connection with her and so had his parents. In their seventies by the time of the murder, they had not so much been shocked by the scandal involving their ten-year-old granddaughter as withered into submission. They had shrivelled behind closed curtains, their faces wrinkled tight like milk skin, their mouths set and stubborn. Toby hasn't spoken to them in nearly twenty years. He suspects they are in a nursing home now, if they aren't dead, and he feels nothing about it. A state of being that he experiences about most things these days.

Defending Laurel was, in Toby's life, as seismic an event, as immaculate, as the Rapture. After the trial, all ten weeks of it, he had no longer been the same man. And he would say the same of the majority of the solicitors, social workers, policemen and women, and even Mr Justice Follett, who had all gazed down upon little Laurel as she sat in an adult dock, playing with a rubber band in her lap, her lips trembling. Her dedicated social worker had had to help her to stand to hear the jury's verdict. When it was relayed, in a shaking voice by the foreman of the jury, that she had been found guilty, with malice aforethought, of the murder of Kirstie Swann, she had cried at last. Eyes that had been dry for the whole trial now sprang forth a well of tears; her knees buckled as she was led down to the cells.

Gregor had been at the trial although Amy hadn't managed it. She was surviving on a cocktail of Valium and antidepressants. They had thought she would make it that morning. Toby had begged her, telling her Laurel needed to see her, needed to say goodbye to her mum. But Amy had faltered at the front door, at once nervous and resolute. 'I can't go through with it,' she had said, her expression mulish. 'I can't have them all looking at me like that, with such hatred. It'll break me, Gregor.' She had clawed at her husband's chest and he had submitted, walked on his own to the waiting car, shoulders hunched in the falling drizzle.

After the trial, when Laurel had been taken to the secure unit where she knew she would spend the next eight years, Toby had gone with his brother to a tiny, dark pub he knew, around the corner from the Crown Court. They had sat deep in a corner, nursing pints of bitter, Gregor still in his coat, collar up, shivering from tension.

'She can't take much more of this,' he had said.

'Laurel?'

'Amy. The police say they can move us tomorrow. Somewhere nobody knows us. Give us new identities.'

Toby bit his lip, thinking over what the judge had said at the sentencing, the violence with which he had directed his remarks to Laurel as she had stared at him, uncomprehending.

The shouts from the public gallery, the high fives, the heat of wrath from all those adults displayed towards a ten year old. As Laurel had left the dock, turning onto the stairs and facing the courtroom, someone had shouted from above, 'How do you feel now, you little bitch?'

Toby shook his head. 'If only Justice Follett hadn't identified her,' he said quietly. 'If she was still Child X, you wouldn't need to be so frightened of payback. Of revenge.'

'People know who we are anyway,' Gregor answered. 'Everyone in Grassington does. There's no way we can go back there.'

'But you could live somewhere near Laurel,' Toby persisted. 'Somewhere where you can visit her. See her regularly.'

'Our family has been destroyed because of her.' Gregor shook his head. 'What about Rosie?' he said. 'What about her life? Is she supposed to have that ruined too? It's bad enough that we've lost Laurel.'

'You haven't lost her. She's right here. She needs you,' Toby said.

'But who is she?' Gregor avoided his brother's eyes, staring up at the ceiling. 'I don't know any more. And Amy certainly doesn't.' He forced his eyes to meet his brother's. 'You should never have taken her case.'

'How could we have trusted anyone else?'

'It should have been someone different. Someone not part of our family. Now . . . the whole thing's so messed up.'

'It *is* messed up, Gregor. That's exactly why I stepped in. I wanted Laurel to have the best possible chance.'

Gregor ran his hands over his face. 'I don't know,' he said. 'I just don't know. I'm terrified of losing them too. Amy and Rosie.'

'You won't lose them,' Toby said firmly. 'But if you cut out Laurel, abandon her, that girl will have no one. She'll be on her own in an institution. For all those years. You heard what the judge said. She's not eligible for parole until she's at least eighteen. It will ruin her. He may as well have given her the death penalty.'

Gregor finished his beer in one big swallow and put his glass down carefully on the table. 'She's already been given it, hasn't she? What's her life going to be now? Wherever she goes, people will know. I mean,' he gave a bitter laugh, 'what job's she ever going to get? No one will want her anywhere near them. Her life is over.' He leaned forward, fist tight around his empty pint glass. 'Over.'

Toby pushed his half-drunk pint away, searching his brother's face with bewildered eyes. 'Come on, Gregor. It's bad, I know. But we'll get through this. Laurel's a child! She's your little girl. And she always will be. She needs you to help her.' He laid a hand on Gregor's sleeve. 'You have to be there for her.'

Gregor jerked his arm away, his eyes glistening. 'Don't tell me what I have to do. What do you know about it? Look at us now. Bloody life sentences for all of us. We can't go home. You saw what they did to our house. The graffiti . . . We can't go anywhere without being terrified some psycho's going to kill us. What's left for us, Toby? Everything's gone. Even her, even Laurel. I don't know who she is any more. I mean . . . it's easy for you, isn't it? Sitting there all clever and wise. But it's not your child, is it? It's not your life.' Gregor wiped his mouth, rubbing away spittle.

'No,' Toby had said. 'But she is yours. And nothing's ever going to change that.'

Gregor stared at him for a moment. 'Fuck you,' he said at last, pushing back his stool and leaving the pub with his head down.

'Toby Bowman?' The receptionist calls his name, jolting him back to the hospital waiting room. 'You can go through now.'

That was when it happened, Toby thinks as he hefts himself to his feet. He remembers the day he saw his brother turn his back on his child, and still he feels the guilt, the terrible raw guilt, of it. That was the grenade that pulverised the sanctum of his legal citadel. He had known it was right to fight for Laurel – she, who had no one else on her side. Of all people, she needed someone – anyone – to take her case, to speak for her. But in doing so, in doing what he knew was the right thing, he had lost his brother, and his parents, forever.

Even if his niece was as innocent as the driven snow, the decision he had made that day had changed his view of the law. Suddenly, it became something not only rational but emotional. Suddenly, it was not just about due process, it was about what was right. And that had shifted his perspective. If it's not about due process, you can't be dispassionate, you have to take a view, and this was something that before his niece's case Toby had been certain was wrong. Previously, he had wholly believed that the law should be an impartial master, weigh only in fact, not feeling.

This change had made him hate Laurel just a little bit. Because even if she hadn't killed that child, he could never know the truth for sure. She was the first one to make him see, to cause the scales to fall from his eyes.

See that the law has nothing to do with the truth.

God . . . he thinks as he leaves the hospital eventually, with his prognosis tucked next to his newspaper, inside his satchel. He desperately needs a coffee to deal with his bounding, leaping thoughts.

. . . the law has nothing to do with the truth.

CHAPTER THIRTY

The car edges its way across the icy gravel away from the hotel. Jonny is at the wheel, staring grimly ahead of him. Evie is in the passenger seat, clicking her tongue against her teeth, her long legs bunched up to her chest.

'There they are,' Jonny murmurs, changing gears and pressing down on the accelerator. 'Vultures.'

Expelling frosty breaths into the air are a huddle of photographers and journalists. One man in fingerless gloves holds a bulky television camera at his thigh. Others smoke cigarettes and crack jokes, their gaze never leaving the façade of the hotel. They are craggy and worn, with beer-flushed faces and eyes as sharp as flint.

On the backseat of the car, underneath a pale blue blanket, Hazel keeps her eyelids tightly shut, feeling the warmth of her breath against the wool pressing down on her nose. She senses the car speed up, the sound of its tyres spinning over the frozen ground.

'Nearly there,' Jonny mutters. 'Get out of the way, you idiots!' He beeps quickly on the horn and a woman in jeans and a Puffa jacket hops out of the way. 'Piss off,' he says to her through gritted teeth.

One of the journalists bangs the car roof as they pass and Hazel flinches in her hiding place. It is only after what seems like hours, when Jonny finally tells her that it is safe and they have left the hotel grounds, that she risks uncovering her face, blinking in the bright of the day.

There is so much to say that there appears to be nowhere to begin. The three of them are silent, digesting the earlier controlled chaos with the arrival of the paramedics and the coastguard helicopter that was commandeered to speed Georgie to hospital. Once she had been found, it had seemed they were free to tell Hillier they were leaving, bundling their possessions into the car, taking Max's advice to hide Hazel from the waiting press. Now they sit quietly, watching the countryside race past them, thinking of all that has transpired in the last twenty-four hours and how it will affect them.

Hazel's shoulders are hunched inwards, as if she is trying to hide from the two people who sit like Sphinxes in front of her. Jonny looks washed out, freezing in his shirtsleeves. His normally confident face is moon-white, his usually neat hair dishevelled from his agitated raking of it. Evie's expression alternates between scorn and anger; her chest rises and falls rapidly as if struggling to contain the violent tears which lurk beneath the checks of her lumberjack shirt.

'Look,' Jonny says at last, 'the girl has been found. Thank God.' He licks his lips, checking Hazel's reflection in the rear-view mirror. 'Going home is the right move now. We can talk about things properly there, without the police looking on. Work out what to do.' He flicks a look sideways at his daughter. 'And sort things out with you, Evie. Most importantly.'

'Yeah, thanks,' his daughter replies. 'It would be nice to have *some* idea of what's going on. Why Hazel's hiding under a blanket, for instance?' She studies her own reflection in the wing mirror. 'Is it because of that woman who attacked her by any chance? The mum of the girl who went missing.'

Jonny can't speak for a moment, scanning the road ahead as he drives. He clears his throat and places one hand on his daughter's knee. 'Evie darling, yes, I'm afraid it was. And this is exactly what we need to talk about. It's not only about the attack. It's because ... well, it's because ...' He glances at Hazel in the mirror. *What should they say?*

'Evie ...' Hazel begins. 'A long time ago ...'

'In a land far, far away?' Evie laughs. 'Oh, don't worry. I know all about it. I know about you, Hazel. I know who you are.' She lifts her head, staring out at the frigid fields, her jawline set. 'I'm not an idiot, Dad. I know she's one of the Flower Girls.'

The car swerves across the white lines in the middle of the road. From the backseat, a despairing moan emerges from Hazel's mouth as tears spring to her eyes.

'How?' Jonny exclaims. 'How did you find out?'

'Oh, please,' Evie says, twirling a piece of her hair around her index finger, pushing out her bottom lip until she resembles a sulky toddler. 'Everyone was talking about it in the hotel. It doesn't take a genius to work out who they meant. Two clicks on Google and I brought up her school picture.' Evie jerks her head backwards in Hazel's direction. 'It's not like she's had plastic surgery or anything, is it? Although she might need it now, with those scratches on her face.'

Jonny's words trip over themselves as he scrambles to recover his composure. 'Oh, God ... Evie. I'm so sorry, sweetheart. I know we should have told you. But ... we never thought . . .' His voice tails off and he runs a hand through his hair again in frustration.

'Never thought she'd be found out?' Evie scoffs and raises an eyebrow at him.

'No, not that. But it never seemed . . . I mean, well, obviously this is a shock.' Jonny grips the wheel tight. 'For all of us.'

'Not for Hazel, though, is it?' Evie puts in. 'She knows exactly who she is. She's known forever.'

'Look, Evie,' he says in a level voice, trying to recover some control. 'The fact is we didn't tell you, rightly or wrongly. And I'm sorry about that. I really am. We certainly would have told you – in the future – when the time was right. But now . . . obviously, all this has happened. And you mustn't conflate the two things. It was simply a terrible coincidence. Georgie probably just slipped and fell down the cliffs. In which case, this will all blow over very soon and we can get on with our lives. But, right now . . . what's important now . . . is that we need some calm. Some peace and quiet so we can gather ourselves and work out what to do. Don't you think, Hazel?'

She sways on the seat behind them, her gaze vacant. She stares through the back of Evie's head as if the girl isn't there.

'And, of course,' Jonny goes on, gathering confidence as he speaks, 'we need to figure out whether we talk to this Max guy. I mean, personally, I think that could be a good thing, don't you?'

'What Max guy?' Evie whips her head round to face him. 'What else is going on, Dad? What else aren't you telling me?'

Jonny pats her thigh, staring at the road ahead. He seems lost in himself, dipping in and out of a dream. 'It'll be OK, Evie,' he says. 'I've always looked after you, haven't I?'

'Yes ... but, Dad?' she says and, for a moment, she sounds like she did only a few years ago, before her hormones popped and fizzed inside of her and she stopped being his little girl. She remains entirely still until he removes his hand and something streams across her face, an alchemy of fear and confusion.

'Now people know,' Jonny says, 'they'll hound Hazel. They'll come for all of us.'

Neither Evie nor Hazel says a word.

'Max Saunders is a journalist, an author,' Jonny continues. 'He thinks he can help us put Hazel's side of the story across. Explain that she was only six years old when Kirstie Swann was killed, that she had nothing to do with the murder. He wants to write a book about her. Laurel Bowman – Hazel's sister – she's already had a chance to put her side of the story across in court. Why shouldn't Hazel? he says. After all, she's the innocent one.'

Hazel takes a breath to speak, leans forward in her seat.

Evie stiffens as if she can't bear to hear the sound of Hazel's voice. 'Oh, for God's sake, what?' she snaps. 'What is it *now*?'

'There's something else,' Hazel says. 'Something I've not mentioned ... I've had emails, Jonny. And cards. Just in the last few months. Things sent to me, threatening me.'

'What do you mean? You never said.' His voice is raw, his stare drilling into the tarmac ahead.

'The emails ... they've come from an account. A fake account. But the name of the sender is Primrose Bowman.'

Jonny frowns. 'You mean . . . ?'

'Someone has been sending me emails telling me that they know I'm a Flower Girl. Pretending to be *me*. Pretending to be Primrose Bowman.'

'But who knows? Who has known before me?' Jonny sounds bitter.

'I don't know, Jonny. I got the first one a couple of months ago. And then I've had about one a week. I've had dead flowers sent to me too. At the flat. At work. And cards. The emails are always just a sentence or two. Nothing more. But frightening. Upsetting. They say they know who I am. That they're going to . . . hurt me.' Hazel is practically whispering.

'I don't understand. Why didn't you tell me about this?'

She twitches involuntarily. 'I didn't know what to say, I suppose. I was scared. I didn't want to worry you.'

'For fuck's sake,' Evie blurts out, folding her arms. 'Is it that much of a surprise? That someone is threatening you, wanting to punish you? It's not exactly quantum physics to work out the reason why, is it? Given what you did.'

'Watch the language, Evelyn,' Jonny says.

Evie tosses her hair. 'Yeah, all right. But it's true. And once more people find out, they're going to go mad, aren't they? Look at that little girl's mum. She wanted to scratch your eyes out. And I can't believe you're not the same, Dad. In all honesty. That once you found out about Hazel, you would have . . .' She pulls back, her lips pursed.

'What?' he asks tersely.

'Nothing.' Evie refuses to look at him. 'Nothing!'

He drives for a minute before speaking. 'You're just upset, sweetie,' he says then, sounding as if his throat is constricted. 'We need to work out a plan of action, that's all. There's a lot to think about. But attacking each other, saying things which could damage *us all*,' he swallows and his voice eases, 'isn't going to help. And these emails,' he says, flicking on the indicator to change lanes, 'are plainly blackmail. We should tell that policewoman about it – Hillier. Definitely we should.'

'It's irrelevant now, though, isn't it?' Hazel's tone is bitter. 'It's like Max said. Now the Greenstreets know, the press will know.' She puffs out air, the beginnings of an emotional storm creeping into her voice. 'They'll find out where I live. Where you live. Where Evie is with her mum.' She shakes her head violently. 'It's no good, Jonny. I don't want you or Evie involved with this. It's not fair on you. Just take me back to the flat and leave me there. This is my problem and I'll deal with it.'

'I agree totally,' Evie says drily. 'Home is where the heart is.'

'Evie, I mean it . . .' Jonny warns.

'No, she's right,' Hazel says, a strange smile on her face as she looks at the teenager's blonde hair, twisted into its glossy ponytail. It occurs to her that both of them are Matryoshka dolls in their stealthy concealment. 'We have to think of Evie. We have to protect her. The journalists will be brutal, like they were before.' Her voice cracks. 'Someone's already bullying me with the emails and that's only going to get worse. It's not right that you'll both be exposed to it as well. Why should you be?'

'I knew about this,' Jonny says. 'About you and your sister. I knew about it before – it didn't matter to me. I loved you anyway.'

Evie wrinkles her nose, concentrates on pressing her fingernails deep into her palm.

'I knew about it and I took it on. I won't abandon you, Hazel.'

Evie looks at him. His cheeks are flushed and he is turning to Hazel, not her, not to his daughter. Despite everything she's done for him. As he speaks, drops of rain spatter against the windscreen and the sky darkens and Evie feels that pull of sadness that threatens to take her over all the time these days. That longing for it all to be over.

'Please,' she says. 'Can we just go home?'

But Jonny and Hazel are silent, locked into their own thoughts as the rain begins in earnest. Neither of them seems to notice that she's said anything at all.

CHAPTER THIRTY-ONE

Max is at the kitchen table back in Birmingham. *The Buccaneer's Daughter* is nothing but a few thousand words saved on a memory card now, destined to be forgotten forever. He senses the looming headlines that, any day, will violently mushroom from the tabloids – a thrilling story in this slow news period – about a girl going missing and being found in the same hotel where Flower Girl Rosie Bowman was staying. But he ignores it and tries to breathe as his fingers fly across the keyboard, creating the thing of beauty that will be his book proposal. Ever since he recognised Hazel for who she actually is, he has had an electric current sparking through him and he shifts on his seat as he types, unable to sit still, wanting to burst through the door and run and run.

Georgie has been found, he reminds himself whenever he feels a dash of guilt that he is manipulating this situation to his advantage. The child is safe in hospital and everything he has planned for Hazel is for her own good. Underneath all of the coal of Georgie's disappearance is the diamond that is Rosie Bowman. And he, Max, has found her after scrabbling around in the dark for all these years: wrestling storylines from flickering images that scamper through his mind on train rides, the moments just before sleep, or those luxurious seconds just after an orgasm. It's no way to conjure up stories or ideas.

But *now* ...

Now he can forget *The Buccaneer's Daughter.* Whatever the tabloids will claim to be the truth, *he* is the one who has a vulnerable and lost Rosie Bowman in his palm. Since he had his epiphany in the hotel lounge, Max is clear-headed about his purpose. What he wants will not harm Hazel. It will help her.

As it will help him.

It feels almost too easy. Like one of those mythical moments he has heard other writers describe. The magical muse that sits on your shoulder and dictates the best-selling book to you; those characters that appear fully formed. Not that Max has had any experience of this but he feels it now, reaching towards him over the deep and vast boundaries of the mind.

The Flower Girls: Their True Story.

It's too good.

Max likes Hazel, he tells himself. He feels protective towards her and, it is his view (he types), that this is the best solution for her, in order for her to move forward and go on with her life.

The problem is – and here, he reluctantly takes his hands off the keyboard – that Hazel cannot remember what happened on that terrible afternoon when Kirstie Swann was murdered, and if she can't recall the details, then there won't be enough information to fill a serialised run of newspaper articles, let alone the eighty thousand words required for a book.

And so – Max jerks his attention back to his proposal, mouth twisting with excitement – he has come up with the idea that the Flower Girls should be reunited.

As the words appear on the screen, his heart begins to pound. Such an idea! One that came to him after he'd left Hazel and Jonny. He had halted midway up the stairs to his room, picturing the possibility of the two women meeting for the first time since one was ten and the other six.

Max's hands drift over his keyboard, thinking about Laurel, about what she must have experienced. Had she tried to contact her family? Had they contacted her? In his cursory research so far, he has discovered that Laurel's lawyer was a Toby Bowman, her uncle and Gregor Bowman's elder brother. Why had he stepped into the breach when the parents appeared to have wanted nothing more to do with her?

All this was yet to be discovered.

But it was clear to him that if he could arrange for Rosie and Laurel Bowman to be reunited, to nudge the memories in Rosie's brain . . . it would be the story of the century. Myra Hindley meets Ian Brady. Maxine Carr goes to visit Ian Huntley.

Max presses the save button, his pulse fizzing, pins and needles in his fingers. Alison will be back from her parents' tonight with the girls and they can celebrate. He will go to the supermarket now to buy some well-deserved champagne.

Hillier sits staring at the white vinyl floor in the hospital, imagining the millions of germs that are crawling over it unobserved. She is warmer now, at least on the outside. But despite the four plastic cups of sugared tea she has already been given, she feels as though, inside, she will never again be anything other than ice.

She runs through it in her mind over and over again, like rain pouring off a drainpipe into a bucket. The heavy weight of the child, the pinch in her shoulders where Georgie's fingers grasped like iron. The numbness in her toes, the shivering and trembling. And the terrible stillness in Georgie's face while she lay rolled up in blankets, dying right before their eyes. The previous twenty-four hours have been so centred on the fixed point that is Georgie that it seems impossible she might soon no longer exist. She looms so large in Hillier's head that even now the physicality of her remains. She had *felt* Georgie. She was alive in Hillier's arms. She had a pulse, faint and tricksy under the fingertips, but it had been *there*.

Hillier looks at her fingernails, at the dirt collected under them, the red of her knuckles, swollen with cold. She will never come to terms with this job if she's honest. The swing and shift of it from a dark blanket of nothing for months and months only to be thrust into a tunnel of blazing adrenaline that, when you exit, disappears behind you as if it had never been there in the first place. They'll be wanting her to go for counselling, she thinks with rueful resignation. Especially if the girl is dead.

Dead.

If a child dies, what's the point? Hillier thinks. If she's dead, what's the point of the five years she lived? Because it's not this. It's not any lesson that they've learnt from this miserable episode. All today carries with it is sorrow: dragging, weighty sorrow. And Hillier doesn't know if she can cope with that in the days to come. She can't let herself think about Georgie's parents. Her mother, who bore her from her own body. Who held her in her arms when she was born. Did she know then? Hillier wonders fleetingly before pushing the thought away. Did she know then that she would only have her daughter until she was five?

Hillier feels faint, her legs weak, but she forces herself up from her chair, to walk along the hospital corridor, to breathe in the disinfectant, the smell of stew or whatever foodstuff it is they're boiling the nutrients out of. She walks towards a door at the end of the corridor beyond which shapes converge and dissipate in patterns of urgency. Mr and Mrs Greenstreet are tucked away from her, in another room, cushioned by police officers who will catch them when they fall.

From behind her comes Detective Sergeant Gordon's voice.

'She's out of the woods.'

Hillier whirls round. 'What did you say?'

'She's going to be OK. They've stabilised her. Her temperature's up. She might lose her right big toe and the tip of a finger, but she's going to live.'

Hillier drops, her knees buckling, her open mouth making no sound.

'Here, here, I've got you,' Gordon says, bending to grab her under the arms, hoisting her over to a chair. 'Come on, put your head between your knees.'

Hillier does as she is bidden, pushing her face down, watching the tears drip onto the floor.

'It's all right,' Gordon says gruffly. 'No one can see. Here you go,' he says, handing her a tissue.

Hillier sits up and blows her nose, wiping her eyes with the back of her hand. 'Fuck,' she says. 'Sorry, Sarge.'

Gordon nods, looking straight ahead.

'Ah,' Hillier says, exhaling and leaning back. 'Thank God.'

'It was dodgy there for a while. Thank the coastguard for the chopper ride to the hospital.'

'Was she in that cave? The one I could see?'

'They don't know for sure. It's certainly possible. She must have sheltered somewhere. She would have died otherwise.'

'Would being in a cave have been enough to keep her warm? It was bitter outside. Minus four the coastguard said.'

Gordon exhales, staring at the ceiling. 'Maybe she had a blanket or coat?'

'She didn't have one when I found her.'

'Perhaps she left it behind? You said she was gripping on to the bodies of the kittens. If she dropped it, though, it'll have gone out with the tide by now.'

Hillier is silent, considering this. After a minute she asks, 'Can she speak?'

'No – it'll be a day or so before she can. But she will eventually. We'll have to take it easy, though. She's so little.'

Hillier sets her chin. 'Yes. But then we'll know.'

'What happened?' Gordon asks.

'Who did this to her,' Hillier says.

A flicker of respect flashes over Gordon's face. 'You don't think she just got lost? Wandered off with the kittens and couldn't find her way back in the storm?'

'No, I don't,' Hillier answers. 'No, I don't. Someone is behind this, Sarge. Someone took her. And I intend to find out who.'

CHAPTER THIRTY-TWO

The milk is sour and thick and Hazel holds her breath, her nose wrinkled as she pours the lumps of congealed dairy down the plughole.

She's only been gone from the flat for four days, even if it does feel like years. But the one-bedroomed space seems musty and close, as if it has been shut up and empty for much longer. For once, she wishes that Jonny lived with her, that she didn't keep putting off moving in with him. She has always resisted the suggestion, saying she needs her space. But tonight she feels too alone, too susceptible to her thoughts.

She turns the tap on and watches the water flush away the rancid milk, and then stands for a while gazing down at the liquid swirling in the sink. Finally, she shuts it off and turns to face the small kitchen. The sun has cracked like a yolk onto the horizon. She hasn't switched on any lights and the place is lit only by the street lights by the windows with the blinds still up. The night outside is amber and glowing, filled with noise from the never-sleeping city.

When they left Devon, she had to give the police her address and contact details, her work phone number, her mobile. She had done it – would have done anything to be gone from that place – but the fear remained, cold and slippery as a stone inside of her, that she was still far from out of danger. That even though the girl had been found, the police still suspected Hazel of having something to do with her disappearance. When Jonny had dropped her at her flat, she had almost expected swathes of reporters to be waiting there but the street was empty. They hadn't found out where she lived.

Yet.

She had let herself in and stood in the middle of her living room, watching the gated gardens down below, listening to the thud of footsteps in the flat above, the murmurings of their television, the roll of a car engine outside – listening to it all, but never moving, standing quite still as if a spell had been cast upon her. After a while she had moved at last and gone into the kitchen, opening the fridge and letting the cold light fall on her face.

How strange it is, she thinks, looking at her kitchen walls, the landscape print, the photo of her and Jonny on a beach holiday last summer, how all of her possessions look exactly as they did before when now – in reality – everything is entirely changed. The turmoil might be yet to come, but it hangs above her like a spider waiting in its web. As soon as the lights are turned on and everyone knows who she is, it will begin to crawl slowly down until it engulfs her life and her sanity.

She looks back at the hallway in the centre of the flat. Lying on the seagrass carpet are a few envelopes, the final bills and statements of the year. There is a thick white envelope that must be a late Christmas card from her accountant. Hazel blinks, considering it as it lies on the floor. She doesn't get Christmas cards from anyone other than businesses, hotels she has stayed in, her local Chinese restaurant. Apart from the odd amicable acquaintance, she doesn't have friends in the way people in her office do. Their desks seem to be wall-papered with cards, hundreds of jaunty, colourful missives, packed with exclamation marks and wishes of the season. Her desk is always empty. Since Jonny's arrival in her life, she has adopted his friends as her own, meagre in number though they are. Before him, there was no one. No one that she could ever let her into her life, allow close to her.

When will it start? she wonders. The abusive mail, the smashed bottles through her letterbox. She has saved the stash of hate mail she has received from her anonymous sender: the dead pressed flowers; the cards containing violent messages. She has printed off the emails from the Primrose Bowman account. She doesn't know what to do with them. Show them to the police? Now they know who she is, they will revile her just as much as the people who sent those things.

She accepted a long time ago that it was impossible for her to have a real relationship with anyone. There would always be the dread that one day they would find out who she was. They could be in a Starbucks, or having lunch, or drinking in a bar, and then her old school photograph might pop up on the news and they would glance at the screen, shoot a quick look at Hazel. Realisation might pass over their brow, sudden nausea be apparent on their face. And then they would wear the expression she'd seen many times before. On the faces of people interviewed on salacious documentaries she has tortured herself watching on YouTube and online.

That look.

The look that says: *You're not human.*

You're wicked.

She has never wanted that moment to arrive with anyone she's classed as a friend. And so she has protected herself from it by shutting herself off. The only person who has ever managed to get through the barrier is Jonny. And she can't bear to lose him, to lose the companionship.

She doesn't think she can live like that again, so lonely and spare. Is this what this journalist Max is offering her? A different way of living her life? A path she can take where she doesn't have to hide any more. Where she could actually be herself. Not Rosie Bowman, because Rosie doesn't exist any more. But Hazel. Legal secretary, expert Thai cook, a faster-than-average swimmer. Can she be her? Can she be allowed to live that simple life, without the hatred, the disgust, the malice thrown at her? Will the world accept what she could tell them?

Hazel sinks to her haunches, a twist of despair coiling inside. Sometimes she thinks she knows the truth about that afternoon, that she can grasp it, slippery though it is. But other times it slides away from her, leaving her scrabbling at its smooth and undefinable shape. She had been six years old, and her brain had hardened around that day like a turtle shell, wrapped around the soft tissue of those memories, preventing her from prodding them, rousing them from their sleep. Now they – Max and the police and all the panting journalists – are asking her to poke a stick into those memories. After all this time. They want her to force her brain to split open the shell. And she's not sure she really wants to do that. Not now.

Hazel gets to her feet and moves to the desk in the corner of the room where her handbag sits. She reaches inside for her mobile and dials a number. She is about to give up when her father finally answers. He sounds breathless.

'Hello, Dad,' she says softly. 'How are you?'

'Hazel? Is that you?'

'Yes, Dad. It's me. Are you all right?'

'Oh, yes. Just a bit puffed. Nice to hear from you, Hazel. Are you well down there?'

From where she stands, Hazel can see the top third of the lofty plane tree that overhangs the gardens her windows overlook. She studies its shape in the darkness, the street lights pooling their shadows at the foot of its great trunk. Without warning, a wave of tears rises up within her and she hiccups, taking a ragged breath to stop the sound from spilling out of her.

'Hazel? Are you all right? What's that noise?'

She tries to breathe, to calm the storm inside. In through her nose and out through her mouth.

'Hazel? Come on, now. What's wrong?'

'Oh, nothing, Dad,' she forces herself to say. 'Just had a bad experience, that's all.' She looks again at the plane tree, its black branches. 'I wanted to tell you. Oh . . .' She stops talking, not sure how to say it, how even to start. 'Dad, I'm sorry. I really am. But there's going to be stuff about us. In the papers. About me and Laurel—'

'Laurel?' Gregor interrupts, his tongue tripping over the two syllables. 'What about her?'

'I've been in Devon, Dad, and a little girl went missing. The police came, and when they did, they interviewed us all. And they . . . they found out who I am. Who I was. Before.'

'What have you done, Hazel?'

'Nothing! I haven't done anything, Dad! I swear . . .'

159

Hazel can hear Gregor's harsh breathing down the phone line. She puts up a hand as if to comfort him.

'Daddy?' she says. 'I'm not Laurel, Daddy. I'd never hurt anyone.'

He is silent and Hazel watches the plane tree, those immense branches reaching into the sky. She says nothing, trying to feel the tree rooting her in history; feel that she witnesses it today like hundreds and thousands have done before her. She is connected to those people in history because she observes the same tree. Her life is not a game to be played at the expense of her sanity. She is real and she is valid.

'As you say,' Gregor finally responds. 'So, going to be a lot of funny business, is there now? Lots of press and what have you?'

'Yes,' Hazel whispers. 'I'm sorry, Daddy.'

'Right then. Well, if that's it . . . ?'

The tree is a gnarled and weary skeleton. Stripped of colour by the winter, it reaches its fingers into her flat, pointing at her, whispering: You. *You are to blame.*

'Yes, Daddy, that's it.'

'Look after yourself then. All right?'

'I will. You too.'

Hazel stands, waiting for something, but there is only the white noise of the phone line in her ear.

'Hazel?' her father suddenly blurts out.

'Yes?'

He releases a long sigh, filled to its edges with frustration. 'Night-night, girlie.'

'Night, Dad.'

Hazel puts the phone down and leans against the wall as a sound leaps into the room, growing louder and louder.

For a moment, she can't work out whether the noise is real or in her head, and then she realises that it is the sound of her doorbell, buzzing incessantly at the same time as her phone begins to ring. She traces her fingers over the wall by her shoulder, standing in the darkness, the sounds of city life filtering in underneath the clamour of the phone and the doorbell.

So it begins, she thinks. *Now they have come.*

She thinks of her mother for the first time in many months. Of the way she would stand at windows herself, always looking out, always searching for something better.

'One day, your prince will come,' she'd sing softly to Hazel as she sat in her nightdress, brushing her dark hair. 'He'll come right up to the house on a white horse, sword in hand. And he'll swoop you away to live in the fairy palace where the roses grow and nobody ever gets old.'

Hazel drops to her knees, blind with tears. She thinks about Max and what he is offering her with the book. How it could mean she might finally be free from her past. But then she thinks of her father, sitting in his cold armchair in his cold house with his cold, stitched-together heart. And she thinks of the pack of wolves that will descend on them all, picking over her bones, tearing at the sinews of their lives.

And then she thinks about Jonny and who he is and what that means for her.

Mummy, she thinks, as the doorbell continues to ring and ring and her phone vibrates with endless calls on the carpet.

Oh, Mummy, what should I do?

CHAPTER THIRTY-THREE

Georgie sits in the middle of the hospital bed. Her face is washed out, her lips still pallid, her black hair an indelible stripe down the starched white of the pillows she leans against. A thick white bandage in the middle of her forehead covers the stitches she needed for a gash to her head.

Jane Greenstreet sits to one side, her hands on Georgie's arm, her chair pulled in as close to the bed as possible. Declan Greenstreet is on the other side, his expression dark. At the end of the bed stand DS Gordon and DC Hillier, who is suddenly conscious that, in comparison to the tiny girl, they look like giants, rearing up from the ground like leviathans.

'Let's sit,' she says to Gordon, gesturing to the chairs on the other side of the room. They pull them over, sitting down primly together, outwardly relaxed.

'How are you, Georgie?' Gordon's voice is level and kind. 'Bit warmer now, eh?'

The little girl looks at her mother, who nods at her reassuringly. 'Yes,' she answers in a small voice.

'You had us all really scared for a while back there.' Gordon smiles at her and Jane. 'But you're safe now and that's the main thing.'

'Thankfully,' Declan murmurs.

'And now you're feeling a bit better, we just want to ask you a few questions about what happened to you there, at the hotel. Find out how you came to be outside in that weather. Do you think you could answer some questions about that for me?'

Again, Georgie glances at her mother, who squeezes her hand. 'It's all right, darling. I'm here. Just try and think back to what happened. Tell the nice policeman.' As she says this, though, Hillier catches Jane glancing at Gordon, sees how an unchecked glint of fear moves across her face while she thinks she's unobserved. As quickly as it appears, however, it is gone.

Gordon settles in his chair, shoulders back, relaxed and easy. 'Georgie, sweetheart. Have a think. Can you remember what you did with your mum and dad on New Year's Eve? Were you having a nice time in the hotel?'

Georgie nods, her face serious, her brow crinkled with the effort of concentrating. 'Yes. We went down to the beach but it was cold. So we came back up to the room where there was the fire and I went on the iPad for a bit. Mummy and Daddy had a drink and Charlie was having his nap. And then . . .'

'That was when you remembered the kittens, wasn't it?' Jane cuts in. 'Right during Charlie's nap. The kittens in the kitchen?'

Hillier looks at Jane, willing her to keep quiet. They need Georgie to tell them in her own words what happened that afternoon. 'Had you seen the kittens beforehand, Georgie?' she asks.

'Yes. They were so cute.' She slides her eyes towards her mother. 'Mummy and Daddy were talking and I didn't want to play or watch the iPad any more so I went to find them.'

'We said she could,' Jane interjects, and it occurs to Hillier that she is embarrassed that they were drinking in the afternoon and letting their children run amok in the hotel unsupervised. Is that all it is – shame for a momentary lapse of attention? Or is there something else Jane Greenstreet is reluctant for them to discover?

'We thought it would be safe, didn't we, Declan? The kitchen is only just down the corridor from the lounge. I feel so bad about it now, of course,' Jane says, her voice breaking, shaking her head.

'Don't you worry, Mrs Greenstreet,' Hillier says, her face the picture of reassurance. 'You aren't to blame in the slightest. Why would you imagine anything could happen to Georgie in the hotel? It was a safe enough place.'

Jane looks down at the hospital blanket on the bed without answering, her fingernails white where she is digging them into her palms.

'So, you wandered along to the kitchen,' Gordon continues. 'And did you see anyone in there?'

'There was a man dressed in white. With hair like this.' Georgie touches her shoulders.

'Long hair? Longer than mine?' Gordon asks.

'Yes.'

Kaczka, thinks Hillier.

'He showed me into the cupboard where they keep all the food. And there was the box with the kittens in.'

'And did the man stay with you?' Hillier asks, her heart-rate increasing a little.

'No.' The child shakes her head. 'He gave me some milk to put down for the kittens and then he went outside and left me there to play.'

Hillier nods. 'And then what happened, sweetie? How long did you stay there?'

'Don't know. One of the kittens was crying and they'd drunk all the milk. They needed more.'

'From the kitchen?'

Georgie nods.

'So you left the pantry. The cupboard.'

'I picked the kitten up and came outside. But they were shouting in the kitchen. I didn't want to get in trouble. And the man was gone . . .'

Hillier's thoughts hover over the image of Kaczka's face, questioning whether this means he's out of the frame or whether he came back, after Georgie thought he'd left.

'. . . So I wanted to find Mummy and ask her. But then I walked out of the door and I couldn't find my way back. 'Cause I was in the room where we eat and I didn't know which way to go.' Georgie is crying now, tears falling down cheeks still raw and red from the ice storm.

Jane Greenstreet shifts abruptly on her seat, her hands picking at the bedclothes. 'Is this really necessary? Georgie's tired. She's exhausted. Look at her. You're upsetting her.'

'It's all right, Georgie,' Gordon says. 'I know it's hard remembering. You were frightened, weren't you?'

'We do need to ask these questions, Mrs Greenstreet,' Hillier puts in. 'I'm sorry but it is important.'

'I realise that,' Jane says, her fingers now tight on Georgie's arm. 'But I don't want her distressed any more than she already has been.'

Hillier says nothing. After a beat, Gordon nods at Georgie encouragingly.

'The kitten was crying,' the girl continues, 'it jumped out of my hands and ran off and then the other ones came and followed it because it was miaowing, making this funny noise. I picked them up and I tried to find the first one but he was gone and then I was outside and it was cold and dark.' She breaks off, her face crumpling in a sob. 'And I just wanted Mummy.'

'That's enough,' Jane says, getting to her feet. 'I'm sorry but I'm going to have to ask you to leave. Georgie is OK now. She's safe and I won't have her terrified in this way. It's not on.'

'Mr Greenstreet?' Gordon turns and appeals to Georgie's father.

'You heard my wife,' Declan adds. 'Perhaps it's better if you come back another time.'

Gordon and Hillier exchange glances.

'Mr and Mrs Greenstreet,' Gordon says. 'It's really in Georgie's best interests that we find out what happened. If there's someone out there who wants to hurt . . .' His voice trails away as he takes in the child looking at him wide-eyed from the bed. 'Well, maybe we can wait a little bit. Just until she's feeling better.' He looks at Hillier nonplussed.

'Good,' Jane says as she moves to the door and opens it for them. 'What Georgie needs now is rest. She doesn't need to be reminded of this . . . this terrible time.'

'All right, Mrs Greenstreet,' Hillier says, bringing herself to her feet. 'As you wish. We'll come back soon.'

She leaves the room after Gordon, closing the door behind them. Outside in the corridor, they look at one another.

'Odd,' Gordon says.

'Odd?' Hillier replies, a frown creasing her face. 'Sarge, odd isn't even the half of it.'

166

CHAPTER THIRTY-FOUR

1997

Laurel sat opposite the police officers. She swung her calves rhythmically, hands tucked under her thighs, chin raised a little in the air despite the tears staining her cheeks.

'I don't want to stay here any more,' she said. 'I want to go home with my mummy.'

'I know you do, Laurel,' the lady police officer said softly. She looked tired, they all did. Last night, Laurel had slept in a small detention room in the empty police station, which had been cleared of other prisoners, sent away to holding cells in the environs. Social Services had brought a thin mattress, blankets and pillows from somewhere and Laurel had curled up on them under high walls, her father dozing over the end of the bed, his hands resting on her ankles.

In the morning, they had brought Laurel a bacon sandwich and a glass of Fanta. When she had finished her breakfast, she had rubbed her eyes and asked Gregor when she would be allowed home.

'Not until you answer all of the police lady's questions,' he had said. 'You must tell the truth, Laurel. You must tell them what you know about baby Kirstie.'

'I don't know anything about her,' Laurel kept saying. There, in the detention cell, and now in the interview room.

She sat in between her uncle, who was also her solicitor, and her father. The two police officers – a man and a woman – were on the other side of the table. A tape machine ran in the middle of them, whirring silently for forty-five-minute bursts. After each period, Laurel would be allowed a short break.

'Tell me about the playground,' the male police officer said. 'You went there with Rosie and what did you do?'

'We went on the slide and the old rocking horse. Then we went off. We didn't see the baby. I wouldn't hurt a baby,' Laurel said firmly.

'All right. But let's take it one step at a time. Now, you know what true means, don't you, Laurel?'

She nodded.

'If I said there are ten people in this room, would that be true or a lie?'

'A lie.'

'Right, because there are only five of us, aren't there?'

'Yes.'

'So you were at the playground, weren't you? With Rosie.'

'Yes.'

'And we know that because you were seen there, Laurel. You were seen with Rosie, playing on the horse and on the swings, so we know that you were there.'

'We went there in the afternoon. We were playing Mums and Dads. It was just a game.'

'Right. And we also know you were there because we got something called a fingerprint of yours on the metal horse. Do you know what a fingerprint is?'

Laurel looked down at her hands and held one up. 'Like from here?' she asked.

168

'Yes. When you touch something, you leave a special mark that belongs only to you. So when you came here last night, to the police station, do you remember putting your fingers in the black ink, and then pushing them onto the paper?'

Laurel nodded.

'That gave us your special mark, that can only come from you. And we also found it on the horse. So we know that you were there. We can see that you were.'

Laurel looked in panic at her father. 'I didn't take the baby, Daddy! I swear it. I didn't. I wouldn't hurt the baby.'

'Shush, shush, little one. I know you didn't. I know you wouldn't.' Gregor put his arm around Laurel, squeezing her tight, tears in his eyes.

She leapt up from her chair and climbed onto his lap, burying her head in his shoulder. 'Tell them, Daddy. Tell them I want to go home. I want to see Mummy. I don't want to be here any more. I didn't hurt the baby, I swear. Please . . .' Her voice rose to a wail, her fists curled and tight.

Gregor looked over at Toby. He tried to convey his anguish, his desperate need to get his daughter out of this nightmare and bring her home.

Toby nodded. 'Laurel's very distressed. I suggest we take a break.'

'OK,' one of the officers said, after a slight pause, and the tape was switched off. 'Would you like a drink, Laurel?'

She said nothing, sobbing into Gregor's chest, her hands white and clenched on his shoulders. After a moment, the police officers stood. 'We'll give you fifteen minutes,' they said before leaving the room.

Gregor closed his eyes, stroking Laurel's hair. 'Shush now, baby. Shush now. Everything will be all right.'

'The special mark, Daddy,' Laurel said, her voice scratched and hoarse. 'The special mark of mine that they've got. They'll say it was me, won't they?'

'No, no. Not if you weren't with the baby, sweetheart. They can't say something's there if it's not.'

'But supposing it is,' Laurel said, sitting up and wiping her face. 'Daddy, supposing they find it? And . . .' stopped, looking deep she into Gregor's eyes. 'Daddy, can the special mark be found on somebody's skin?'

CHAPTER THIRTY-FIVE

Laurel stares up at the ceiling of her cell. They call it a room but it's a cell all right, even though the door is open onto the corridor. Coming from beyond it, shouts and scuffling, explosions of laughter and swear words from the other women assail her ears every minute of every day. The open door only leads to further confinement, to a rat-run of closed-off spaces denied natural light and fresh air.

This box of a building has been her world for over ten years, since she moved here from Oakingham Young Offenders' Unit with her tiny bag of possessions: a few T-shirts and pairs of jeans, a copy of *Anne of Green Gables*, and her old cassette player. She knows the cracks and the ripples in the plaster by heart now: the bed as hard as a concrete floor; the square of window that hovers enticingly close to the ceiling; the desk in the corner next to the aluminium toilet bowl. Her duvet cover is garish, depicting a yellow, one-eyed Pixar minion. Toby had sent it to her years ago, trying to encourage her to take an interest in her 'bedroom', as he called it. He used to send her posters, prints of landscapes, beaches and mountain tops. When she finally told him that she either used them to barter with the other inmates for ciggies, or just bunched them up and threw them in the bin, he stopped. Sometimes, a flicker of something inside her makes her feel bad about that. But then she moves on.

It is never quiet in prison. Doors slam, televisions propagate any kind of silence with inane music and the peppery, jaunty trumpeting of news programmes and magazine shows that no one cares about. The air is thick with the smell of boiled vegetables from the kitchens. The canteen is a full ten-minute walk from the sleeping quarters but the funk of it has weaved its way along the corridors for so many years that the stench of cabbage and potatoes is as layered onto the paintwork as the scrawls of the inmates. The place hasn't been decorated since Laurel has been here. In the shower stalls, tags of inmates past are still indelibly marked on the walls, the names indicative of the era they were written in, Shazza and Julie giving way to Jamie and Kylie. Now the names are less nouns than adjectives, guttural sounds that people have thought fit to give their children as monikers – Unique, Des'Ray, Beauty. Laurel shuts her eyes for a moment, turning her head to find a patch of coolness on her pillow. Her name is a constant thorn. A fucking stupid, prissy name that has no place inside of prison. She calls herself L and when the other girls ask her what it stands for, she tells them it's for 'Leave me the fuck alone'.

She swings her legs to the floor and comes to standing. She needs to go to the gym, to burn off the constant rage that carves solid grooves right through the middle of her, ball-bearings of anger that sink into her stomach, one after the other, making her feel heavy and sick all the time. Only sweat and effort and the relentless refrain of *I can* give her any kind of mental clarity, of peace.

She changes into her kit and walks along the interminable corridors, past the TV room, the kitchen, avoiding the eyes of anyone in her way. She pushes into the gym, the smell of body odour, of stale oestrogen, a vague comfort, and gets on the treadmill, ramping the speed up to maximum, pounding her feet until her hair is wet and her vision blurred.

The crappy television hoisted on a stand up in a corner of the gym is showing some programme Laurel is barely cognisant of as she runs. Then reality slams into her face and she hits the emergency stop button and halts, breathing hard.

Rosie.

Right there in front of her. The old photograph of her in her school uniform. Then, a photograph of a different little dark-haired girl appears. She is hugging her parents in the snow.

Laurel jumps off the treadmill and stands underneath the television, squinting up at the images.

The other girl is called Georgie Greenstreet and – the reporter says – she is now happily reunited with her parents. Despite losing her right big toe, she has miraculously survived a night in one of the worst storms to have hit the Devon coastline in over a hundred years. The image changes to show a reporter standing on a windswept cliff, a hotel behind her lit up with Christmas lights.

'But there are further developments in this breaking story,' she continues in a Welsh accent. 'A source at the Balcombe Court Hotel has revealed that, when Georgie went missing, one of the guests at the hotel was the other – less famous but still notorious – Flower Girl, Rosie Bowman.' Here the reporter pauses, as if anticipating the intake of breath across the country.

173

'It's certainly a coincidence, Roger,' the reporter slyly suggests to the anchor in the news studio, 'that a young child would go missing at the same time as the sister of a known child kidnapper and murderer was staying there.'

'A big coincidence indeed,' Roger back in the studio answers, nodding sagely.

Laurel realises that her jaw is slack, the sweat turned cold on her face. The door to the gym opens and, gathering herself, she reaches up and switches off the TV.

'What's your problem?' asks the woman who has just come in, her tattooed arms bulging. 'I was going to watch that.'

'Fuck off,' Laurel snaps, pushing past her. 'Just fuck right off.'

CHAPTER THIRTY-SIX

Two weeks later and Hillier and Ellis sit in the small canteen at the top of Brixham police station, rolling a Trebor soft mint back and forth between them.

'Georgie's going home today,' Hillier says, catching the mint and popping it into her mouth. 'Back to London.'

'That was mine!' Ellis exclaims, shaking his head. 'Cheers very much. Another coffee, boss?'

Hillier doesn't answer, her mind turning yet again to Georgie and what happened to her on New Year's Eve. She has been debating going one last time to the hotel the Greenstreets have moved to in Brixham while Georgie has been recuperating. 'It's not right,' she says as Ellis returns to the table with a polystyrene cup. 'DS Gordon should be insisting on her parents coming in to make statements. All the money we've spent looking for her, the resources . . .'

Ellis sits down heavily, sipping on his coffee.

'OK, I know it's not the resources that bother me really,' Hillier admits. 'I just don't like it. Why is Jane Greenstreet being so evasive?'

'You think she had something to do with it?'

Hillier sighs. 'Not really. But it's weird. And I don't like weird. What reason could she have for not wanting to find out what happened to her daughter? It just bugs me that we still have no idea what happened to her in those twenty-four hours.'

As she hears herself say the words, her cheeks flash hot with frustration. Why are they talking about this case as if it's done and dusted, in the past? They should be down at the hotel, talking to Georgie again, trying to wheedle those frozen hours out of her memory.

She had tried for the last time yesterday, only for Jane Greenstreet effectively to ask her to leave. It was too upsetting, she had said. For all of them – having to relive what happened over and over again. Georgie was safe and that was the main thing. Now they just wanted to go back home and forget the whole episode.

Hillier pushes back from the table in exasperation. 'I just can't work it out.'

Ellis shrugs. 'You know what I think. The kid wandered off. Got lost on the cliffs and found that cave to shelter in. The weather was that bad you could hardly see in front of your face. She's so small, she wouldn't have had a clue where she was going. Once she got beyond the lights of the hotel, she would have been in all kinds of trouble.'

Hillier looks at him without replying. The silence seems to mount in the room until Ellis shifts in his chair and Hillier finally says, 'But then why doesn't she tell us? Why doesn't she just say that? What is it that's making her mother keep her quiet? Or maybe the mother's got nothing to do with it. Maybe it's someone else.'

'Someone like who?'

'Kaczka, with his liking for young girls? Or what about Hazel Archer? Look at what's been in the papers about her. There are just too many questions . . .' Hillier murmurs, chewing on her mint, looking out into the fading light of the afternoon '... that haven't been answered.'

'I'm off, Hillier,' Ellis says, picking up his keys and coffee and scraping his chair back. 'I've got real work to do.'

'If you took a child, Ellis ...' She holds up her hands. 'Just bear with me a minute. If you did take a kid, why would you let them go? Having risked it – the fact you might be seen, the fact the kid might scream and resist – wouldn't you want to deal with said kid?'

Ellis puts his coffee cup to his mouth without answering.

'Wouldn't you want to hide the evidence? Be absolutely certain that child wouldn't rat on you. Tell the police, her parents, what had happened? Point their fingers and say: he's the one who did it.' Hillier's eyes flame at Ellis. 'Would Kaczka have killed her? Possibly. Caught up in the moment, thinking he'll get caught. Or Archer? She's seen torture and murder before, that much we *do* know. But who's the most likely to have let Georgie go? It doesn't make any sense that she survived. Unless ...'

'What?'

'Unless the person who took her couldn't go through with it.'

'The parents?'

Hillier shrugs. 'It's the obvious answer.'

Ellis tosses his keys in the air and deftly catches them. 'You know what the obvious answer is, boss?'

She lifts her eyebrows.

'The kid wandered off and got lost in the storm. End of.' He gives her an apologetic grin and heads out of the canteen.

Hillier watches him go, tapping her nails on the table. She thinks about Georgie's little body, coming through the snow with the corpses of the kittens in her arms. She thinks about the night she went missing; the panic in the hotel; the reactions of the guests to the news of the missing child. She thinks about Marek Kaczka working the afternoon shift, and Hazel Archer hiding herself for all these years.

She thinks about them long after the canteen gradually empties and the day turns from dusk to black outside.

CHAPTER THIRTY-SEVEN

'What everyone wants to know is the truth.' The barrister uses words like a masseuse uses her hands: strong but silken; persuasive but never too obvious. There is never a suggestion that the arguments posed are anything other than a conclusion that only the most intelligent can perceive. Toby watches the back of counsel's horsehair wig, the tiny ribboned pigtails hitting his collar as he turns this way and that.

Outside the court he had managed to fight his way through the press cordon, where photographers scrummaged in front of the barriers the court had erected to corral them. He had kept his head bent low, ignoring the hoarse voices shouting Laurel and Rosie's names. He tried to keep calm, tried to put out of his mind the call he had received on route to the court from a writer called Max Saunders.

'I'd like to bring them together,' the man had said.

'Laurel and Rosie?' Toby had asked, amazed, struggling to hear what Max was saying over the thunderous traffic that surrounded him.

'Laurel and Hazel, yes. I think it's in Laurel's interests. It could help in her parole application if she has the support of her family. She hasn't had that for all the years she's been in prison, has she?'

'No,' Toby admitted, hurrying round a corner as the Royal Courts of Justice came into sight. 'But I'm struggling to see how it would help. Neither of them has ever spoken about the crime. Won't it just open up Pandora's box? Our position in the parole process is that Laurel has been rehabilitated, no more and no less.'

'Yes, yes,' Max had countered. 'But what support does she have on the outside? What kind of community? She needs that, doesn't she? Maybe Hazel could offer it to her?'

'And she's willing?' Toby had asked, slowing down as he approached the mass of people waiting on the pavement outside the court. He halted, trying to think, to compute the benefits and disadvantages that this proposal could have for his eldest niece.

'Well, I'm getting there,' Max told him. 'But I thought we should start the ball rolling with Laurel. There's no point to any of this if she won't agree to see Hazel.'

Inside the courtroom, the panelled walls stretch high above them and natural light is minimal. The colour palette is all reds and browns and blacks, and the antique cream of the wigs that bob before the judge on his bench at the front. Toby sits directly behind the barrister, his head permanently down as he scribbles notes on the legal pad before him. This is Laurel's application and so her barrister is up on his feet first. Then it will be over to the parole board's legal team to try and oppose her application for a judicial review of their decision.

Through it all, Toby can feel the eyes of Debbie Swann's sister, Joanna Denton, boring into the back of his tired old suit from a few rows behind in the courtroom's mahogany seats. He understands why she needs to be there, that Kirstie's family should be represented at the hearing. And he accepts, too, the awful symmetry of them both being relations of the protagonists of this drama. Nevertheless, he wishes it were not Joanna who was here. Today, with his bloated stomach and ever-present nausea, he feels more in tune with the grief of Debbie Swann than the white-hot rage of Joanna.

'We would say, quite categorically, that in light of the negative press that has surrounded Ms Bowman for many, many years, the Respondent parole board has paid *far too much* attention to the wishes of the public and, as such, has failed to apply the presumption in favour of release, on terms that we say, my lord, are unacceptable and, quite frankly, wrong in law. We submit, to the contrary to the Respondent's recent decision . . .' here, the barrister waves a piece of paper in the air at which the judge raises one grey eyebrow '. . . that in light of the rehabilitation work the Applicant has achieved; the undertaking of her recent GCSE course; and her work in the prison library, she no longer faces the insuperable obstacles that disqualified her before.'

Fifty minutes later the hearing is over. Toby gathers his papers and shakes the barrister's hand vigorously, unable to quell the adrenaline surfing through his bloodstream. He can't wait to leave the court and call Laurel in prison. Tell her that, for once, things have gone their way. Their application for a judicial review of the decision of the parole board has been granted and a full oral hearing where that decision will be analysed will be held very soon.

He pushes out of his mind for the moment that he is also obliged to tell her about Max's phone call. Give her the news that, after all this time, her sister may be paying her a visit.

'Congratulations!' Joanna's voice coming from behind him is laden with spite. 'Off to let her know the result, are you?'

Toby looks at her briefly before picking up his briefcase. 'Ms Denton,' he says politely. 'How are you?'

'Pretty disgusted with today's outcome, as I'm sure you can imagine.' Joanna stares at him, cheeks sucked in as if she has swallowed a glass of bile. She throws a glance at Laurel's barrister, chatting amiably to his opponent. 'It's a disgrace,' she hisses. 'The parole board are perfectly within their rights to make any decision they see fit.'

'All due process, Ms Denton. As you know,' Toby says lightly. 'Everyone is entitled to a fair hearing.'

'My niece didn't get one, did she? Little Kirstie hasn't had her say.'

'I'm not going to debate jurisprudence with you here, Joanna. I think the court has just done that.'

He turns his back on her and squeezes out of the row of seats.

'Life should mean life,' she calls after him, her voice rising, uncontrolled. 'Kirstie was a baby. A baby ... How *can* you help her killer? She bit the ear off a toddler. You disgust me, Toby Bowman. You make me sick!'

Toby bows his head and continues on his way. He doesn't respond.

CHAPTER THIRTY-EIGHT

Evie stands in the school playground alone. It's cold but this morning she, along with all her classmates, rolled her skirt up high above her knees and her legs are bare apart from the white socks that reach midway up her calves. She folds her arms across her chest, pursing her mouth as she waits for her mother to arrive to pick her up.

She is late.

It's three-fifty and the playground is empty. Evie turns back to look up at the school building behind her, its windows vacant, the doors shut. Inside, she knows there are teachers to whom she could go, ask them to call her mother. But something in her resists. She is pissed off. Pissed off with her mother. Pissed off with everything.

How can Mum be late after everything that happened down in Devon? Isn't she worried that Evie could be taken just like Georgie was? How can she seem not to care?

Because she doesn't love you, the voice whispers inside of her. *That's why she's late. That's why she isn't bothered about Devon, why she sent you there in the first place. She just doesn't care.*

This voice.

It has been growing louder and louder inside of her for the last few months. It started long before her father took up with the sister of the most infamous female murderer since Rose West. It shelters inside of her, fading away, and then booming out when she least expects it. It tells her vile things; things she doesn't want to think about.

Ever.

She wants to shut it out entirely but then, perversely, forces herself to think about her dad. How popular he is at school. How he's the one who always comes to the quiz nights; the school fetes; and the parents' evenings. Always smiling, always bounding around as if nothing's ever wrong. Her friends ask her why it is that, after the divorce, she chose to live with her mum. Vanessa. The parent who doesn't give a shit about Evie and wouldn't notice if she never turned up again.

What can she say? The answer never comes fully formed. It sticks in her gullet like the first hard bite of an apple that scratches your throat on the way down.

And as for Hazel . . . Evie shakes her head, trailing her foot across the asphalt in the playground, scuffing her shoe. Her expensive shoe that her mother moaned about when she bought it at John Lewis, telling her this kind of expense was something her father should be responsible for.

Whatever.

Hazel is practically her own age. Evie had nearly spat out her Coke when she'd first met her, seen how young she was. All she does is trot around after Dad, doing everything he says.

It's all so fucked up, Evie thinks, raising her head to a sky banked with clouds that dip close to the ground. Even in the city, you feel it. You know that you're only a step, a moment away, from death. Those clouds, they could come down at any time. Rain hell upon you, wash you away, drag you from everything you know. The threat is there all the time. Hovering over you.

Droplets of water start to fall and Evie lowers her gaze. She looks at the school gates where a car has pulled up silently. A woman opens the door and steps out. She has a mild-looking, friendly face. Mousy hair tied up in a pony-tail, jeans and boots and one of those cool jackets that Evie's school friend Arabella was given for Christmas.

'Hello, Evie,' the woman says in a cheery voice. 'Weather's looking bad. Can I offer you a lift?'

Evie looks at the car. Inside she can hear The Chain-smokers' latest song. She stares up at the darkening sky and down again at the hard drops of rain hitting the ground beneath her feet and wetting her hair. She turns her wrist to see her watch. Her mother is over half an hour late.

She doesn't love you, the voice whispers again. *She doesn't care.* Evie sniffs, a hot kamikaze-like feeling stealing over her. Suddenly the anger feels good, like she's the one in control. Maybe her mother will finally get it if she arrives at school and Evie has gone. See that, for once, she hasn't waited around like a fucking loser. Maybe that'll make her realise what a failure of a parent she is.

'Yes,' Evie calls to the woman, slinging her bag over her shoulder and moving towards the gate. 'That would be great, thanks.'

CHAPTER THIRTY-NINE

'I cannot fucking believe it,' Joanna says, pushing a twenty-pound note across the bar. 'Permission granted? What are they thinking? I can't bear it. Toby Bowman standing in the court like a prince, smiles all over his face. How *dare* they?'

The barmaid takes the money and hands her the change before moving a glass containing ice, gin and lemon with a small bottle of tonic towards Joanna. 'Here's your double,' she says, flicking a quick troubled glance at the expression on her customer's face, the violence that seems to throb beneath it, the unhealthy sheen over her features.

Joanna pours the tonic into the glass and takes a huge gulp.

'Cheers,' Will says, his pint held lonely in the air as Joanna downs her drink.

'Oh, sorry,' she says. 'Here, I'll get another one. I need it after this week.'

'Let me,' he answers, catching the barmaid's eye and gesturing for the same again. He looks at Joanna and wonders, not for the first time, whether this is really what they should be doing. All this effort expended to keep one woman locked up in prison. Something about it seems wrong, as if they are the ones being punished and not Laurel Bowman. His cheeks burn as he notices Joanna stare at him, as if she can read these disloyal thoughts running through his mind.

'What?'

He shrugs. 'Nothing. Just tired, I suppose. It's only permission, Jo. The real hearing could easily agree with the parole board not to release Bowman.'

'Yeah, but it's a risk, isn't it? I feel like she's slipping and sliding towards the exit doors.' Joanna puts her head on one side and reaches for the new glass that has appeared at her elbow. 'Thanks.'

Will surveys their local. The one they like because its clientele consists more of old men and less of the faux-ironic hipsters who slouch in bars further along the road, stroking their beards and ordering craft beer. An elderly man sits in the corner, his eyes closed, a half-pint glass of bitter on the table next to a folded copy of the *Sun*. The photograph of Rosie Bowman as a schoolgirl stares up at him from the front page.

'What about that?' he says to Joanna, tipping his glass in the direction of the newspaper. 'Talk about timing.'

Joanna shakes her head and rubs the back of her neck. 'Unbelievable. Seems unlikely, though, doesn't it? That she had anything to do with that kid going missing? She'd have to be mad to try anything dodgy, with her background.'

'Unless she couldn't help herself,' Will points out.

Joanna looks at him. 'I'm going to go up and see Deb tomorrow,' she says as if she has just reached that decision. 'See if she needs anything. If she wants to come down and give some interviews maybe. Try and get some leverage to swing the coverage back to Kirstie.'

Will takes a swig of his pint and glances back at the old man. The thought hovers just within reach that he will never be that man. By the time he is the same age, pubs like this will be long-since gone. He sighs. Life just gets more and more complicated and, lately, the relentless ethos of Bang to Rights is wearing him down.

'Wears what?' Joanna asks. 'What did you say?'

Will laughs uncomfortably. 'I didn't realise I'd said anything out loud.'

Joanna doesn't reply, holding up her hand for another gin.

'You're drinking a lot,' he observes.

'Thirsty, tired, and grieving. No better reasons.' She studies his face while she waits. 'Well? Wears what?'

'Oh, nothing. Just thinking about us and what we do and what we'll do in the future.'

'Carry on fighting the good fight.' She gives him an angry little smile. 'Making sure people who can't speak for themselves have a voice.' She shakes her head vigorously. 'As if suddenly it's acceptable to be a child murderer? As if you can be rehabilitated from that.'

Will doesn't answer but stares down at his beer.

'Jesus, Will. What is it? I know it was a shit result today but you look like your puppy's just been run over.'

Will lifts his eyebrows and presses his lips together, debating with himself whether to reply. 'I just don't know, Jo,' he says finally.

'What is it that's wearing you down?'

'I don't know if it's what I want any more,' he says simply.

Joanna's eyes narrow.

'I mean . . . it should feel good, right? Even today when we essentially lost. But we had our submissions considered. The court *is* listening to us. We *are* making a difference. But . . .'

'But, what?'

'But,' he scratches the back of his neck nervously, 'I don't feel like that. I just feel really sad about it all. Like no one's a winner really. That it's all so miserable while we argue with each other. And nothing gets better. We only make sure it stays exactly the same. All the hatred, you know? There's so much of it.

'And then I go home and I look at my daughter, and I think, what kind of life is it for her? To grow up in such a depressing world where all we do is argue and try and keep people locked up. Not help them. Not help anyone. Because, you know,' he stares at Joanna earnestly, 'I don't think even Debbie and Rob are happy about this. After all this time, how does Laurel rotting away in prison help them move on? How can you move on? Because, you know . . . wouldn't it be better if you could?'

Will's voice trails away and the silence between them lengthens. He swallows, watching Joanna, but her face is blank.

'Don't,' he says, pushing his glass away. 'Don't do this. I just mean . . . it's something I've been thinking about. I don't want to end up in a pit of resentment, stewing in my own anger. Not forever, Jo. And I don't want you to do it either.'

Joanna gives a short nod. 'And . . .' she runs her tongue over her bottom lip, eyes fixed on the condensation moving down her glass towards her fingers '. . . what would you do instead? What would you do?'

'I don't know. I'm not saying I've planned anything. I'm just talking. About how I feel sometimes. Not all the time. You know what I think about Bowman. It's not that I'm saying we should forgive . . .'

Joanna bangs her glass down on top of the bar. Her knuckles wrapped around it are red. The barmaid jerks her head up at the sound. 'That *is* what you're saying, Will. If you don't keep her inside, what else is there? You *have* to forgive. You can't say – oh, yeah, come on out, come and have a nice council flat, enjoy your NHS medical card and the rest of it. Oh, and by the way, I still think you're a murderous lying cow, but never mind! It's about time you were out and living amongst us all. Please don't kill anyone else, though! That wouldn't do at all.'

'You're being facetious. That's not what I mean and you know it.'

'I'm serious, Will. If you let her out, you have to *forgive*. What's the point otherwise?'

'What about saying that she's served her time? That she's a different person from who she was before? That the ten-year-old Laurel has gone. This is someone who won't hurt again because she's learnt her lesson?'

Joanna seems frozen, her mouth open a little, her eyes fixed on Will's. After a second or two, she tosses her head. 'You're a fucking idiot,' she snaps, picking up her bag from off the floor. 'You're an idiot if you think that someone like that can change. They never change. Ever.' Joanna wipes her mouth with the back of her hand. 'I'm going now. Because I'm feeling pretty sick.'

'Don't go, Jo. I'm sorry. I don't want to upset you. I wish we could talk about it.' He reaches out and touches her arm but Joanna looks down coldly at his hand before shifting away and it falls into empty air.

'There's nothing to talk about. You can take your paid notice. It's two weeks, I think.'

'Oh, Jo. Come on . . .'

'And then you can get your stuff and get out. Got it?' Joanna backs off, an expression of disgust contorting her face, before she turns and slams out of the pub.

CHAPTER FORTY

1998

The courtroom in the Old Bailey was stuffed to the rafters with a roiling mix of legal arguments, rhetoric and latent violence. The dark-panelled walls seemed to push in on the inhabitants, sliding them in towards each other, the ceiling pressed down flat on top of them, stifling them, compressing the air until it was heady with the might of justice.

Laurel sat in the dock, her chin level with the balustrade around it. Her chair was perched on a wooden block, which had been purposely and hurriedly made over the weekend when it was discovered that she would not be able to see over and into the courtroom otherwise.

She wore a plain white shirt and her school tie. Her hair was brushed back from her face in a simple ponytail. Her eyes were big and round, staring straight ahead, focused away from the gallery above her, to her right. There sat Debbie and Rob Swann, holding hands, flanked by a bristling and tear-stained Joanna. Their faces were grey, washed out. Debbie's chest rose and fell quickly with her rapid breathing. Rob's lips were drawn tightly together, dark shadows under his eyes.

Along the wall opposite Laurel were the press. Amongst them sat the courtroom artist, his eyes fixed on her, committing every detail of the scene to memory, to be scratched down as soon as he left the courtroom. He would draw her image as if blocked by her barrister, his wig concealing the detail of her face. Because her identity was shielded. She was no longer Laurel Bowman. She was Child X.

Mr Justice Follett entered with mistral force, his red robes swept back behind him as he sat, his face stern and heavy with duty. As he spoke, the journalists hunched forward with their pens raised, nibs at the ready. Counsel for the prosecution spoke first, addressing the jury of seven women and five men, who still seemed stunned to find themselves here in this courtroom. They averted their eyes from the huddled shape of Laurel in the dock. Several jurors held crumpled tissues in their hands, looking desperately up at Debbie and Rob Swann as they heard what had happened to their daughter.

The learned counsel spoke at length in his opening speech, reeling in the jury and the others packed into the courtroom like reams of nets packed and jiving with the silvery skin of fish. He spoke of wickedness, of pure and unadulterated violence. He spoke of cruelty and torture and the desperate cries of a mother when she realised that her child was missing. Of little Kirstie, and how she did not deserve her fate. How her end was all the more shocking, perpetrated as it was by someone who should still be innocent, beyond the realm of such atrocities.

How was it? he pondered aloud. How was it that such depravity could exist in one so young? Was it a sign of our times? An indication that this new generation had bewilderingly embraced unfathomable violence? Had exposure to violence on television and film meant that the mind of a ten-year-old child could become addled, tainted with poison, until she could no longer see straight, could no longer discern the difference between right and wrong? Or was that all an illusion? Was that merely a puff, an excuse? Here, Counsel paused and half-turned behind him, towards the occupants of the gallery straining to follow his words.

Or was it, instead, that Child X was very simply, very plainly, wicked?

Wasn't that the most likely explanation? Because how could one quantify the effect of violent films or games on a brain? Scientists grappled with this problem on a daily basis, and perhaps the equation was within our grasp in the course of our lifetime. But not today. Not as Child X sat in this courtroom. Only she could explain the dark forces that must have been at work inside her when she decided to kidnap Kirstie and take her by the hand down onto the canal path. Only she knew why she had beaten and tortured her. Only she knew those secret places where her thoughts lay within her, tangled like weeds.

It is not, he said, for us to try and understand. It is necessary only to agree that she is indeed guilty. That she, with malice aforethought, did take the life of Kirstie Swann. A chilling and abominable intention indeed. One that very few of us in this world will ever be able to understand. Even she – and here he pointed at Laurel, her head dipped low – even she does not accept the evil inside of her. She claims to be not guilty. She says she did not kill Kirstie and yet she offers no other explanation for the little girl's death. She suggests it was a mistake, but she will not tell us in what way. After this *explanation* – counsel's disdain for it was

194

clear – she is silent. She will not be drawn on that afternoon. That beautiful summer's day when a child's innocent life was cruelly, and violently, robbed from her.

Counsel reached the end of his speech, his voice hoarse from the passion with which he had spoken. Laurel's head remained bent. She avoided the laser stare of Joanna Denton, the slow hot tears of Debbie Swann. She stared down at her hands in her lap, feeling her buttocks numb beneath her, her expression frozen. She had been sitting on her hard chair in the dock for four hours.

Tomorrow her barrister would begin her defence.

Laurel did not listen as the judge explained this to her at the end of the day.

She had not been listening for hours.

CHAPTER FORTY-ONE

Lying in her cell, Laurel links her hands behind her neck and shuts her eyes for a second. She thinks back to the conversation she has just had with her uncle, to the staccato pleasure in his voice as he excitedly fired information at her about the court hearing and how they had won. Laurel sniffs, unable to take the news in. She's annoyed with herself that, on the phone, she had felt seeds of hope take root in her. Now she concentrates on angrily telling them to fuck off and die.

Her pulse has finally slowed from where it had ratcheted when she first heard the news and now she is back to her normal self. She'll put that information somewhere else in her head. She'll think about it later when she can believe that it will mean anything for her future.

Now, though, she's focusing on what else Toby had told her. As she lies there, dwelling on it, Fritz shoves her head round the door.

'Fucking Cags has broken the fucking remote and it's stuck on shit-balls *Bargain Hunt*. I cannot take any more of that orange wanker.'

Laurel licks her lips and squeezes her eyes shut, tries to stay with one foot in the past and keep from bringing herself back to her present.

'L?' Fritz says. 'D'you hear me? Cags again. I swear, this is the last time . . .'

'Piss off,' Laurel snaps.

'Eh?'

'Fuck off, I'm busy.'

Fritz falls silent. Laurel raises her head, seeing the hurt in her friend's eyes. Her only friend, if you don't count Toby, which she doesn't most of the time. Fritz and she have been together since they were fifteen when they both wound up in Oakingham. Fritz was locked up for breaking into a house on her own estate, tying up a seventy-year-old woman in her armchair in the lounge for six hours while Fritz ransacked her cupboards, ate the contents of her fridge and watched an Alfred Hitchcock DVD. When she had finally left, she had stuffed a pair of flesh-coloured tights into the woman's mouth before letting herself out by the front door, her pockets filled with the woman's pension. It was only when she was arrested that she learnt the victim had suffered a stroke whilst Fritz had been busy watching *Rear Window*. She was now entirely paralysed down her left side and reduced to living in a care home for the rest of her days.

Fritz had attached herself to Laurel from the first day she'd met her. She had never mentioned the murder of Kirstie Swann and Laurel never asked her about the old woman. They bumbled along together, watching telly, playing cards and sharing jokes that nobody else seemed to get. Fritz is long and lanky with a greasy mullet haircut that renders her face even thinner. She has deep green eyes and focuses them reproachfully on Laurel as her friend tells her to get lost.

'What is it?' asks Fritz, folding her arms, her voice petulant.

Laurel sighs, her face bunched in a tight, unhappy scowl. 'My sister,' she says.

Fritz says nothing for a second. Then: 'Rosie?'

'The very same.'

'What about her?'

Laurel leaps up, rubbing a palm across her face and pushing past Fritz as she leaves the room. 'Nothing,' she says as she goes, 'forget it.'

They swing into the recreation room, which Laurel crosses before smacking the television into oblivion.

'You'll regret that,' Cags remarks from her corner, hunched up in a saggy blue chair. 'You'll be back cleaning the bogs now, I'll bet.'

Laurel straightens, rubbing her fist where it smarts from its contact with the TV casing. 'Lucky it wasn't you instead, eh? What's that?' she says, whipping round, her stomach convulsing at the sight of the spittle at the edges of Cags's mouth, the crust of green around her nostrils. 'What did you say?'

'Nothing.' The girl shrugs and gives a mean little smile. 'I'm just saying.'

'Well, don't fucking say, right?' Laurel walks over to where Cags's legs stick out straight in front across the stained carpet. She looks down at the girl's slippers, the folds of her tracksuit bottoms, and wrinkles her nose at the smell of stale sweat, a sweet and fertile odour, emanating from the other girl. 'Don't you ever wash, Cags?' She kicks at one of her ankles. ''Bout time you cleaned yourself up, I reckon.'

From her sentry post in the doorway, Fritz gives a low chuckle.

Cags's smile freezes and a pink hue rises up, mottling her chest and neck. Laurel leans down and sniffs theatrically. 'You fucking reek.'

When the guards arrive, Laurel is sent to the toilets with a toothbrush. As she scrubs the tiles and, later, when she is back in her room, she still struggles to get her head around what Toby had told her.

Rosie wants to visit her, in here?

Laurel hasn't seen her sister since the night she was taken away from her parents. For nineteen years, apart from one drawing right at the beginning of her sentence, she has heard nothing from her although Laurel thinks about Rosie most days.

The request from Toby thrums in her head, pouring into the room along with the shaft of sunlight that floods through the high window, hot against her legs. She remembers her sister's face. Her dark hair, the tiny mole on her earlobe, her brown eyes, quick and watchful. The way she hummed as she moved, unaware of the music that danced through her, tapping her fingers against her thighs. Laurel focuses on the edge of a crack in the wall, the way it fragments the light, splits it into two when she half-closes her eyes, watching the colours fracture through her eyelashes.

Her eyes open wide as she suddenly articulates the thought that has been beetling around inside her head since she'd spoken to Toby.

Every bone in her body knows that Rosie should not come here to prison. Knows that she should not look her sister in the eyes. That her life – such as it is – should remain untouched and unscathed.

Setting scorpions running across her toes with visits, court applications . . . all talk of these should be banned from between these walls because hope is never welcome here.

But she is battling with another emotion just as strong.

She loves her sister.

Laurel is shamed by it. Has tried to kill it in all the cells she's sat in, through all the loathing she's faced.

But there it is.

And she cannot help herself from seeking to find out if that love is returned.

CHAPTER FORTY-TWO

Jonny brings the roast to the table with that air of bashful pride so common in those who cook well. The beef is pink and fulsome and Max salivates, fingering the stem of his wine glass. Hazel is sitting next to him. Evie's absence isn't mentioned and hovers in the corner with the other elephant in the room: the articles spread all over the recent papers. Evie's interview with a journalist has been repeated ad infinitum, pouring petrol on the bonfire that is Hazel's public persona. The mainstream media directly links the unsolved disappearance of Georgie Greenstreet with Hazel's presence at the hotel.

As Max read the papers, his heart had fluttered more violently than usual, ambition mixing with frustration inside him in a slurry of panic. The vultures were flying ahead, rushing information out and causing a perfect storm of anger, fear and visceral hatred towards Hazel. The timing of the story too, happening just as Laurel Bowman's appeal against the parole board is being heard in court, has whipped the public into a frenzy. The Flower Girls are all anyone is talking about, from print media, to morning television, to the radio. Max's mind is whirring as he bends his head closer to Hazel, listening to her talking without really taking in the words. This is his story, he keeps telling himself. He found Hazel. It is up to him to show the world Rosie Bowman.

If only he can persuade her to meet her sister.

But he must breathe. Drink his wine. Take things slow. He doesn't know how he's going to get Hazel to that point because she has yet to be persuaded actually to do anything. This lunch will be crucial to that end. Because if he gets Hazel into that prison with Laurel then he has won. Any deal he'll make will blow the rest of the scavenging journos out of the park.

'This looks delicious,' he says, moving to pick up a serving spoon. 'Good enough to eat.'

Jonny grins and sets down a china dish of parsnips. 'Try the gravy. It's a family recipe. You'll like it.'

'Jonny is a fabulous cook,' Hazel says with a smile although her hand trembles a little as she pours Max more red wine. 'One of his many qualities.'

They begin to eat, a soft silence settling around them with the aromas from the food and the wine. Jonny's place is bigger than Max had expected: a mansion flat in West London. He's obviously doing well for himself. It has high ceilings with ornate dado rails and floor-to-ceiling windows. As Max gets to know Jonny better, he understands that the man has two levels of energy: high and higher. He can't stay still. Even sitting with a plate of food in front of him, he is constantly checking Hazel and Max with his eyes, roving his hands across the table like a conductor, offering, serving, never motionless.

By contrast, Hazel has an air of childlike serenity about her, despite the stress she must be under at the moment. Her smiles are warm, her touch is kind. She seems to know exactly the right time to offer a second helping, or a top-up of wine. Max can discern a clear tension underneath but she seems to be coping well and, he's pleased to see, is responsive to his suggestions.

'I saw,' she begins tentatively. 'I saw that Laurel won her hearing. Does this mean she will be released from prison?'

Max shakes his head. 'No. Not yet at least. I'm no lawyer but, from what I've read, it means that the parole board will now have to argue in front of a judge that they're right to have decided she needs to serve more time, that she shouldn't be released yet. Whereas she's saying their decision is unreasonable and irrational.'

Hazel nods. 'But she could get out eventually?'

'I would imagine so. She's served eighteen years, Hazel. I'd think they'd struggle to keep her in for the rest of her life. She was so young when she killed Kirstie.'

Hazel bites her lip and reaches for the remote control to turn up the music. 'Sorry,' she says abruptly. 'It's hard for me to talk about.'

'I understand,' Max says, patting the tablecloth as if it were Hazel's hand. 'What is this music?' he asks after a moment. 'It's beautiful.'

'"Dido's Lament",' Hazel replies. 'Jonny hates it. It's so sad. I love it, though.'

Jonny raises his eyebrows. 'I'm more of a guitar and drums sort of a guy. A bottle of wine and this kind of stuff and I'm fast asleep.'

Max lifts his head towards the Sonos system fixed in the corners of the dining room where they sit around a mahogany dining table. He falls silent as Jonny moves the conversation on, listening to the notes floating high above them. As the lament ends, he is bewildered to discover that he has tears in his eyes.

'"Remember me,"' Hazel murmurs to him, causing Jonny to halt mid-sentence. '"But forget my fate."'

'What does it mean?'

Hazel averts her face as she thinks, half-closing her eyes. 'Dido lost everything she had ever loved. She was betrayed by the person she most trusted. So, I think she's asking for her place in history but to be remembered well. Not as a victim, but as a woman who loved.'

Max watches Hazel as she speaks, the music rising above them. The wine is warm in his stomach and he is suddenly deeply and completely content.

'Max ...' Jonny's voice cuts in, scattering his thoughts. 'We need to talk about Evie and what she's done. Talking to that journalist. All the things she said about my relationship with Hazel. I can't believe she spoke like that.'

Max raises his shoulders along with his glass. 'Ah, yes. The shame of it is that we didn't control it ourselves, prep her to say more positive things. At this stage of the game, people will read into absolutely anything. Or nothing.' He drinks from his glass.

'Well, I'm hugely concerned. All that attention on Evie is really not good. It's interfering with her schoolwork. I don't understand how her mother could ever have let this happen.'

'We don't blame Evie, of course,' Hazel interjects. 'The poor thing was tricked by the journalist, it's obvious. She's only fourteen, after all. Something should be done about these papers. They're out of control.' She dips her head as her voice falters. 'They're trying to take photos of me, out on the street. No one's protecting me, everyone knows who I am. All these years I've been someone else, and now it's all out in the open. I don't understand why they don't stop them, put a ban on it. You don't know what it's like, reading things about yourself that are so untrue. So vile. The other day,' she looks from Jonny to Max, 'I had to go to the chemist to get a prescription. The doctor has prescribed me some anti-anxiety pills,' she explains softly. 'And as I went in, someone actually spat at me. It landed on my sleeve. I'm not Laurel.' She wipes her eyes and a smear of mascara stains the top of her cheek. 'I'm not her.'

Max shifts in his seat, sensing his opportunity. 'I agree that things have been blown up out of proportion,' he says. 'As I warned you down at Balcombe Court, once the press got wind of who you really are, Hazel, they were bound to run with this story. That's why I want some damage control. I want to try and rein this in before it becomes something beyond any of us.'

'Isn't the damage already done?' Jonny reaches over to wipe away the mark on Hazel's face. 'After what Hazel's just said? Added to which, she's getting more letters, more hate mail.'

'From the same person as before?' Max asks.

'Maybe.' Hazel's voice trembles. 'I'm not sure. The ones I had before New Year were . . . different. They all had the same quality about them. These ones seem . . . erratic. As if they're coming from all kinds of nasty people. And there are photographs of . . . terrible things.' She presses the knuckles of one hand into the palm of the other. 'They say they want to kill me. Make me pay. Accuse me of taking Georgie. Even though she's been found!'

Hazel puts her hands over her face, her voice becoming muffled. 'Of course I didn't hurt her,' she says desperately.

'I was so relieved when she was brought back safely.' She releases her hands and stares wildly at Max. 'I am NOT Rosie Bowman! I haven't been for nineteen years. I am Hazel Archer. THAT is who I am. Not that child . . .' she begins to cry gently '. . . not that child. I'm not her any more . . .'

Jonny gets up quickly and comes to stand behind Hazel, leaning in over her chair to put his arms around her. He buries his face in her hair, whispering, 'I know, I know . . . I know you're not, my darling.'

Max says nothing for a moment. His mouth is dry.

'Do you know how stressful it is?' Jonny turns to him angrily. 'Leading a double life? I know . . .' he taps his chest '. . . what this poor woman has been going through.' He strokes Hazel's hair. 'I know, my darling. I'm here.'

Max clears his throat and fingers the stem of his wine glass. 'Well, yes. Of course it's been terribly difficult for you. All of you,' he says, looking apologetic as Jonny glares at him. 'But . . . you must appreciate . . . what I've been reading . . . And then the interview with Evie . . .' He hesitates, tracing the edge of his coaster with his fingertips, gathering his thoughts. 'I really think you should consider doing what I've been asking.'

Hazel's crying quietens and eventually she stops, reaching forward to sip from her wine glass.

Seeing Jonny open his mouth to speak, Max jumps in again to maintain momentum. 'So, I should tell you that I have already contacted Toby Bowman, your sister's solicitor – your uncle, Hazel, I believe? He's been in touch with Laurel. He's on a high after winning the hearing. And . . .' Max reaches over the table as if to touch Hazel's arm but drops his hand at the last second, resting it on his placemat '. . . she has agreed, Hazel. Laurel will see you.'

Hazel gazes down at her lap, saying nothing in response.

'And you think that bringing them together will stop the bad press?' Jonny asks, returning to his chair, buzzing with a vitality that even Max has noticed is blurred by red wine. 'I mean, call me an idiot, but why would it?'

'Because it might jog Hazel's memory. It might enable her finally to know what happened that afternoon with Kirstie. And if she does, then she might be able to help Debbie and Rob Swann get some closure. Which, frankly, will improve her popularity with the public no end.'

'Right. I get it,' Jonny says, looking over at Hazel. 'What do you think, darling? Can it hurt?'

The edges of her mouth twist, as if she is in pain. 'No,' she says at last. 'I suppose it can't.'

'So you'll go?' Max says, his heart thumping. 'Because, in actual fact, there's a window this week. On Thursday. Toby can arrange a visit then.'

Hazel looks at him, thoughts playing out across her mind. Finally she gives a short, swift nod.

'Yes,' she says. 'I'll go.'

CHAPTER FORTY-THREE

Debbie is only three years older than her sister, but side by side the gap between them could be more than a decade. Debbie's hair is grey and her face is scored with the grief of nearly twenty years. She cannot drink alcohol; she refuses even to take headache tablets. For her, the pain is what makes her daughter real. If she blocks it out, Kirstie will be gone.

'She'd be twenty-two in September,' Debbie says, a cigarette smouldering in an ashtray at her elbow. Joanna sits opposite her at the kitchen table, cups of tea in front of them. 'So . . .' Debbie sighs, looking down at her wedding band. 'What does this latest court thing mean?'

'It means,' Joanna replies, 'that Laurel Bowman has been given a chance to argue in front of a judge that the parole board were wrong to deny her release.' She closes her eyes and exhales up towards the nicotine-stained ceiling. 'I can't believe it either. It never ends, does it?'

Joanna stops talking, her eyes fixed on her mug. After a moment, Debbie pushes back her chair with a groan and walks to the sink, keeping her back to Joanna.

'Deb?' she asks. 'Are you OK?'

After a moment, her sister turns round and gives her a sad smile.

'Yes. I'm OK.'

'This is a shock, right? But let me tell you . . . we will not give up. We are not going to let this happen. We will honour Kirstie, we *will*.'

Debbie smiles again and lights another cigarette, breathing the smoke deep down into her lungs. She studies its lit end for a moment before speaking.

'Nineteen years ago, when it first happened, I wanted to die. You know, you were there. Even though I was pregnant with Ben. Even then. I couldn't see . . . I couldn't see how I could go on without her. Without my Kirstie.'

'Of course, Deb,' Joanna whispers. 'No one can imagine . . .'

'Everywhere I looked there were reminders. The house. The garden. The street. The corner shop. All her toys everywhere. Her bedroom. The smell of her pillow, her clothes. Even Rob's face.' Debbie coughs, taking another drag. 'She was the spit of him. So I couldn't bring myself to look at him some days. He thought I hated him. Sometimes I do ...' She grimaces, leaning forward and stubbing the half-smoked cigarette into the ashtray.

'But through all of it, my main thing was ... like you said . . . to *honour* Kirstie.' She looks directly at Joanna. 'To keep her alive in people's memories. To tell the world how beautiful she was, how innocent she was. How she should never have died.'

She nods a few times.

Joanna can't breathe, can't move.

'And that's what we've done, isn't it? All these years. All of us. Me, Rob and Ben. And you. You've fought like a Trojan, haven't you, Jo? More than anyone outside of here, outside of our home. And we've kept together as a family, haven't we? We made it. Not many people would.' Her eyes are bright blue and fierce on Joanna's face in the winter sunshine coming through the window. 'And I thank you for that. Really I do.'

It's there in the room, Joanna can feel it as strongly as the warmth of the mug in her hands.

The *but*.

'But sometimes . . .' Debbie reaches for her pack of cigarettes again and sighs, her voice trailing off.

'Sometimes?'

'Sometimes I wonder if the memories of Kirstie are getting . . . *tainted* by all this fighting. Keeping that woman inside. Making everything about her. It's all about Laurel, isn't it? Not about Kirstie any more.'

Joanna swallows. 'But it *is*, Debbie. It *is* about Kirstie. It's about getting her justice. Why should Laurel be allowed to get away with—'

'Get away with it?' Debbie interrupts sharply. 'She already has, hasn't she? She *has* got away with it. She did the moment she killed my baby. I'm not getting Kirstie back, am I? What punishment can make up for that?'

'The sentence . . .' Joanna tries.

'Ben's having a baby. I'm going to be a granny,' Debbie says, folding a tea towel and placing it on the counter. 'There must be *some* happiness we can have, mustn't there? Waiting for us in the future or even here *now*. Where we're not always fighting.' She comes back to the table and puts her hand on Joanna's. 'I want to remember Kirstie as she was. Not as a rod to use on someone else's back. If we carry on, all the months ahead – more fighting – I don't think I've got the energy for it, Jo. I really don't. The only thing I care about now is Kirstie and my family.'

*

210

The rhythm of the train back down to London feels like a cradle to Joanna, the sensations of rocking and speed lulling her into calm. Her breathing has lengthened from the agitated state she'd been in on leaving Debbie's house and she watches the fog-covered, tawny outline of the Yorkshire Moors stretch past her with a growing sense of detachment. Here she is, about to witness Laurel Bowman's release, and everyone around her has given up. They've all stopped caring.

But why does she care when even her sister is moving on? Why can't she let it go?

Joanna traces with her finger a bead of condensation falling down the window and brings a can of lager to her lips. Here she is again. The one on the outside. Even when they were kids, she would barrel into anyone who dared have a go at her sister. Debbie was always the popular one anyway. She was happy and easy, and people generally just seemed to do her bidding. Joanna would stamp her feet and demand that people did what she said, even though they never would.

When Kirstie was born, Joanna had held her in her arms and she had felt such a burst of love and of pride that this little girl was part of her, her family's blood. And then to see that blood spilt on the ground ...

But *Debbie* is the one who bore her. *Debbie* the one whose genes spiralled through Kirstie like strands of fairy dust. So why is she able to accept a future without her? How can she let her go when, for Joanna, it seems impossible?

Kirstie is dead. And Debbie's right, nothing is going to bring her back.

So it's not that Joanna can't accept that Kirstie has gone.

211

But to abandon the fight against Laurel seems only to offer the prospect of a life without any kind of meaning.

God, am I that selfish? she wonders, resting her forehead on the glass. Has it all just been selfishness, a way to avoid her own failings? Without the fight to win justice for Kirstie, Joanna fears she will be untethered. Her anger keeps her on the ground. Without it to anchor her, there is only a void.

Suddenly Joanna feels cold, wrapping her arms around herself. Suddenly she feels very alone.

The train pulls into a station and someone sits down opposite, throwing their newspaper onto the shared table in front of her. There they are, the Flower Girls, captured for eternity in those two photographs.

Laurel and Rosie Bowman.

Joanna turns away and considers her reflection in the window as rain begins to spatter the glass.

What now? she thinks. *What now?*

CHAPTER FORTY-FOUR

Toby waits for Laurel in the private room he has requested for the purpose, away from the cacophony and chaos of the main prison-visit cattle pen. The room has walls painted a dirty cream; the table is stained and chipped. It is at least quiet, overheated but calm. Outside, a downpour is reaching biblical proportions. The sound of it is a white-noise hum, washing against the wrap-around window that runs around the top of the walls. The halogen light above emits a stark, unattractive glare. Toby's bald head is illuminated like the top of a boiled egg, his jowls and eye-bags cast into sinister shadow.

'Jeez, you look rough, Uncle Toby,' Laurel observes accurately as she enters the room. 'I thought I was the one who should be shitting themselves about today: not be able to sleep, off my food . . . I'm all right, though, as it goes, but you . . .' Her voice trails off as she sits down opposite him. 'Well, let's just say, you're not going to be winning any sexy solicitor contests any time soon.'

Toby sighs, leaning back in his chair and crossing his arms. He knows he looks a sight. Ever since his last hospital visit, on the day of Laurel's hearing, when he was told there was no hope and that the cancer had progressed too far, weight has seemed to drip off him like candle wax. His face is haggard and sunken. It is as if his body overheard what the consultant said and has immediately put the truth of it on display. Rogue thoughts of food, which used to dominate his waking hours, now make him irreversibly nauseous.

'It's only a joke,' Laurel says. 'I'm being a bitch. Sorry.'

'It's fine. Don't fuss yourself. How are you feeling about today?'

Laurel shrugs. 'Don't feel anything.'

Toby raises his eyebrows.

'Seriously. Now I've got used to the idea, it's all right. It's about time, I suppose.' Laurel's lips are thin, her eyes dark as currants.

'You know, I'm still not entirely convinced it's a great idea. What with the full hearing of the judicial review happening soon, I don't want anything to jeopardise that.' He leans forward, frowning. 'But look ... maybe it might help to have her on side. To resolve things finally. Anyway, I suppose, you're damned if you do, damned if you don't, right?' He gives a short laugh then stops abruptly as Laurel looks at him, her face expressionless.

'It's just ... you have to be calm, Lulu. Right? The purpose of the visit is closure. Or that's how she's presented it. She misses you. Wants to see how you are. You don't have to fight her—'

'Why would I fight her?' Laurel interrupts. 'She only hasn't bothered having anything to do with me for nearly twenty years.'

'This is what I mean.' He wags a finger at her. 'I know you have a lot of anger. But if you don't deal with that – *demonstrate* that you've dealt with it – you're really going to struggle with the parole board. They need to see that you *are* now rehabilitated. That your demons have been exorcised and you're ready to return to society.'

'Rehabilitated?' Laurel says. 'I haven't been in a supermarket since I was ten years old. I can't drive a car. I don't know how to use a bank account, for fuck's sake. How am I supposed to *return to society* when I was barely in it to begin with?'

Toby purses his mouth, looking at her. 'And that is exactly the kind of thing you have to stop saying, Laurel.'

'My name is L.'

'L, then. L!' Toby slaps the table with both palms. 'Please! Work with me here, L. I'm trying to help you. The advice I give you, it's not to piss you off. It's not to try and make your life even worse. It's to get you out of this place. On the outside . . . where we can help you. Help you adjust to living. But first I need to get you out! If you stay in here for the rest of your days, what's the point of any of it? Come on, you know that. Please.'

They sit in silence, looking at each other. Laurel takes in Toby's appearance, his normally mild-mannered face now creased with worry and strain. This man who has come every month without fail to visit her. Brought her presents, sent her Christmas cards. He has never been paid, he has never asked to be paid. Laurel feels her stomach dip, an unfamiliar contraction in the back of her throat, and wonders, surprised, if she is about to cry. Because it is Toby who has been her father all of these years. Her own father, long-since disappeared, went scurrying off with her mother to burrow down into the dank earth, far from their responsibilities, from what they had produced. But Toby has always remained.

'You're not going to be there, though, are you?' Laurel says at last. 'On the outside.' She juts her chin at him. 'I mean, look at you. How long have you got?'

He glances down at his lap. 'I'm having an operation,' he lies. 'Soon. The prognosis will be good after that. I still have hope.'

'You don't look very hopeful,' Laurel observes with her sharp eyes fixed on him. She throws back her head, gazing up at the ceiling and exhaling in a whoosh of air. 'Fuck, this place is shit, isn't it?' she says, looking back to meet his gaze. 'I'll be a good girl,' she says at last. 'For you.'

'I'm glad to hear it.'

Thunder rolls above them and the rain hardens as she says, 'May as well bring her in then. Let the fun begin.'

CHAPTER FORTY-FIVE

Joanna sits by the window in a café, a chipped white mug of brown tea slowly cooling between her hands. She takes no notice of it, nor the pieces of toast dripping with butter on the plate in front of her. Her eyes are fixed on the block of flats opposite, still visible despite the steam rising up the window which, every so often, she wipes away with a sleeve.

Days later and she still can't get the image of her sister out of her head. She hasn't slept and every thought in her brain feels like a hammer. Added to which, it's been over a week since she had the fight with Will and she still hasn't spoken to him. The sadness she feels that her oldest friend has betrayed her is incalculable. So she does what she always does when she feels overcome. She buries her feelings.

She has been in the café for nearly an hour. As she has sat there, the number of photographers and journalists across the street from her, outside the flats, has steadily increased. There are now at least twenty of them, chatting and smoking; frowning at the faint drizzle which drifts down from the sky.

Other punters in the café have noticed the throng on the other side of the road and periodically gesture over to it, clearly wondering which celebrity is staying in the flats. She has already heard the Eastern European waitress state with utmost certainty that she saw Keira Knightley go in there earlier. But Joanna knows this isn't true. She knows the flat belongs to Rosie Bowman.

In her handbag is yet another copy of the *Sun* with Rosie's photograph on its front page. It seems fated that Rosie should appear like this – pop up in the world after being hidden for so long – just as Laurel may finally be close to achieving her freedom. After everything that has happened in the last week – the court hearing; the fight with Will; seeing Debbie – the lure was irresistible. Joanna had called an ex-boyfriend who works in communications for the Met Police. She hated herself for it, had avoided the mirror this morning, but she had done it. It had cost her six pints of bitter last night, a considerable amount of flirting and the promise of dinner next week, but she had managed to get him to drunkenly look up Hazel Archer's address.

As she arrived at the block of flats, she realised she has been unusually naive. The press pack have zeroed in on the youngest Flower Girl like snipers. They hover around the door, cameras flashing whenever a delivery arrives or another inhabitant braves the throng in order to leave their flat.

She's not sure why she's here, why she wanted Rosie's address in the first place. She's been trying to work that out as she sits here in the fug of the café. She isn't even sure what she'd say to the woman, if she met her face to face. She has imagined countless conversations where she confronts Laurel Bowman, makes her realise what she's done, makes her cry heavy, heartfelt tears over Kirstie's grave. Makes her finally say how sorry she is, over and over again. But Rosie has always remained a shadow. Six years old, too young – according to the system – to be cognisant of a crime. Too on the cusp of what it is to be human to be able to have developed a mind that desires harm, that actively seeks it out.

Joanna has read a great deal of criminal psychology, particularly in connection to young children. She has read Jean Piaget, scoured books on the mental development of children. She has sought to understand what drove Laurel Bowman to commit the atrocity that she did. There are more child murderers than perhaps society likes to acknowledge, she has discovered. The famous ones: Mary Bell; Robert Thompson; Jon Venables. The lesser-known: Jesse Pomeroy, Barratt and Bradley, Hannah Ocuish. Children who have come from broken homes, from situations of horrific abuse, but also those – like Laurel – who have committed an aberration, travelled so far out of character and what would be considered normal with regard to their background, that their behaviour seems alien: it becomes inexplicable.

Joanna presses her fingertips into her eye sockets, shutting out the noise of the café chatter, the clinking of cutlery. She breathes in the smell of soap from the shower she took this morning, washing off the hangover from the night before. She thinks about Rosie and her development levels aged six. The ego is rampant at that age. The world turns around, and according to, the child.

A truck rumbles past, disrupting her thoughts. Joanna pushes away her tea and gets to her feet. As she does, she sees the door of the building opposite open slowly, inch by inch. Hazel tries to keep her head down, a hood covers her dark cap of hair. But the cameras flare and flash as she emerges and she has to lift her head to find her way. Joanna freezes as she watches, unable to move, to do anything, her mouth open as if ready to call out Hazel's name, call her back, as she jumps quickly into a car that pulls up at the kerb. Joanna follows her with her gaze, taking in everything about her as the car swerves away, its tyres spinning fast and splashing water over the paparazzi as they snap endless footage of the second Flower Girl leaving her home in the rain.

CHAPTER FORTY-SIX

Hazel and Max arrive at the prison and wait silently in the reception area, ignoring the stares of others around them. They sit on bucket seats nailed to the wall in a small, grey room where a heavy gunmetal-coloured door stands guard between them and the prison interior. Hazel's hands are red and chilled from the air outside and she shivers, not with cold so much as anticipation.

She is finding it hard to breathe. Being in here. Hearing the clank of locks and keys, the slam of heavy doors swinging into place. Then the dark, the claustrophobia. And, very faintly, the call of the birds outside, circling the skies, so far away through the glass and the brick that confine her.

She is picturing her sister. Recalling her face before they were separated, before Laurel was taken away: on the beach, her blonde hair wrapped around her face by the wind, her mouth curved in a huge smile, cheeks bronzed by the sun. Snow-White and Rose-Red. That's what their mother had always called them. Her two princesses. Laurel looked more like their father with her fairness and her height whereas Hazel was her mother's image, dark and slim and contained in a way that Laurel never was. Her sister was clumsy, forever tripping over, dropping things and breaking them, her arms flailing in enthusiasm for whatever was around her, for what the day held. Hazel and her mother would watch her sometimes as she sprinted across the garden in the rain, her face lifted up to the skies, relishing the feel of the water on her skin.

And now Hazel is going to see her again. After nearly twenty years. What will she look like? Will her face be as unguarded? Or will it reflect the vitriol and bile she must feel towards her sister? Will she have forgiven her? Hazel shakes her head, feeling the leaves on the bud of fear inside her beginning to uncurl. She clenches her fists and breathes. One, two, three. She is strong enough to cope with this. She has to be.

Next to her, Max sits with his legs spread wide, the confident position belying his nervousness. He can feel Hazel trembling beside him and glances at his watch. They were early and now have been sitting here for over thirty-five minutes. He can still taste the hurriedly swigged coffee that passed for breakfast, the bile from his ever-present heartburn searing his throat. For want of anything better to do, he lets out a little laugh.

'This place is pretty horrendous, isn't it?' He turns to Hazel. 'How are you feeling?'

'Oh,' she sighs, scuffing the toe of her boot along the floor. Her hood hangs over the collar of her coat, making her seem much smaller than she is, ducked down and hidden. 'Pretty scared. Nervous. Terrified actually. I don't really know what to expect.'

'The main thing is to try and establish a relationship with Laurel. Take things easy, one step at a time. You may find,' Max's voice rises a little with the energy of his thoughts, 'that just the very fact of seeing her after all of this time will trigger things you've forgotten. Memory is a funny thing.

You can never tell what will bring stuff to the surface. A smell, a sound. It's been so long . . . if you've pushed things down for all these years, you might be surprised what comes up.' He stops, as if he has suddenly heard what he is saying. 'I mean . . . Hazel, I don't want you to get upset. I'm sure ... I *know* this will be very traumatic for you. I'm sorry, I've put my foot in it. It's just, I'm *so sure* that this is the right thing we're doing. That you're doing. I really hope – want – you to get some closure here.'

Hazel runs her hands over her face. From somewhere outside, a drain gurgles with water as the door into the prison opens. 'I know, Max. Don't worry,' she says, lifting her head. 'Hello, Uncle Toby,' she says, seeing him suddenly appear in the doorway, his face pale. He is with a female prison guard, a heavy blonde woman with a large chest, buttons straining on her shirt, the colour of which reminds Hazel of limp and flabby oysters seeping juices over their shells.

'Rosie,' Toby says, coming forward, his hands outstretched. He halts as if stung by an electric fence. 'I mean, Hazel. I'm an idiot. I'm so sorry . . . You look so . . .' He flashes her a smile. 'It's been a long time, that's all.'

She nods her head and takes his hands. 'It's good to see you.'

Toby kisses her on the cheek, closing his eyes briefly as he does. Then he straightens and turns to Max. 'Toby Bowman. We spoke on the phone.'

'Max Saunders. Thank you for all of your help with this.'

They are similar in stature, in build and age, Toby observes, but he is the thinner of the two, he notes with a mixture of gratitude and fear. Max has the stomach of a man who likes good food and wine, much as Toby used to do but, in all likelihood, will never do again.

They appraise each other as subtly as is possible under the glare of the unforgiving strip lighting.

Max, as the author, wonders if Toby the lawyer has realised the symmetry. A Flower Girl each, Max thinks. And immediately pushes the thought away, slightly sickened by it.

'Laurel is waiting for you,' Toby says.

'We need you to go through security here,' the guard states.

'A couple of things before you do,' Toby says, ignoring the barked instruction. 'Laurel likes to be called L now. I'd call her that if I were you. Also . . .' He fidgets with something in his pocket, flicks a glance up at the ceiling. 'She isn't in a good place, Ros— Hazel. She's been incarcerated for a long time. She may exhibit some anger.' He pats Hazel's arm. 'I'm not saying she will be angry with you, but try and be understanding if you find her behaviour challenging. Be patient. This is a difficult thing for L to do. She had to be persuaded. Her view of your – of *our* – family is not entirely charitable, I'm afraid.'

Hazel nods, her face meek and flat. 'I understand,' she says. 'I'll be careful.'

'OK, good,' Toby answers, and moves aside to let her pass.

CHAPTER FORTY-SEVEN

1998

'This was an act of unparalleled evil and barbarity. On the fifteenth of July last year, Child X purposefully abducted two-year-old Kirstie Swann and yet she has consistently denied culpability for her crime. Furthermore, she is silent as to the course of events and thus Kirstie's parents are unable, at the very least, to try and fathom the motive behind the brutal attack on their young daughter. At this juncture, I should like to say that in the absence of any explanation from the Defendant, it is beyond us, as sentient adults, to fathom why on God's earth this crime should ever have taken place.

'How it came about that a mentally normal girl, aged ten, and of average intelligence, committed this crime is hard to comprehend. It is not for me to pass judgment on her upbringing. In fairness to Child X's father, it is very much to his credit that he made every effort to get his daughter to tell the truth. But the people of Grassington who have been involved in this case cannot ever forget the tragic circumstances of Kirstie Swann's murder. I would like to make a special point here of saying that I am sure everyone in court today will especially wish Mrs Swann well in the months ahead and hope that her new baby will bring her a measure of peace and happiness.

'I am required by the law, with such a verdict as I am given by this jury, who find Child X guilty of abduction and murder, to sentence her to Detention at Her Majesty's pleasure, and this I accordingly and rightfully do. In view of the seriousness of this crime, and the incomprehensible nature of it given Child X's apparently stable upbringing, I would recommend a tariff of no less than eight years until she reaches the age of eighteen. Then she will, of course, be subject to the rigours of parole.

'I now turn to the application made on behalf of the Newspaper Group that the identity of Child X should be revealed. I have given this matter considerable thought. I am aware of the high level of interest in this case on a national and indeed a global level. It is my considered view that Child X's detention will be for such a period – and indeed I have recommended thus – as to render the revelation of her identity benign, in light of the passage of years that will have elapsed by the time she is released from detention. I also consider that her identity will be important to scholars of jurisprudence and those who interpret the law, in their attempt to make sense of this crime. As such, I rule that her name shall be unredacted in my judgment, which will be published in accordance with the usual timetable.

'Finally, I would like to extend my utmost gratitude and heartfelt thanks to the seven women and five men who have sat on the jury during the course of the trial. This has been a truly dreadful task we have asked of them and yet they have fulfilled their duty admirably and without fault. In doing so, they have had to witness unspeakable horrors and hear of behaviour quite unnatural. The interests of justice have been well served by them.

'Court dismissed.'

CHAPTER FORTY-EIGHT

The door opens and Hazel sees Laurel sitting with head bowed behind a table set in the middle of a small, low-ceilinged room. Light from the narrow wrap-around window above seems to frame Laurel's head with a crown of grey; thorny with the dark of the glowering skies outside.

The thunder rumbling above matches the unease in Hazel's chest and her breathing is short when Laurel lifts her head and her eyes meet her sister's. Where once she was soft, now she is callused. Her blonde hair has a brassy tinge, nothing like the flyaway buttery yellow that used to frame her face. Her skin is grey, purple slashes underneath her eyes, which are themselves like flint, slitted windows in a castle keep.

But then, as she meets those eyes across the table, something in Hazel lets go and relaxes. She feels the steel bonds of the tension she has been holding in her shoulders, her facial muscles, even the way she is clenching her fingers. She feels all of that and then feels it dissipate. As she stands there, observing her sister, the moment stretches into something timeless, unquantifiable. It could be hours that they gaze at each other. Eventually Hazel sits down, slowly taking the chair opposite Laurel. Her heart-rate begins to slow and her breathing lengthens. *It's going to be all right*, she thinks.

Laurel looks comfortable although her arms are crossed, one leg balanced over the knee of the other. It occurs to Hazel that this body language is to be expected. Laurel is on guard, she is protecting herself from something she expects to come from Hazel. *That's OK*, Hazel thinks. *I am benign.* She decides to speak first. Breaking this silence will be like throwing a stone into still water. If she is the one to cause the ripples, then she will be in the best position to see how far they reach.

'Thank you for agreeing to see me,' she says. Her voice is calm, its timbre low and easy. 'I'm sure the request came as a shock to you.'

Laurel shrugs but Hazel sees a flash of pain shoot across her eyes. For some reason, this relaxes her even further.

'Not much to do here, you know. Everyone's welcome to come.' Laurel's smile is acid; her words tinged with sharp metal. Hazel feels the bitterness of them as a clear precursor to an attack, but still, she remains untroubled. She moves her head from side to side as if limbering up before entering the ring.

'When did you come here?' she asks. 'When did they move you from . . .' In a sliver of panic, she cannot remember the name of the secure unit for a second. 'Oakingham.' She reaches for it with slippery hands, manages to keep the conversation in her grasp. 'When did you leave Oakingham?'

'When I was eighteen, Rosie,' Laurel says. 'Nice little present for my eighteenth, wasn't it? Got to move to big girls' prison. Have myself a cheery little room, with a sink and everything. Bars on the windows, of course, and just a small risk of getting fingered in the shower, but otherwise, happy fucking days.'

Hazel nods, taking it on the chin. 'You know,' she says, her eyes burning into Laurel's, 'I'm not here to apologise.'

Laurel laughs, a sound like china smashing on tiles. 'Right. 'Course you're not. Why would you be?'

'I know you're angry. With me. And with Mum and Dad.'

'I don't have a mum or dad,' Laurel cuts in. 'My only family is Toby. And even he's on his way out.'

Hazel frowns.

'He's got cancer, didn't you know?' Laurel spits the information out with relish. 'Hasn't got long on this earth, our Toby. So I may as well get used to no more visits from him. Not that we have that much to talk about. *Have you got me parole? No, I haven't. Oh, all right then. See you next month.*'

This knowledge about Toby drifts like a feather inside Hazel. She beds it down, to deal with later. 'You've got a court case coming up, haven't you?' she asks instead. 'Are you confident?'

Laurel leans forward then with an aggression Hazel notes but is not surprised by. 'Are you having a fucking laugh? Confident? I've had thousands of hearings in the last ten years. I've lost all of them. The only reason we've got this one is down to Toby and his bloody castles . . .' she swipes her hands across her in a slicing motion, close to Hazel's face '. . . in the air. I haven't got a fucking clue. I sit in here and get told what's what. Show me some fucking respect, Rosie. Please.'

Hazel forces herself not to withdraw from the proximity of Laurel's hands. 'I understand. I'm sorry. I just . . .' She lifts her chin and glances up to the ceiling as if choosing her words.

'How's your life anyway?' Laurel's tone is acerbic. 'Married, are you? Kids?'

Hazel swallows. 'Yes. I mean, not married. But I have a partner – Jonny. He has a daughter, Evie.'

'How nice. No kids of your own?'

Hazel shifts on her seat, ignoring the question. 'Look, I need to talk to you. About what happened. And . . . that's hard. Because – well, because I haven't seen you. You've been here alone.' She stops suddenly.

'What?'

'Mum and Dad. Don't hate them forever, Laurel . . .' Hazel sees her sister work her tongue into her cheek. 'I'm sorry. You like to be called L.'

Laurel raises her eyebrows.

'I know they let you down. And I don't understand why. Or maybe I do. Maybe we both do . . . But Mum's gone now, hasn't she? And you wouldn't recognise Dad these days. He's nothing like before. I don't think they really knew what they were doing when it happened, during the trial and after. They were frightened and worried about everything. And Dad was sick, with his heart. They just . . .' Hazel dips her head. 'Look, I know they did wrong. But I also know that Mum loved you. That Dad still does, in his own way.'

Laurel sits perched forward, her chest heaving behind the edge of the table. She spreads her fingers very deliberately and slowly on the table top in front of her. 'I don't think,' she mutters through her teeth at Hazel, her expression rigid as stone, 'that I have ever known a more selfish act.'

Hazel nods again. Somewhere in the back of her head, she pictures her mother standing at the sink in their old house, before everything changed. The sun glinting on her hair and suds on her wrists, filled with the light of rainbows. 'Don't you remember?' she says. 'What it was like before?'

'No,' Laurel replies thinly. 'I don't.'

'In the house. With the garden and the game. You remember the game, don't you?'

'The judge said we watched violent films,' Laurel snaps. 'He said I was depraved by them. That they made me evil.'

'No, we never watched television. Just played games in the garden. Out in the sunshine, chasing each other under that big tree. We used to get that sticky stuff from its leaves on our skirts and Mum would go mad. Don't you remember? She'd send us up to the bathroom. Stick us in the bath and the window would be open and the breeze coming in. Sitting there, with you in the bath. It was so light outside we could never sleep properly. The hours we spent, lying hot in our beds, talking to each other.'

'Stop it!' Laurel says, her fists curling tight on the table. 'Just stop. What do you want here? What is it that you want?'

Hazel halts, her eyes moving back to Laurel, the memories popping like soap bubbles in the heat of the tiny room. She can smell Laurel's body odour, her own fading perfume. She looks down at her fingernails, acting out a mantra she used to say to herself as a child. *I am here, this is happening now,* she whispers silently to herself. *I am here, this is happening now*. Over and over again.

'You just want to go out there,' Laurel flings her arm towards the door, 'and tell them all that you've seen your evil sister and now you can remember. And everything's all right, because you didn't do anything wrong. It was all Laurel Bowman. That evil cow who killed the baby. And now you can finally set out your side of the story, tell the public all the fucking gruesome details they want to hear. Go on some TV show, dip your head and bat your eyelashes. Poor baby Rosie. Poor innocent child caught up in her despicable sister's games. Just so you can get on with your life. And meanwhile? I'm sitting on my arse in here. I will fucking *die in here*. Don't you get it? I will *fucking die*.'

'No. You won't.' Hazel's voice is firm. 'Things are different now. Time is a healer, you know?' She gives a little smile. 'And . . . I want you to know that I'll speak for you, at your hearing. If you like. If you want me, I'll be on your side. From now on. I'll make it up to you. All the silence, the estrangement. Before . . . I know you're angry, but you must understand a bit of it at least.'

Hazel's voice cracks a little, causing Laurel to bite her lip. 'When it happened, suddenly I wasn't Rosie Bowman any more. They took everything from me. My house, my school, my name. You didn't see what it was like. The press, the terrible things they said. The abuse we got. Shit poured on our front door. Bottles smashed on our car. I was only six, Lau— L. I just did what I was told. And then, when I was old enough to make my own decisions, I was scared. Scared that if I came here, people would find me out. Work out who I was and then my life would be a nightmare all over again.'

'Get me a fucking violin, Rosie,' Laurel says, her expression cold and hard. 'Selfish, selfish, selfish.'

'Even now, even before that girl went missing in Devon, I was getting anonymous letters. Someone had found out who I was. Sending me hate mail, trying to scare me. Telling me I had it coming. Look at my face.' She touches her cheek.

'This is where the mother of that girl who went missing attacked me.'

Laurel remains impassive, unmoved.

'Yeah, maybe you're right,' Hazel goes on, her voice rising. She needs to bring her sister back. She had her for a moment, but she has gone, darting underneath the water like a tiny fish. 'Maybe it *was* selfish. But . . .' she opens her hands to the room '. . . here we are, L. And if we don't move on, what's left? It's always going to be hard, isn't it? Being you and me. We're never going to be on the Queen's Honours list. Right?'

Laurel doesn't smile, but her face softens. Just a fraction.

'And at least now . . .' Hazel pauses, catching her breath, her lashes wet with tears. 'At least now we'll have each other. Won't we? Couldn't we?'

Laurel dips her forehead to her fingertips, pressing hard with their pads on her skin, leaving white pressure marks behind.

'I don't remember, L. What happened with the baby . . . I remember being at the park. Playing on the roundabout, the swings, the horse. And then we went over the top of that bank, and down. And after that it's like a train coming in fast, right through my head. I don't remember anything else. Just flashes of that hotel they sent us to. People shouting at us on the street.' A tear falls onto the table and Hazel wipes it away angrily, annoyed with herself for crying. 'I know you're being punished. What you've suffered. But what can I do? It wasn't fair perhaps. But I *just don't know*. Please, L. Let me help you now. Please.'

Laurel stares at her sister for a good long minute. At last, she pushes her chair away from the table and stands. She comes over and, for a second, Hazel thinks that her sister is going to embrace her. Laurel hitches up her jeans on her skinny frame, pulls down her grey sweatshirt, crusted with ingrained dirt, and walks to the door. She raps twice and it opens and she is out of the room before Hazel has realised that their meeting is over, before she understands that her sister has truly gone.

CHAPTER FORTY-NINE

Hillier notices Karen, the waitress from Balcombe Court, as soon as she enters the bar. It's hot inside and Hillier removes her jacket as she walks in past garish orange walls, the music reverberating in her chest. As she hoists herself up onto a stool next to Karen's, Hillier feels suddenly ancient, a relic of something even she can't remember.

'Bloody dark in here, isn't it?' she says, passing her badge across. 'My ID, if you're interested and can see it. Drink?' she says, raising a hand to the barman.

'Vodka and soda, please.'

Hillier orders it and an orange juice for herself. 'Thanks for agreeing to see me,' she says.

'S'alright,' Karen replies, sipping at her drink. 'I did talk to the police already, though. When the girl went missing?' The waitress has an open face and Hillier feels haggard just looking at her bright eyes and unlined skin.

'Yep, I know. You were interviewed by one of my colleagues after your shift at Balcombe Court had finished.'

'So how can I help now?'

Hillier pushes her glass away from her a little. 'I just wanted to check on the timings with you. About that afternoon. You said in your statement that you left the hotel at three o'clock. Is that right?'

'Yes. I was on the early shift that day as it was New Year's, so I would have left at three.'

'And you saw Georgie, did you, before you left?'

'Yes. She'd come into the kitchen to see the kittens that I'd found on the beach. Poor little things. I couldn't believe someone would just abandon them like that. Left all alone in the freezing cold to die. Shameful.' Karen's eyes are wide and tragic.

Hillier smiles. 'So, your . . . boyfriend? Marek Kaczka . . .'

'He's not my boyfriend.' Karen's interruption is firm.

'Well, your colleague then. Marek,' Hillier says. 'He had put the box of kittens into the pantry?'

'Yep. After I brought them up to the hotel. I gave them something to eat. We had a tin of tuna and some milk. And then Georgie came in, wanting to see them, so I showed her where they were and then I left.'

'And you're certain it was three o'clock?'

'Definitely. Shift ended at three and I could see the time on the clock in the kitchen.'

Hillier looks hard at her.

Karen nods. 'Swear on my mum's life. Clock said three and three it was.' She puts her head on one side. 'If you don't mind me saying, why are you asking about this? The little girl was found, wasn't she? I mean, do you think someone took her on purpose?' Her eyes widen again. 'Not Marek? Do you think it was Marek that took her?'

Hillier gets down inelegantly from the stool and shoots Karen a quick smile. 'We're just making enquiries,' she says. 'Thanks for your time.'

'He wouldn't have hurt her,' Karen says earnestly. 'He's not the type. He's a sweet guy. Wouldn't harm a fly.

He's ... well, he's just not my type is all. But not because he's dodgy. It was me that was the problem, not him. He's only left Brixham because of all the talk. You know, about what happened to him before. It's not fair, really. That girl was asking for it. She lied to him about her age and then he gets the blame.' Karen's face crumples with loathing.

'Kaczka's left Brixham?' Hillier asks, her lips suddenly dry. 'You mean, he's quit up at Balcombe?'

Karen nods, taking a sip through the straw in her glass. 'He jacked it in a couple of weeks ago. Couldn't hack what everyone was saying. That's it, isn't it? If you get accused of kiddy fiddling, you can't ever shake it off. I feel sorry for him, if you want to know.'

'Where's he gone then?'

The girl shrugs. 'I dunno,' she says, refusing to meet Hillier's eyes.

'Not in touch with him?'

'Nope.'

'I see,' Hillier says, putting on her jacket. 'Well, thanks for your time anyway.'

'Bloody dead in this town. Nice to have a bit of excitement in all fairness.'

After Hillier has left, banging the door behind her with a cold gust of January air, Karen takes out her phone and taps out a message. The reply comes back before she has even ordered another drink.

CHAPTER FIFTY

'It's time,' Max says as they walk away from the prison. Hazel shivers as she stands by the passenger door, waiting for him to retrieve his keys from his coat pocket. 'I think it's time,' he says again, clicking the lock and hefting himself into the driver's seat. The pain in his gullet is so bad today, he can hardly swallow.

'Time for what?' asks Hazel. She can't get the visceral image of Laurel's rage out of her mind. She plays another old game where she puts the confusing thoughts into a Perspex box in her mind. She watches them rattle around inside, jiggering and scuttling like trapped angry beetles. In the box, they are separate from her; that is the game. She can watch how they move, how they clatter, but keep them away from inside of her where it must be peaceful and safe.

The game.

There are so many games, Hazel thinks. The games they used to play together as children. The games her mother taught her. You can call them games but, ultimately, they're really about survival.

'BITCH!!' The cry comes from across the car park like a banshee's wail. 'YOU SHOULD ROT IN HELL!'

Hazel jerks round to see a woman in a denim jacket a few yards away, her face fixed in a snarl.

'Come away, Hazel,' Max says urgently. 'Get into the car.'

She climbs in hurriedly, pulling her collar up around her ears, pushing her chin into her chest. They are everywhere these days. Ghouls and monsters, lurking in the shadows. Leaping out at her with teeth bared, drooling hatred. She fears them with an intensity so raw it is as if her skin has been flayed. Every approach, every word, is like a scald. *Leave me alone!* she screams inside her head. *Leave me alone!*

'Just ignore it,' Max says, his voice shaking as he starts the engine. 'Let's get out of here.'

Hazel is silent as the car makes its way through the wet streets. The hush of the rain washing across the windscreen and the squeak of the wipers have a near-meditative effect on her. They echo the rhythm of her thoughts.

'I've set up a meeting,' Max says after a while. 'It's all a bit cloak and dagger.' He shrugs wryly. 'That's just the way of the business.'

'What business?' Hazel asks, moving her head from side to side, trying to focus, erase the thoughts of Laurel and what she said, how she abandoned her own sister in the visiting room.

'The publishing business,' Max replies. 'I've got a meeting with Romilly Harris. She's a huge literary agent. Massive. She's read my proposal and loves it. Wants to send it out to numerous publishing houses. She's hopeful for a bidding war. But we have to keep it secret for the moment. We mustn't let the papers get hold of the same idea.'

Hazel stares out of the passenger window as if she isn't listening.

'Hazel?' Max says, glancing across but she still doesn't answer. He sighs, staring out at the darkening skies. 'Look, can they really hate you forever?'

'I don't know,' Hazel says, understanding what he means. 'They hated Myra Hindley until the day she died.'

'But you're not her. What she and Brady did to those children was depraved. It was deliberate and sadistic. But you and Laurel . . .' Max exhales loudly. 'I don't know. It's not the same thing. You were so young. I mean, you wouldn't have had the capacity, would you? To know what you were doing? And what Laurel did, it was an . . . an aberration, wasn't it?'

Hazel says nothing, stares straight ahead at the reds and greens of the traffic lights gleaming through the fading afternoon light.

'It was play that went wrong. And you were just a bystander. And in any case, you can't remember.' Max shrugs, keeping his voice low as if he's convincing himself, running the patchwork of the story through in his mind. 'The shock of what your sister did paralysed you, sent you catatonic. Six years old. The damage caused on that day has had far-reaching consequences for everyone involved. But now it's time to move on. Maybe you will regain some memories. Maybe it will come back to you some day . . .'

Hazel remains quiet, watching the wet streets out of the window. She thinks of the plane tree outside her flat, the way its falling leaves drift down in waves, spreading in a carpet over the ground.

'Don't you think?' he says. 'What do you think?'

Hazel nods, folding her hands in her lap. 'The thing is . . .' she says at last, before faltering.

'What?'

'I think . . . I think some things are coming back.' She looks over at him.

'What things?' he asks, a pulse point quickening in his temple. 'Memories?'

'Yes,' she answers slowly. 'I think I might be starting to remember.'

CHAPTER FIFTY-ONE

1996

The cat lay prone on the stoop of the back door, which led out onto the garden. It was fat and ginger with white paws and a pink nose. It didn't belong to the Bowmans. Their mother used to chase it away if she saw it in the garden. Amy Bowman hated cats, they made her sneeze. It belonged to one of the neighbours whose garden ran alongside theirs. All the gardens lay in a straight row at the back of the terrace like a line of verdant soldiers.

The cat would bound through one of the holes in the trellis face and walk languidly over to the step where the sun would hit most afternoons, creating a warm patch in which it liked to sleep.

Laurel and Rosie sat cross-legged on the grass, watching the cat in slumber. They sat quite still, their eyes steady on the animal, on his ginger paws crossed in front of him, his whiskers twitching in the soft breeze.

After a while, Laurel held out her hand, her fist closed, her arm straight and stretched out. A moment later Rosie did the same, her clenched first alongside her sister's. As if to a beat that only they could hear, they bounced their fists once, twice, three times over the grass before opening their palms simultaneously. Laurel's fingers formed a V-shape whereas Rosie's hand was flat. Seeing this, she nodded and climbed slowly to her feet.

Carefully, she walked across the grass to where the cat lay. She made no sound, her bare feet quiet on the warm grass. Laurel continued to watch in silence as Rosie picked up the cat by the scruff of its neck. It opened its eyes in surprise but it was impossible to wriggle out of the girl's grip. She held the cat out to one side as she made her way round, past Laurel and down to the end of the garden where the blue hydrangeas were.

Laurel lay back on the grass, stretching out her toes and feeling the caress of the sun on her face. As her mother looked on from the kitchen window, she counted the clouds in the sky, floating past on the current of the earth. A shadow fell briefly over her as Rosie came back to join her, lying next to her sister without speaking. They lay there for a while, softly breathing before getting up and going to sit on the now empty stoop.

CHAPTER FIFTY-TWO

Joanna sits on the sofa in the midst of the detritus of Will and Lucy's house. It's a small terrace in Hackney with an even smaller mortgage thanks to Will's last few City bonuses. She'd sat on a wall on the other side of the road for what felt like forever, watching the windows until the lights began to pop on. Eventually, Will had come to the door, held it open and inclined his head, a glass of red wine in his hand. Joanna had slid off the wall and crossed the road. At the gate, she'd paused, looking at him.

'Just come in, Jo,' he'd said. 'You can come in.'

It felt almost impossible to Joanna, those steps up to the door. As if she were climbing an Everest of her own resentment, her own conviction that she exists only on the periphery. Will is one of the few people she has ever admitted to herself that she loves. Other than Debbie and her family. It seems to Joanna as she crosses the threshold into the house that to show anyone love is immediately to make yourself vulnerable to them taking it away from you. And for a moment she hesitates, scared once again. But then she straightens her shoulders and continues, because she can't be that pathetic. Not she, who is so strong and so able to fight.

'You've never been here before, have you?' Will says, ushering her inside and into the small sitting room. He hands her the wine and Joanna sits on the sofa underneath the window.

'I thought I had,' she answers.

'Nope. We've offered.' Will smiles. 'But, you're busy. I know . . . Lucy's upstairs reading to Jemima. *The Gruffalo*. Takes forever. All the characters have different voices,' he explains, sitting forward, holding his own glass between his knees. In the background, a radio is playing.

Something about the place feels utterly familiar to Joanna as she sits inside this warm house with its brick-coloured walls and antique mirrors. It is filled to the brim with finger paintings, recipe books, tins of Heinz baked beans, spices on the shelves. And then she realises that it's because it feels like home. It reminds her of her childhood house, of Debbie and herself coming in after school, chucking their bags down in the hall, their mum bringing them jam on toast in front of the TV.

Joanna has none of this in her flat. Everything there is impermanent, as if she could pack a bag and be off in a matter of hours, nothing left behind to show she was there other than some rumpled bedsheets and a few half-finished bottles of Grey Goose.

She shakes her head and takes a long sip from her wine.

'What?' Will asks.

She looks at him. 'I went to see her, you know. The other day. Rosie Bowman.'

'Where? God, really? Did you talk to her?'

'No. She was heading off somewhere, surrounded by photographers. They were mobbing her, going to swallow her up.'

Will leans back in his armchair. 'Laurel's oral hearing has been set for next month,' he says. 'You haven't been answering your emails. I didn't know if you knew. It's a closed proceeding. We can't attend.' The sound of laughter trickles down from upstairs and he glances up at the ceiling. 'So, what was she like? Rosie?'

Joanna shrugs. 'I don't know. Different from Laurel. She's tiny. She had a hood on, I couldn't really see. It was pointless, going there. But . . . I'd been to see Debbie.'

'I know. She called me.'

Joanna lifts her eyebrows. 'Yeah, well. She's moving on. She says she's not got the energy to stop Laurel being released. She wants to remember Kirstie in peace. *No energy.*' She gives a wry laugh. 'Anyway, it appears that I ...' she looks down at her wine glass '. . . still seem to have *lots* of energy for it. And also,' she shuts her eyes briefly, 'I've been making some really bad decisions lately. I'm sorry,' she says. 'About what I said in the bar that day.'

Will nods but doesn't speak.

For a while they sit in silence, hearing the creak of Lucy's footsteps above them, a few tiny cries from Jemima as she settles in her cot.

'How would you react, do you think?' Joanna says at last. 'If something happened to Jemima?'

Will sighs. 'God, Jo. I have no idea. It's too horrific even to contemplate.'

'Yeah. But it's weird, isn't it? Don't you think? I'm not a parent. And yet, I'm so intractable, I can't let it go. Whereas Debbie wants to move on. It's like she's reached her limit.'

'But this has been your life, your job, for so long,' Will says. 'It's been the reason you get up in the morning. And also,' he puts his glass down on the carpet, 'a lot – and I mean *a lot* – of people agree with you. They don't want

Laurel Bowman released. They think she hasn't been punished enough. Supposing she reoffends once she's out? Supposing she hurts another child?'

Joanna frowns at him. 'Now you're sounding like me.'

'Yeah, but I'm only playing devil's advocate because I don't think it's good for *you*. All this haranguing of the Bowmans, the appeals, the interviews. I think it's wearing you away.'

Will gets up and comes and sits next to Jo on the sofa, takes her hand but she won't look at him.

'It's OK, you know. To let her go. You've done more than anyone has – to defend Kirstie, protect her memory.'

Joanna shakes her head as tears spill onto her lap. 'I haven't . . . there's always more. I just wish I could bring her back. For Debs . . .'

'Come here,' Will says, drawing her head onto his shoulder. 'You've done everything you can. Let the courts decide now, Jo. Give it up to them. Everything you've done for other victims as well as Debbie and Rob. All the support you've given, it's been so valuable. But it's not worth killing yourself over. Drinking yourself into a grave for . . . Don't you think?'

'But when you have something to fight for, it's almost easier, don't *you* think?' Joanna gives him her glass and sinks back on the cushions behind her, palms over her face. 'Because what am I going to do now, Will? Once all of this is over. What am I going to do?'

CHAPTER FIFTY-THREE

They sit together on facing sofas in Jonny's flat. Max is opposite Hazel, who has her head bowed, hands in her lap, Jonny's arm curled protectively around her back. The room has the weighted stillness of tension. Jonny has made coffee but it remains untouched on the side table, its aroma vaguely nauseating in the overheated space.

Max is aware of the traffic noise outside. In the distance, a jackhammer is ploughing up a road. He squeezes his palms together, trying desperately to quell the adrenaline, to remain calm and not frighten Hazel with his eagerness. She is sunken and pale from the prison trip yesterday. When she had confessed to Max that her memories were returning, he had driven her to Jonny's straight away. They had run the gauntlet through the camera flashes of the pack of paparazzi, who waited outside Jonny's flat just as they lurked outside her own. Once inside, she had trembled as if she were cold, as if she could never be warm again. Jonny had looked over her head at Max in concern as he led her inside, sat her in an armchair with a blanket over her knees.

'She needs to rest,' Max said quietly to him in the hallway. 'She thinks she can remember what happened on that day.' He looked over Jonny's shoulder to where Hazel sat. 'Keep her calm tonight and I'll come back in the morning. Just let her sleep. She looks exhausted.'

Jonny had nodded. 'Right you are.' After Max had left, he had given Hazel a bowl of chicken soup and they had eaten together in silence. Then he had run her a bath and washed her back slowly as she stared down at her knees.

'I'm sorry,' she had said at last. 'I'm so sorry to have involved you in this. To have involved Evie. The press. It's all so horrible. You can't know how much I wish that things were different.'

'It's not your fault, babe,' Jonny had replied, lifting her chin to look her in the eye. 'You're just as much a victim of this as anyone.' He nodded at her, swirling his hand in the water. 'Hopefully now, though, we're on the way to sorting it all out. Making everything better.'

Hazel had given him a sad smile.

'What's that for?'

'You look after me, don't you, Jonny?' she had answered. 'I don't know what I'd do without you, that's all.'

'You don't have to do without me. And do you know why?'

She had shaken her head.

'Because once all of this has gone away, been dealt with, we're going to get married. You and me against the world. Just us two. And Evie of course. And maybe,' he had said, his voice faltering a little, 'a baby of our own. What do you reckon?'

Hazel had reached up a hand covered in soap suds and stroked his cheek. 'Yes,' she had said. 'That's all I want.'

Max looks over at her now and wonders, not for the first time, how much a person can take. How much pressure can be loaded onto Hazel before she snaps, needs more qualified help than either he or Jonny can provide.

'Hazel,' he asks gently. 'Are you feeling a bit better? After yesterday?'

She nods. 'Thank you for looking after me,' she says. 'I felt so strange in the car. As if I were . . . outside myself. I couldn't think straight at all.' She shakes her head. 'Thank you for bringing me home.'

Jonny's chest puffs up a little at this. His hand doesn't leave Hazel's thigh, stroking the wool of her skirt repeatedly. 'We had a quiet night last night, didn't we, babe?' he says.

'I spoke to my father,' Hazel says, tears brimming.

'Oh?' Max lifts his head. 'How is he? It must be a shock for him to know that you're back in contact with Laurel.'

Hazel nods, giving a thin smile. 'He's not well, Daddy. He . . . can't take the strain of this really. I feel so guilty that it's all being dragged up again.'

Max's mind is whirring. Unable to stop himself, he asks, 'Would he consent to being interviewed, do you think? For the book?'

An expression of fear passes across Hazel's face. 'No!' she blurts. 'Please don't speak to Daddy! We must leave him alone. He can't take the strain. It's going to kill him, all of this.'

Max bites his lip, sitting back. 'OK, of course. You mustn't worry, Hazel. Please. I'm here to look after you—' He breaks off as if a thought has leapt into his head. Tense silence fills the room as he shifts in his seat and crosses his legs. He smiles wanly at her, taking off his glasses, polishing the lenses with the edge of his jumper.

'You look worried suddenly, Max,' she says. 'What's wrong?'

'Well . . .' he hedges. 'Something's just occurred to me. About your memories coming back, that's all.'

'But it's good, isn't it?' Hazel asks. 'If my memory is returning? It will help with the book, won't it? With the publishing deal?'

Max nods, replacing his spectacles. 'Yes, yes. It's good for the book. It's just . . .'

'What?' she says, moving Jonny's hand away and leaning forward. 'What is it? Tell me.'

Max blinks and rubs the back of his neck. 'It's just . . . I've realised you might be testifying soon, mightn't you? If the court allows it. At Laurel's court hearing.'

'What about it?' Jonny asks. 'Why does that matter?'

Hazel pushes back into the cushions, comprehension dawning on her face.

'Hazel?' Jonny says. 'I don't get it. Why is this a problem?'

She holds Max's gaze as she answers.

'Because it will matter to Laurel what I say,' she says. 'It will make a difference to her parole.'

CHAPTER FIFTY-FOUR

As March comes in like a lion, Toby sits opposite Laurel, who stares up at the ceiling, chewing gum. From her studied lack of interest, he knows that she is deeply upset. He shifts on his seat, trying to ignore the pain in his lower abdomen. He can't help himself, though. Inside of him, he can feel the cancer growing, multiplying in mushrooming nodules. Sometimes, he feels it actively crawling upwards, sideways and along his organs. It has become part of him and he is no longer certain where the cancer ends and he begins. It has crept over him, carpeting his insides with a stealth that leaves him breathless. He looks gaunt, the flesh around his cheeks hanging down in chalky-coloured folds.

His operation was cancelled at his last consultation. The cancer has spread to his lymph nodes and liver. But, looking at his fingernails, calcified and worn, in truth he had known even before then, without articulating it, that it would not be an operating table he would lie on soon.

'I saw a rainbow this morning,' he says. 'Did you manage to see it?'

Laurel's eyes remain looking upwards and she does not respond.

'Funny the things you realise you'll miss.' Toby sighs, leaning forward across the space between them. 'I'll miss you, L. I really will. I feel ...' He grimaces, his mouth contorting uselessly, trying to articulate what he means. 'I feel I've let you down.'

Laurel chews on her lip, working at it so forcefully that Toby is worried that soon she will draw blood.

'Stop it, L. Please. Don't hurt yourself ... We have to talk. We have to prepare ourselves for next week. For the hearing.' He rubs the back of his neck. 'Your sister's offered to speak on your behalf. To help you in the judicial review.'

Laurel's head snaps up. 'Is she allowed?'

'Yes. It's not common. But we've made the application and the court just agreed. We argued there were extraordinary circumstances. New evidence might come to light, which could influence the parole board. It might help you to have some familial support. Some back-up. All these years, you've never had that, have you? And from what Rosie said when I saw her here ...' Toby tries to catch Laurel's eye but she ducks her head. 'What do you think?' He shrugs helplessly in the silence which thickens around them. 'L? What do you think?'

He looks at her, at the harsh set of her face, and wonders again why she cannot speak, why she cannot help herself.

'Could you talk to me, L? Could you? Just because this might be the last time we see each other before the actual day of the hearing. And there are so many things that I feel are unresolved. Could we try and deal with them today?' He waits, but no answer comes from her. 'Has she been in touch?'

'Rosie? No. Not since her visit.'

'No letters or anything?'

'No.' Laurel eyeballs him. 'You trust her, do you?'

He thinks about it. 'I think she's frightened. She's been brought into the public eye because of this Devon thing. She never wanted it but now she has to deal with it, make the best of it. I think she cares about you, yes. Do I trust her?' He expels a long breath. 'In all honesty, I don't know. But I feel very strongly that time is running out and we should take the opportunities that present themselves.'

'Running out for me? Or for you?' Laurel looks at him, blinking slowly. Her hair is greasy and her skin a greyish colour. Toby feels his heart constrict as he notices the boniness of her wrists, the pulse point in her temple, flickering rapidly.

'For both of us,' he says softly.

Laurel raises her arms above her head, and cracks her knuckles. 'What if I told you that I had proof Rosie was involved?' she says lightly.

'What?' Toby sits forward. 'What proof? Involved in what happened to Kirstie? What are you talking about?'

Laurel shrugs. 'Nothing concrete. But something that would harm her. Make people wonder. About her. About what was going on back then.'

'I'd want to see it. Right now. And I'd wonder why you hadn't shown it to me before. Why you've waited all this time to say something.' Toby's voice is sharp, his blood pumping. He stares at Laurel. Her eyes are dark, fathomless, but just for a second he sees a light pass across them. An open duct of longing, of desperate pain.

'Have you ever been frightened?' she asks him. 'Really terrified? So scared that you think you're going to die, that your heart might stop?'

'No,' he says, wondering where she's going with this, his forehead creased with concern. *What proof does she have? Why won't she tell him?* 'Not really. Anxious, worried. But not frightened like that. Not like you mean.'

'Not even now? Not even when you're facing . . . death?' She whispers the word as if afraid she might summon it.

Toby shakes his head. 'What happens in death has always been something I've thought of as being out of my control,' he says. 'I've lived my life.' His lips twist sadly. 'I've done my best. What will happen . . . afterwards, I don't know. But I'm not scared of it.'

Laurel nods. 'But you're a man,' she says, as if this is an answer. 'You're a grown-up.'

It breaks Toby's heart to hear this, as if she has never left her ten-year-old self behind. Stuck forever down on that canal path, the wind in her hair. She cannot see herself as an adult. She has never had any barometer of her worth.

'If you know something, L,' he pushes on regardless, 'you *must* tell me. You must help yourself. Speak! Tell us what you know and then we can help you. I can't help you if you keep me in the dark.' He rubs his face in frustration.

'I know I've been here all this time,' Laurel says. 'Never been to school or anything. But I'm not an idiot. I know what the law is. Even if I knew anything about that day, what would have been the point of saying it? They were never even going to arrest her. She was too young. She was six. They wouldn't have done anything. And . . .'

'And?' Toby prods, his cheeks hot with a terrible growing fear that he has misguided her for all of these years. That she has been under a horrific misapprehension, something so utterly wrong, and the reason for it is entirely his fault.

'. . . And what would it have done to my mother?' She looks at him, appalled. 'How would she have dealt with ... with anything else? She was so fragile, Mummy. It was impossible. Just impossible. Everything was. All of it.'

Laurel breathes in deeply through her nose and rolls her shoulders back as if hefting away all these thoughts. 'I've sent something to your office,' she says. 'Something I want you to pass to that writer bloke who's helping Rosie.'

Toby clears his throat, his mind spinning. 'What? What is it?'

'Call it a form of protection. Promise me you won't open it.'

'Laurel . . . please. What protection? This is insane. I think I've misled you. I think you've got things wrong.'

'I haven't got anything wrong,' she retorts. 'Nothing at all. But you have to promise.'

'Look, time's running out. What can we do? Help me here. Let me help you.'

She ducks her head but not before he has seen the flash of fear pass across her face again.

'I'll stop it.' He stabs the table with a finger, the muscles in his jaw clenched. 'I'll stop her testifying if you think it's wrong. We won't have it.'

Laurel pushes her chair back and the smile she gives him then is so sweet and pretty that, for a moment, he is back in the garden in Grassington, watching his nieces play on the lawn, running through the sprinkler with dappled sunlight on their backs.

'Thank you for everything, Uncle Toby,' she says as she stands up and moves to the door, tapping at it with scabbed knuckles. 'I'll always remember it, really.'

'Laurel . . . please . . .'

But she is gone. And Toby is left alone in the room, his heart hammering in his chest, feeling absolutely spent. Thinking about those two little girls, Rosie and Laurel, playing games in the fading summer light.

PART THREE

CHAPTER FIFTY-FIVE

1999

Dear Rosie,

They say they are sending my letters but Mummy hasn't written back. Is she still cross with me?

Daddy hasn't written either so I'm writing to you because you sent me that picture when I first got here and I know you aren't mad with me. How did you send it? Did Uncle Toby help you?

I miss you.

It's all right here. We do school and on Fridays they let us watch a film. Last week, we made popcorn. We're working on an art project. It's about lightning and conduction. We have to make a model of a storm. Do you remember that big storm we had last year when the tree outside rattled the windows and we hugged each other in bed because we were scared?

You can't act scared here. If you feel it, you have to hide it deep inside. If they know you're scared, they laugh at you, and one girl, who's always crying, got pushed into the wall because they knew she wouldn't tattle-tale. I don't cry here. Only sometimes at night, in bed, when it's dark and they can't see or hear me. That's when I miss you the most. And Mummy and Daddy.

I've got a nice teacher. Nicer than Mrs Brooking at school. She lets me get three books out of the library instead of two. I got out *Horrid Henry* the other day because it reminded me of you. But then that made me sad so I took it back again. Now I'm reading *Black Beauty*. It's not bad.

Anyway, I hope you write back. And that you come and see me some time.

Love,

Laurel xxx

P.S. Do you still play the game?

CHAPTER FIFTY-SIX

Hillier gets out of the Tube at Clapham South and takes stock of where she is. To her left is Clapham Common where joggers are already puffing around the perimeter despite the early hour. Opposite her is a little line of shops: kebab restaurants, fried chicken takeaways, a newsagent and a local Sainsbury's. She looks down at her pocket A–Z and heads over the road in that direction.

She turns up another road at right angles to the row of shops. The street is empty; a Sunday quiet fills the air. The houses are decent-sized Victorian semis with tiny gardens and identikit stained-glass panels in the front doors and white slatted shutters in the windows. She thinks back to her little sanctuary in Brixham with the view over the hills and the patch of grass out the back. She had left while it was still dark this morning. It seems a world away from here, where the main road bustles noisily with traffic, where empty cans of lager are abandoned on a wall she passes. She wouldn't live in the city if you paid her the three million that you'd need to afford to buy something here.

Halfway down the street she finds the house she's looking for. Number ninety. The door is a deep red colour and the stained glass around it cobalt blue. The garden is tidy albeit sparsely planted. Hillier hesitates at the gate and looks at her watch. It isn't even eight-thirty and she wonders if she should wait, head back to the high street and have a coffee before she knocks.

As she stands there debating this, the curtains in the lower front window twitch and a moment later the front door opens. Jane Greenstreet stands there in jogging bottoms and a grey T-shirt.

'You coming in then, or what?' she says.

'You won't let it go, will you?' Jane asks, ten minutes later, as she bangs a mug of coffee down in front of Hillier, the liquid sloshing onto the island countertop. She gets a cloth and wipes it away. 'You're lucky Georgie isn't here or I wouldn't have let you in.'

'Thanks,' Hillier says, ignoring Jane's mood. She can mollify her. She pulls the mug towards her and blows on the coffee. 'Where is Georgie?'

Jane lifts her eyebrows and delays speaking for an antagonistic second or two before giving up and replying. 'She's with her dad at my in-laws.' He took her there for the weekend but it's too much of a faff lugging everything that Charlie needs so we stayed here.'

Hillier looks across the kitchen to where the baby sits in his highchair carefully throwing one Cheerio after another down onto the floor. She smiles at him. 'He's bonny.'

Jane sighs, capitulating, and takes a seat opposite her. 'So?' she says. 'Why *are* you here?'

Hillier nods. 'I know you think I won't let it go. But I can't. I don't understand it – what happened to Georgie. I don't understand why you wouldn't let us talk to her. Properly, I mean. Really question her about what happened—'

'I'm allowed to protect my daughter,' Jane cuts in. 'At the very least – after everything that's happened – you can give me that.'

'I get it, I really do. But I don't understand why you – and your husband – aren't more . . . *curious* . . . as to what happened. If someone had wanted to hurt my child, I wouldn't rest until I'd found out who it was, and why.'

'She just wandered off,' Jane says in an exasperated tone. 'Why does there need to be any other reason?'

'Mrs Greenstreet – Jane – with all due respect, Georgie's five years old. She'll be led by you. At the moment, you won't let us anywhere near her. We can't ask her proper questions about whether she saw anyone, spoke to anyone, whether anyone tried to hurt her. You're being completely obstructive, frankly.' Hillier breaks off, her breathing agitated. She needs to calm down before Georgie's mother throws her out onto the street. She looks down at her coffee mug and bites her lip. 'I'm just saying it's odd. And I don't deal well with odd. I like things clear and tidy.'

Jane Greenstreet studies her in silence. 'I understand,' she says at last. 'I'm the same, as it goes.' She glances over at Charlie, who gives her a gummy grin before chucking another Cheerio on the floor. 'It's why I don't do so well with this parenting lark. All a bit too messy for my liking. Isn't it, Charlie boy?' She gets up and bends down at the base of the highchair, scooping up the cereal into her palm.

'That afternoon,' Hillier continues, 'you said that Georgie left the bar where you were sitting with Declan at three o'clock. Is that right? That's when Karen the waitress described seeing Georgie come into the kitchen and the sous-chef, Marek, backs her up.'

Jane freezes and a pink flush appears on the back of her neck. 'Yes, it was three. Because that's when Charlie wakes up from his nap. We had him in the buggy in the bar where we were. It was fairly quiet. I think we were the only ones in there.'

Hillier studies Jane, wondering why the woman suddenly appears nervous. Why she has coloured up as if she is lying. 'Everyone can place Georgie in the kitchen at three,' she says. 'And everyone in the hotel is accounted for at the same time. But the timing for Georgie in the kitchen is given by Karen and Marek who were looking at the kitchen clock. Which was slow. By thirty-three minutes.'

'So?' Jane looks confused. 'What does it matter?'

Hillier shrugs and takes a sip of coffee. 'It might not,' she says. 'But, then again, it might. Because if Karen and Marek reckon Georgie came into the kitchen at three on a clock that was running slow, what it means is that Georgie actually came in more around three-*thirty*. So I just wanted to check with you what time you think it was.'

Jane walks over to the bin and drops the cereal inside. She stands with her back to Hillier for a minute and then her shoulders sag. When she turns round, her face is blotchy as if she is trying not to cry.

'What is it, Jane?' Hillier asks gently. 'Do you know something about the timing that you're not telling me?'

Jane rubs a hand over her face and breathes in deeply before coming to sit down. 'The reason we were down in Devon over New Year is that . . .' She glances at Charlie and lowers her voice. 'We haven't been getting on well, Declan and I. In fact, it's been bloody awful. Arguing. Then not sleeping. We're so bloody tired. It's why he's gone to his parents'. We need a break. I don't want to separate but . . .' A tear rolls down her cheek. 'I don't know what's best for the children. Having us together or not seeing us argue all the time.' She takes a look at her wedding ring. 'We went down there to try and have some family time. Have a break from the monotony of it all. You don't know what it's like, being stuck in the house all the time. I used to have a job, a career. Now I spend my days doing washing and pureeing apples. It's crap. Don't get me wrong,' she says quickly. 'I love my kids. But sometimes you need a bit more, you know?'

Hillier nods, her fingers tight on her mug.

'So . . . New Year's Eve. We had a bottle of wine over lunch. Then that turned into two. Then we had a gin and tonic afterwards in the bar. Bad idea as it turns out. Just meant another argument. A nasty one. We said things we shouldn't.' She shakes her head and a sob escapes her. Charlie gives his mother a startled glance from the high-chair and Jane wipes her face hurriedly. 'And so, all that time, we were drinking and fighting when we should have been watching Georgie. We should have been looking after her.'

'Hang on, Jane. What happened to Georgie wasn't your fault,' Hillier says.

'It was,' she insists. 'If we'd been looking after her properly and not getting hammered in the middle of the day, we would have stopped her going out of the room. Or we would have gone with her. What were we thinking? With Charlie asleep in his pram. And – as it turns out – a bloody serial killer staying in the same hotel. It's bloody appalling!'

267

'Hazel Archer isn't a serial killer,' Hillier says. 'Look, these things happen. Children wander off. You can't keep tabs on them all of the time.'

'You bloody well can. It's called parenting,' Jane practically spits.

'I don't think beating yourself up now is going to help anything. Least of all your marriage.' Hillier is rational, cool. She bites her lip, watching Jane gradually calm down, breathe slower. 'And so what you're saying about the time issue is . . .'

'That I haven't got a fucking clue what time Georgie went off. Could be three, half-past, could have been four. *I don't know*. We were arguing and then suddenly she was gone.'

'But why didn't you say this at the time? Tell us that you weren't sure when Georgie went off?'

'Can you imagine the headlines?' Jane exclaims. 'Journalists were swarming round the hotel like bees. They would have had a field day. *Pissed Parents Lose Child*. Think of the accusations they could have made. Look how everyone pilloried the McCanns for having dinner while their kid was getting abducted. And then all that money spent on the search. I thought they might charge us for it.' She shakes her head vigorously. 'Declan's on a warning at work. If he loses his job because he was drinking and irresponsible . . . we're already really struggling. The mortgage on this place gives me a hernia every time I think about it. And what about Children's Services?' Jane stares wildly at Hillier. 'I knew this woman at school who was half an hour late to pick her kids up and they took them away from her. Half an hour! What would they be like if they found out we were both boozing and forgot all about her—'

Jane breaks off, rubs a hand over her face. She swallows, calming down. 'Look, when Georgie was found, I was so relieved. You can't imagine . . . I just wanted the whole thing over. Neither of us has drunk anything since. We can't. We want to put the whole thing behind us. Try and keep together. I didn't want you digging around and stirring things up. Can't you see that?'

Hillier sighs. 'I suppose I can. But from my perspective it still leaves loose ends hanging.'

'She's safe,' Jane says firmly. 'And nothing like that is ever going to happen again.'

'All right.' Hillier's tone is muted. 'And so, just to confirm. When you concurred with the timing Karen gave . . .'

'I said it was the same time as I didn't want to admit the truth.' Jane looks up at the ceiling and then back at Hillier, her face screwed up in self-disgust. 'It sounded possible, so I said it. But if you want the god's honest truth, I've got no idea what time Georgie went missing.'

CHAPTER FIFTY-SEVEN

Hazel stands before the judge, her head bowed. She wears a cream blouse with a Peter Pan collar. Her hair is brushed to one side, her head as sleek as a seal's. Her hands are trembling as she clings to the balustrade of the witness box.

'Would you like some water, Miss Archer?' the judge asks kindly.

Hazel nods and then nearly drops the glass the usher brings to her. She shakes her head, embarrassed.

'I'm so sorry.'

Laurel's barrister smiles at her, leaning easily over the wooden lectern in front of him. The courtroom is small, a single male judge in red robes facing them all. Max and Jonny sit at the back of the room on a bench with green felt cushions. Other than them, the barristers and the clerks, the court contains no one else and is closed to outsiders. The air smells of furniture polish and the foxed pages of legal tomes.

Laurel isn't present. As is normal with a judicial review, she awaits the verdict in her prison cell.

'Miss Archer,' the barrister begins. 'This is a rare occurrence, as you know. But the court has agreed that these are extraordinary circumstances. Oral evidence in a judicial review hearing such as this is extremely unusual. But we have called you here today – and you have agreed – to speak for your sister, Laurel Bowman.

'Perhaps you could explain to the court a little bit about your relationship with your sister.' He waves his hand towards her. 'How you come to be here today and so forth.'

Hazel swallows. 'I haven't seen my sister for many years. We got back in touch just recently because ... uh, well, because my identity became known. For various reasons. And so we thought ... Well, I thought that the time was right to get back in contact.' She inhales deeply as if she has emerged breathless from deep underwater.

The barrister nods. 'And so, Miss Archer, if we go back to the offence for which your sister was convicted, it is my understanding that you have no recollection of that day. That – although you *were* present – given your very young age at the time and the distress rightly caused by the nature of the crime committed, you have blocked out all memory of that day and its transgressions?'

Hazel lifts her eyes to look at the barrister.

The judge pushes his elbows to the front of his desk, peering down to where she stands. The barrister shifts on his feet, waiting. A shaft of sudden sunlight bursts in through the small window at the very top of the courtroom, illuminating dust particles dancing through the air.

'Miss Archer?' the barrister says again. 'Can you answer? Have you any memory of that day in 1997?'

Hazel doesn't speak.

Max is on the edge of his seat, his palms pressed into his knees. The barrister turns with an uncomfortable laugh to the judge, his hands splayed, pleading for assistance.

'Miss Archer?' the judge says kindly. 'I realise this is hard for you. But I must request that you answer Mr Donnelly's question.'

'Yes,' she says. Her voice is clear although her eyes are glazed, as if she is herself transported back to that day when willow leaves spilled down on to the canal weaving its empty way through the trees. 'That day in July. All those years ago. Yes,' she says. All eyes are on her. The courtroom is as silent as if under a spell. 'I have some kind of memory of that day. In fact, now I remember everything.'

'It was the start of the summer holidays. Six weeks in front of us. Nothing to do except play. Be together. We were very close, Laurel and me. I remember . . .

'If we were careful and promised not to talk to any strangers, Mum would let us walk from our garden gate, up the canal path to where the playground was.

'It was hot. One of those beautiful summer days when everything was bright green and yellow and all you could hear were the leaves rustling in the trees and the far-off drone of a plane in the sky. You could hear the birds singing. We were happy. We were playing. Running to the playground together. We loved the roundabout and the swings. Flying through the air. Laurel would push me so high, to the point where your stomach flips. It was . . . fun.'

Hazel pauses, taking a breath.

'We were just kids. Little girls.'

She looks up then, at the tableau of faces before her. Jonny is gazing directly at her. Something in his eyes comforts her, steadies her. She gives him a sad smile before continuing.

'Kirstie was playing on the horse when we arrived. We just started talking to her. Playing with her. Her mother was having coffee, talking to her friends, I think. We didn't notice. We were in a world of our own. That was why it didn't seem strange when we suddenly found ourselves back at the old canal. We often played there, Laurel and I. The woods ran either side of it so it was good for Hide and Seek and Tag and make-believe games . . .'

She hesitates.

'I mean, I know what people say about us watching films and that.' Hazel looks up at the bench. 'The trial judge said it. I read it, later on. But it wasn't true. Really, you have to understand, films and television are nothing compared to what you can have in your head. Willow trees were fairy kingdoms to us. We used to go to a clearing where Laurel had her house and I had mine. Bits partitioned off where we had cinemas and swimming pools and huge master bedrooms with four-poster beds. None of it was real. You know?'

She picks up the glass of water and takes a sip. Her hands no longer tremble. She is calm.

As she drinks, the barrister rouses as if sunken in a trance and forces himself to interject. 'And Kirstie Swann. What happened to her that afternoon?'

Hazel puts her head on one side.

'She didn't fall,' she says carefully. 'She was hit. We were playing Mums and Dads and the baby was naughty and so she was hit. And then she fell.' She looks around the courtroom slowly. 'But that was when I ran.' She shakes her head. 'The blood . . . I didn't like it, I was scared. I wanted my mummy. So I ran. All the way back home.' Hazel wipes her cheeks, which glisten with tears. 'I swear that's the truth. On the Bible. On my father's life.'

The barrister stares at her for a long moment before seeming to shake himself into action.

'Who hit Kirstie, Miss Archer? Who hit her and caused her to fall?'

Hazel looks surprised as she folds her hands one over the other in front of her skirt. 'Well, it was Laurel. Of course it was. That's why she was found guilty.' She frowns as if confused. 'That's why she's in prison.'

The barrister looks at the judge, who leans heavily back in his seat and lifts his chin at the ceiling in an apparent direction to continue.

'Um, yes, indeed. 'The barrister's voice is bewildered, rising as he struggles to think on his feet.' As it was found by a jury of her peers in 1998. And . . . can you tell the court, Miss Archer, are you willing to vouch for your sister now? Are you happy to state that you will be a constant in her life going forward? Provide her with some much-needed familial support if she were to be released?'

Hazel bows her head as the sun reappears. Its light catches the shine of her hair.

'Can you vouch for your sister?' the barrister says again after a beat. 'Can you say that in your view she has been rehabilitated?'

There is no sound for a moment. The courtroom hangs on her words, chests rising and falling inaudibly, as they watch Hazel carefully considering her reply.

'No,' she says at last. 'No, I'm sorry to say that I can't vouch for my sister Laurel. I thought that I might be able to, but from what she told me at our recent meeting, and what I now remember to be the truth of that day back in 1997 . . .' She looks slowly around the room, blinking as if viewing it from behind glass. 'I'm so very sorry but I cannot in all conscience say that Laurel should ever be released.'

CHAPTER FIFTY-EIGHT

In the early evening Max lets himself in to the Airbnb flat he has rented for the last couple of weeks just off Leicester Square. Its sash windows overlook Gerrard Place where people are wandering along to theatres, looking for restaurants or standing in the freezing cold, chatting and smoking outside pubs. Watching them move around, unaware they're being observed, he runs over what happened today, how life for him will soon become completely different, and how all these people will soon be very much aware of the name Max Saunders.

It occurred to him, while Hazel was speaking in court – steadily unsticking the glue from her memories – that she is a natural for this kind of public arena. She speaks well, quietly and carefully, and creates that weird kind of empathy with onlookers not many people have but every celebrity wants.

He goes to the tiny kitchen to pour himself a glass of wine, thinking how, even in the mainstream press, he can see the tide of public opinion turning. He knows that the more Hazel is discussed, the more normalised her situation will become. In the last few days, even before her meeting in the prison with Laurel, she has been approached by a television morning show who want to do an interview with her, and then a fashion magazine who want to feature her in a double-page spread. Of course, Max thinks as he drinks, she is remarkably pretty. That's always going to help.

He takes his glass back to the sitting room, swallowing a little as he goes, grimacing at the cold hitting his stomach. He needs to answer the numerous emails he has received from the literary agent, Romilly Harris, regarding his book proposal. She is straining at the bit to get it out to auction. Thank God, he thinks, the court was closed to the public today. If anyone leaks what happened, they will be in contempt. If there had been journalists allowed inside to witness what Hazel said, his scoop would have been blown out of the water.

He remembers then the packet that a sad-faced Toby had handed him after the hearing. He roots around in his bag and retrieves it. Tearing it open, he pulls out an old cassette tape, its label worn away. He turns it over in his hands and looks inside the package but there is no note, only a compliments slip from Toby Bowman's office. He wanders through into the sitting room, staring down at the tape. Outside, someone shouts drunkenly from the street but Max doesn't notice. He tosses the tape into the air and catches it one-handed.

Tomorrow morning, first thing, he'll go into Soho and buy a cassette player. They sell them in those vintage shops he's often walked past, never understanding how they make any money.

For now, though, he settles himself down in a chair, listening to the sounds of the city rumbling outside, drinking, smoking and thinking about those two little girls, those sisters, who seem so pitched at opposite ends on the spectrum of good and evil.

CHAPTER FIFTY-NINE

1997

'Once upon a time, there lived a poor widow with her two little girls in a cottage by the edge of a forest. In front of the cottage stood two little rose bushes. One bush bore white roses and one bore red, and the little girls were named after them.'

'Like me,' said Rosie, pointing to her chest. 'Rosie.'

'Yes,' said Amy, sitting on the end of Laurel's bed where both girls sat in their pyjamas. 'But your names are even more beautiful. One little girl was called Snow-White and she was blonde like you, Laurel. And the other little girl was called Rose-Red and she had dark hair like you, Rosie.'

The nightlight twirled familiar shapes around the bedroom walls as Amy curled up with her girls. Tiny, glittering stars of light were reflected onto the ceiling. The girls could see their mother's face as she leaned against the pale pink wall, eyes half-closed as she told the story from memory.

'Snow-White and Rose-Red loved each other very, very much and vowed that they would stay together forever.'

'What does vowed mean?' asked Laurel.

'It means a solemn promise. And they used to play together in the forest. Just like you play together in the garden and

277

down where the trees are, outside the fence. They were such good children and they did everything their mother used to tell them to do. Just like you do. Remember?'

Both girls nodded. Rosie moved to curl up with her head on Amy's lap as Laurel watched her quietly from her pillow.

'One day, a grizzly bear came into their cottage. The girls and their mother were terribly frightened. But the bear told them not to be afraid and that he was just hungry and cold. So they brushed the snow from his fur and gave him something to eat. The bear ended up staying with them for days and they played with him and loved him very much.'

'I'd like a bear as a pet,' Laurel said.

'Mummy says no pets, remember?' Rosie replied.

'Animals are nice to look at but not to touch,' Amy said. 'Anyway. A few days later Snow-White and Rose-Red were in the forest when they came across a little dwarf who had got his beard stuck in a log. Immediately, they knelt down to help him but they couldn't release his beard from where it was trapped. So Rose-Red took out some little scissors she always carried with her, and cut his beard free.

'He should have been grateful but he was very angry and stomped around and around, yelling at them for causing him such bad luck by chopping off a piece of his beard.'

'How mean,' Laurel said.

'Yes. Awful. So he gathered up his bag and the girls could see it was filled with rubies and diamonds and pearls. And he marched off into the forest without a word of thanks.

'A few days later, the girls were in the forest once more when they saw the dwarf again. Suddenly, a huge golden eagle swooped down from the sky and picked the dwarf up in his talons. Talons are like claws,' Amy said, seeing Laurel raise her head. At the answer to her unspoken question, she lay down again to listen.

'Rose-Red and Snow-White jumped up and ran over to where the dwarf was dangling in the sky and caught hold of his coat-tails. They tugged and tugged and eventually he came loose and fell onto the ground and the eagle flew away. The little man was even angrier than he had been the time before. "Why did you tug me so roughly!" he cried. "You could have torn my new coat!"' Amy looked down at her girls who were staring at her wide-eyed. 'Just then, a huge bear came ambling out of the woods and the dwarf screamed in terror.'

'The bear!' Rosie gasped.

'The bear indeed. The dwarf immediately fell to his knees, saying, "Please, bear, don't eat me. Take these two girls who are much plumper ..."'

'What's plumper?' asked Laurel.

'Fatter, Laurel. Fatter. Goodness, such a lot of questions! So he said, 'Take these two girls who are much plumper than me and will make a much nicer meal than anything I could provide.' And do you know what the bear did then?'

The girls shook their heads as stars scattered over the ceiling above them.

'The bear took his great paw and swiped the dwarf dead onto the ground. Blood seeped out of his nasty little head until it stained the earth as red as the roses in Rose-Red's bush.'

'Oh, Mummy,' Laurel whispered. 'That's terrible.'

'Well, not really, sweetie. Because the bear then transformed into a prince. The bear was, of course, the same one they had been so kind to. And he told them that the dwarf was an evil little man who had turned him into a bear years ago and robbed him of all his treasure. That was the same treasure as the dwarf was taking round with him in his bag. Now the dwarf was dead, the spell was broken and he could be a prince once again.'

'But the dwarf was dead,' Laurel said, her voice on the verge of distress.

'But, Laurel, the bear turned into a prince. And then he married Snow-White. And Rose-Red married his brother. And they all lived happily together in a big castle with all the treasure they'd got back from the dwarf.' Amy glanced down. Seeing Rosie's eyes closed, her mother gently moved herself out from underneath her, picked her up and carried her over to her own bed. She opened the bedroom door, letting in a shaft of light from the landing. Looking back as she went to leave, she saw Laurel had her eyes open and lay staring up at the ceiling.

'All right, baby? Don't worry. It's just a story.'

'It's sad.'

'Good night, Laurel. Sweet dreams.'

After her mother had left, Laurel lay for a few moments before turning onto her side towards her sister. 'Rosie? Are you awake? Did you like that story?'

Her sister said nothing.

'I don't think he should have killed the dwarf, do you?'

But Rosie didn't answer, for she was fast asleep.

CHAPTER SIXTY

Laurel and Fritz sit in her cell, flicking ash into an empty Coke can. The cassette player scratches out an ancient tape of Patsy Cline.

They are quiet, companionably lost in the weed and their thoughts. Laurel has her head leaning against the wall, eyes closed, trying to palpate the anger which rages inside of her into something calmer, easier to swallow. The weed is helping, transforming the image of Rosie's face into a blurry mash.

Since she spoke to Toby after the hearing, the number of times he has tried to call her back has risen to double figures. But Laurel refuses to talk to him. What's the point? It should have been obvious to Toby that Rosie would do this. Just as it had been obvious to her when she'd heard that her sister wanted to see her. She's still angry with herself that she allowed curiosity to sucker her into the meeting. And then, that her rage had caused her to walk out on Rosie during it. That would have been what prompted her sister to be so cruel. She never did like to be left alone.

Laurel thinks about Toby and the hole that will be left in her life from now on. She would like to talk to him. The desire burns inside her so bitter it makes her sick. But there's just no point. He'd only want to say sorry, and she can't bear to hear any more sadness from that man. He won't last the month, she reckons. About time she gave him a break, let him live out his last days in peace without always having to bother about her.

She can look after herself anyway. She has her mates in here. She has her routine. What was she going to do on the outside? Work for fucking Sainsbury's? And whatever anyone said, she knows what the deal is. Keep your shit private. That shit is worth something.

Down the corridor, a girl screams out and a clash of metal reverberates through the doorway. Laurel opens her eyes.

'Shut the fuck up,' she murmurs, trying to keep stoned and in the place where things make sense, where it's warm and tomorrow doesn't rear up like a slap in the face.

She feels the weight of Fritz, curled up at the end of her bed, like a coil of lanky string. Laurel knows it won't be long until they're separated. It might be years, it might be months, but at some point Fritz'll get parole or she'll be moved to another prison and Laurel will be on her own again. It's the way it has been since that day in the courtroom when she was led away from her parents and sister and they left her in a cell by herself. The only person there was the social worker. Laurel can't even remember that bitch's name any more. She hadn't spoken to the child anyway, just let her sit there on the hard, thin bed, waiting for her mum to come and explain what was going on, for someone to take her home.

Nobody came.

Nobody ever comes to your aid in life because you're on your own for all of it. Birth to death and back again.

Laurel takes another drag and Fritz taps her on the knee.

'What?'

'Why do you listen to this old rubbish?'

Laurel doesn't answer, remembering her mother swaying at the sink with Patsy Cline singing that she was crazy.

They were all fucking crazy. That was the problem.

'Just do,' she says at last. 'Makes me think.'

Fritz nods and falls silent.

'Are you going to see her again?' she asks after a minute.

Laurel knows who Fritz means but she won't say the name. Won't have it said in her presence.

'Bitch is coming next week.' Laurel drops her butt into the can and shakes it, extinguishing it with a hiss. 'Last fucking time. Last fucking time that bitch is coming anywhere near me.'

CHAPTER SIXTY-ONE

Hazel opens the door to Hillier in surprise. So taken aback was she by the announcement of the name through the intercom that she pressed the buzzer with barely a second's thought. Now she is regretting her impetuosity as she steps back to allow the policewoman to cross the threshold.

'Hello,' she says, backing into the flat as if she is a gladiator in the ring. 'What can I do for you?'

'Thanks for letting me in, Miss Archer,' Hillier says as she steps in quickly as if worried Hazel will change her mind.

'Uh, no problem.' Hazel walks into the sitting room and gestures towards the sofa. 'Have a seat.'

'Thank you,' Hillier replies. 'No chance of a glass of water, is there? I'm a bit parched from walking from the Tube.'

'Yes, of course,' Hazel says, leaving the room to go to the kitchen.

The flat has an unused air, Hillier thinks, her eyes scanning the surfaces and walls for evidence of Hazel's past, her character. One wall is covered in bookshelves but there are no photographs or pictures apart from a single painting on the opposite wall. Hillier stares at it. It is small, showing a woman with dark hair, wearing a red jumper, in the middle of a dark green background. The woman has her hands up next to her cheeks and her mouth is open in the circle of a scream. The expression in her eyes is so visceral that Hillier thinks she can hear that scream, feel the pain that lies beneath.

'My mother painted it,' Hazel says from behind, handing Hillier a glass of water. 'Years ago, when I was a child. I always liked it. When she died, my dad gave it to me. I didn't want anything else.'

'I don't know much about art,' Hillier admits, wondering at the same time what could make Hazel possibly like this painting, want to look at it on a daily basis when all it conveys is panic and fear. 'But that is striking.'

'Yes,' Hazel says, taking in the picture as if for the first time. 'I must bring it with me to Jonny's.' She sits down in a leather club chair to the left of Hillier. 'We're getting married,' she says, a faint smile playing at her lips. 'He proposed just yesterday. It's been such an emotional time. We went to court for my sister . . . You'll hear about it soon enough, I would think. I suspect Laurel will be unsuccessful in gaining parole again, sadly.'

'Ah, I see.' Hillier's eyebrows lift, her tone carefully neutral. 'Congratulations on the engagement. Things are really working out for you.'

'I think he meant to ask me at New Year's,' Hazel continues as if Hillier hasn't spoken. 'But, what with Georgie going missing, well, you know . . .'

'Yes indeed,' Hillier says, taking a sip of water. 'May I?' She indicates her jacket and, on Hazel's nodded assent, removes it and places it carefully on the cushion next to her.

Hazel looks at her. 'Have you seen Georgie lately? Is she OK now?'

'Oh, yes. Fit as a fiddle and bright as a button. Apart from her toe obviously . . . She was out of hospital not long after she went in.'

'That's good. And . . . does she remember much about what happened? Must be traumatic for a child as young as that.'

'It was indeed. She remembers parts. Not all of what happened. But bits of it.'

'Oh, that's good. I'm pleased. It must have been so frightening for her parents.'

'Yes, it was.' Hillier leans back with a congenial expression on her face. 'So! Can't move without seeing you on a front page these days.'

Hazel colours. 'I can't say I'm happy about it. It's been very difficult actually.'

'I'm sure. Still,' Hillier says, 'you're quite the person of the moment.'

Hazel's face clouds over. 'There has been a great deal of pressure . . . I'm not comfortable with it, as I said. For poor Jonny – and Evie – as well. It's been a tremendous strain.'

'I can imagine.'

'So, why is it you're here, Detective Hillier?' Hazel asks, shifting on her chair and changing gear. 'What can I do to help you?'

'Oh, yes! Sorry, almost forgot myself,' Hillier says, reaching into her jacket for a small notebook and flicking through the pages, the end of her biro in one corner of her mouth. 'Ah, yes, that's it. Just on the timings. On that afternoon Georgie went missing . . .' She falls silent, apparently reading her notes.

'Yes?' Hazel prompts after a moment.

'Yup, hang on. Here it is. Now, on the day that Georgie went missing, we established that she went into the kitchen and disappeared from there at three o'clock. Where were you at that time, Ms Archer?'

Hazel screws up her face. 'I think . . . I told you this before. I was having tea with Jonny in the hotel lounge.'

'You're sure about that? It wasn't later?'

'I think so. It's hard to remember exactly this far on, Detective.'

'Sure, I understand. And you were together until four?'

She looks unblinkingly at Hazel. Sees the merest second of hesitation before Hazel shakes her head. 'I was with him all the time. We went up to our rooms at five and that's when the hotel manager came and knocked on our door and said that Georgie was missing.'

'Ah, yes.' Hillier taps her biro on the notebook. 'That's right, of course.' She glances up and smiles. 'You're sure it wasn't later? Even by perhaps half an hour? Was it dark outside by then, when you went up to your room? Do you recall?'

Hazel folds her arms. 'I don't.'

'No. That's OK. No problem.'

'Why are you asking me this? Has something come up? Didn't Georgie just go wandering off? Why are you still asking questions?'

Hillier gets to her feet. 'Just a few end-of-the-case enquiries,' she says, reaching for her jacket. 'And Mr Newell? He would corroborate that, would he? That you were together all afternoon? That the timings you mention are correct?'

'Yes,' Hazel answers coldly. 'He did before when you questioned us at the hotel. And he would do so again.'

'Your fiancé now, isn't he?' Hillier says lightly.

'That's right. Is that all, DC Hillier?'

'Yep, that's it. Thanks for talking to me, Ms Archer, I appreciate it. Funny old business, wasn't it? What happened to the little girl . . .'

'Kids will run off, I suppose.'

Hillier looks at her sharply. 'Seem to run off a lot around you, if you don't mind me saying.'

Hazel draws herself up. 'I do mind actually. I think it's better if you leave now.'

Hillier smiles, making her way into the hallway, glancing at a photograph of Hazel and Jonny on the wall. She taps the glass covering his face. 'Nice photo. Seems a decent chap.'

'Goodbye, Detective Hillier,' Hazel says at the door.

'Look after yourself, Ms Archer.'

Hazel shuts the door behind the policewoman, standing in the entryway for a long while before she finally turns and heads back into the body of the flat.

CHAPTER SIXTY-TWO

Max walks through Soho with a pair of headphones over his ears. The Sony Walkman is in his jacket pocket, the volume turned up to maximum. At first, there is just static. Then the sound of two little girls' voices fills his head.

He stops. Lights a cigarette while leaning against a wall covered in fly posters. As he listens, he drops to the ground, sitting down on a doorstep, his head in his hands. When the tape comes to the end, he exhales smoke, squinting up into the sky.

And then he presses rewind.

Joanna runs along Shaftesbury Avenue, rueing the decision to take this route as she dodges past the pottering tourists, the dawdling office workers. Still, she loves this part of London. She loves the mingling of different languages; the way Londoners walk with their heads down whereas the tourists look only upwards; she even loves the rubbish and detritus swept into piles in the gutters, that feeling of everything getting tidied and sorted and washed away clean.

The morning is clear and bright and her lungs drink in the cold fresh air. She carries on into Soho itself, up through Leicester Square, past a man hunched in a doorway listening to his headphones, thinking already of the latte and the sausage sandwich she'll have when she's run her ten kilometres.

It seems a lifetime ago since the New Year. During the last few months – since seeing Debbie and then resolving things with Will – she has to admit that she has felt lighter. Not indifferent, not absolved, but as if a small chip of ice has been dislodged from inside her. She can breathe easier. She has been sleeping better for the first time in years.

They have taken on a number of different cases at BTR. An environmental matter she has really got stuck into, and a case involving a death row inmate in Jamaica. They've nudged her away from Kirstie a little. She's still there but not as visceral. Joanna has even managed to put the date of the judicial review hearing out of her mind.

Perhaps she *has* been wrong all this time, she thinks as she cuts up through Chinatown, breathing in the smell of crispy duck and noodles. Perhaps opening up is good. Maybe she should find a counsellor, someone professional to help her put what happened to Kirstie in a place that hurts her less, isn't so intrusive, so obstructive.

Is it forgiveness she feels? She takes that thought and throws it down on the ground in front of her as she pounds the pavement, runs over it as if testing its strength. From the way her speed picks up, she realises that it's not. She thinks about meeting Laurel Bowman face to face and can still imagine screaming at her, making her beg for forgiveness, for what she's done. But ... and her feet slow a little as she passes the Curzon Cinema and turns onto Frith Street ... is that entirely accurate? Would she actually do that? Or would she rather sit and ask her how this could have happened? Ask her whether she wishes that things were different. Whether that ten-year-old girl exists any more or whether she has been extinguished.

Could she – ever – put the Flower Girls behind her? Could she go back to the person she was before she heard the name Laurel Bowman? That bright-eyed girl at university with all her idealistic dreams. She'd always thought she was going to *be* something, help people. Not fester in a pool of anger and vitriol.

Joanna glances up, to where the glass of the sky is smeared only by the white trails of planes traversing it. She sees that she's outside a newsagent's and feels thirsty. Sweat is coasting down her forehead and she feels warm outside for the first time this winter.

The bell rings as she enters the shop and it is as if the universe is laughing at her. Because there, slapped all over the front pages, are photos and headlines concerning the Flower Girls. Laurel Bowman's judicial review was heard in court yesterday and judgment is expected any day now.

It is as if she can never escape. She feels a searing anger at the injustice of it. Images dance in front of her eyes and she sways in the shop. The sight of her pregnant sister sobbing with pain at Kirstie's funeral; of the sombre police guard holding her tiny coffin; of Toby Bowman making his rotund way into court, dropping papers as he goes; of the judge looking down and making orders that affected everyone but him; of Debbie again, flicking ash into a saucer, pale hands and face, her eyes shrunken and exhausted; of the sounds of Jemima, playing upstairs in her cot; and finally of Rosie Bowman, her hood covering her face as she made her way outside in the rain.

It hits her in a rush, like the curve at the top of a roller-coaster as the car pushes out over the edge. All these images. The last twenty years of her life.

'Are you OK?' the newsagent asks her from behind his counter. 'Do you need something to make you better?'

Joanna whips her head up to look at him and her eyes blaze.

'Yes,' she says. 'I do need something.'

And, in that instant, she knows exactly what she needs to make her better.

She knows exactly what she needs to do.

CHAPTER SIXTY-THREE

The Devon air is brittle with frost as Karen waits in the play park opposite the blocks of flats. The high-rises were built before she was born so she has never considered their incongruity, the starkness of their mean, grey shapes, as if they are famished, starved of warmth against the dome of the sky and the roar of the sea.

Eventually, she can see the familiar shape of Marek as he comes tumbling out of the entrance, his hands tucked under his armpits.

'You've been bloody ages,' she complains. 'I'm freezing.'

'Sorry,' he mutters, sitting next to her on the bench and lighting a cigarette that he passes to her before taking out one for himself. 'Have you heard anything?'

'No,' she says, exhaling smoke into the cold air. 'It's all gone quiet. That policewoman hasn't been in touch since the other week. Who are you staying with anyway? You need to tell your family where you are.'

'No way,' Marek replies. 'As soon as she knows where I am, Mum'll be on the phone to the police and I just don't need that crap. She's never forgiven me for that little bitch from Brixham. Seriously, even the police knew it was bollocks. She looked bloody twenty. But Mum's like, "oh, the shame, the humiliation . . ."' He peers up into the sky. 'I fucking hate this place,' he says.

'Yeah,' Karen replies. 'It's shite.'

'Ta for telling me, though,' Marek says. 'About the copper. Appreciate it.'

She nods, flicking ash onto the ground.

'Might have got something up in London. Hotel out near Heathrow.' He shrugs. 'Agency thing. But at least it'd be away from here. You can have a bit of a crack in London anyway.'

Karen looks over at him. 'So you'll leave?'

'Maybe.' Marek feigns a disinterested study of the swings, under which condom packets, cans of Tennent's Extra and some old sheets of newspaper are strewn. 'I'm not going back to Balcombe, am I? Not with that policewoman sniffing around. What did she say again?'

'Just went on about the timings. What time I left. What time the kid came into the kitchen. Didn't make any sense if you ask me.'

'Kid just fucked off out of the hotel by mistake,' Marek sniffs. 'But I'm bolloxed if I'm going to hang around while they try and pin it on me.'

'Innocent until proven guilty.' Karen gives a disbelieving laugh.

'Yeah, right. Not for people like us. She had me fingered soon as she knew I was a Polski and that the police had talked to me before. It's typical of this place.' Marek sneaks a glance at Karen's profile as she pulls on the cigarette. 'You could come to London with me. If you wanted. It's not like you've got a job any more.'

'Couldn't stay at the hotel without you, could I?' she answers. 'Job was shite.'

'So come to London then.'

Karen looks at him, his cheeks red with the cold, his eyes bright. She gives a laugh. 'And leave all this? Nah.' She gets up and stands in front of Marek and gently kicks his trainers. 'I can't walk out on my dad, you know that.'

'So that's it then?'

She shoves her hands in her pockets and glances over at the coastline, the edge of the cliffs where the clouds cluster low in the sky. 'I'm gonna get going. Go into town. See what's happening.'

'All right,' Marek says flatly. 'See you.'

'Don't get moody,' she says, looking down at him, but he doesn't answer. 'Be like that then. See you around.' She heads across the asphalt back towards the road and a lone bus stop, its dismal light flickering in the gloom.

A few minutes later, the bus arrives and she gets on, sitting down at the front, her head tucked into her jacket. She doesn't look for the departing Marek as he goes back inside the flats and she doesn't notice Hillier, sitting with her back to them on a bench in the shadows of the playground, where she has been waiting in silence, listening to the two of them as they talked.

CHAPTER SIXTY-FOUR

The woman sitting opposite Max in The Ivy brings to mind a hound. She has a long nose and longer chin and her bush of blonde hair, which swirls across her shoulders, calls forth images of recently shorn wool. He widens his smile to dispel the picture and inclines his head.

'Are we drinking, Romilly?'

'I thought champagne would be appropriate?'

'Wonderful. You know,' Max says, after the waiter has taken the order and retreated discreetly, 'I was so delighted to get your call. With all the recent attention Hazel has had, and the way the press has leapt on the story, it's been a tad overwhelming. When you called, it was like manna from heaven.' He raises the crystal flute he is handed and chinks it delicately against Romilly's. 'Cheers.'

'This is where I'm at my most useful,' she says, her eyes trained on Max above the rim of her glass. 'In the eye of the storm, it's easy to lose your bearings. You need a compass, someone to direct you and present the different options. That's how Harris Associates earn our money. We can quieten the racket, pick out the good options, and help you focus on the aspects that will have the best outcome. Oh, just the chef's salad,' she says, without turning her head to the waiter who has deftly reappeared at their table. 'No dressing.'

'The duck,' Max says, pushing the menu towards the table's edge and lifting his glass again. 'Thank you.'

'For example,' Romilly continues, 'this week alone, I've had producers from Netflix wanting to discuss a feature-length documentary on the Flower Girls – obviously focusing on Hazel. Did you see the Amanda Knox one? Propelled her massively in public opinion ratings. I mean, I still think she did it but that's irrelevant. It's what the public think that counts. If Hazel could get just half such a positive response, then we're looking at film deals. Before any of that, of course, we've got the auction of the book proposal. And then once you've written the book – which will need to be done immediately, by the way – there's the submission to media groups for serialisation rights.'

'Which I'm hugely excited by,' Max says.

'Yes, it's great news.' Romilly smiles again. 'These really are happy days.'

Conversation pauses as the food arrives.

'And Hazel,' Romilly says, studying her salad in the manner of a pest-control expert appraising a rat's den. 'How is she coping with it all? With the attention? Is she strong enough to deal with it, do you think?'

Max nods. 'Hazel's fine. I'm sorry she hasn't come along today. She's just got engaged. A little bit swept off her feet, I think.' He takes a sip of champagne. 'One thing I will say about her, though: she looks vulnerable but underneath she's tough as anything. And she has Jonny to support her too.'

'Sure, but we're going to have to move quickly, Max. Once the court judgment is out, all of this will be in the public domain. We have Hazel for the moment. But we need her to sign a contract. Because she's vital. Without her, frankly, we'll have nothing other than the stuff that is out there already. You're positive you have her on board?'

'Yes, yes,' Max says, bristling slightly, feeling a prickly flush creep up the back of his neck. 'Hazel depends on me to advise her. She's vulnerable. I don't think she really understands how to handle it all so that's where I come in. Where *we* come in, Romilly. Don't you worry about her.'

The table vibrates with the buzzing of Romilly's phone. She holds up a hand in apology as she takes the call.

'OK, thanks. I'll be right there.'

Ending the brief conversation, she smiles at Max, bringing her handbag onto her lap. 'I'm so sorry but I'm going to have to dash. Something's cropped up back at the office.' She stands and waves at the table. 'Do let me get this. It's been so lovely to meet.'

Max rises, his napkin in his hand. 'Thank you *so*, so much, Romilly. It has indeed been a delight. And listen,' he continues as she exits from behind the table and makes to leave. 'Please don't worry overly about getting the contract signed.' He kisses her on both cheeks, his hands on her shoulders. 'There's no cause for concern at all. Hazel and I are as thick as thieves.'

He meets her later that afternoon in a bookshop just off Piccadilly Circus. She arrives hand in hand with Jonny and they retreat to a café at the top of the building. Hazel's eyes rove around, taking in the hushed whispers of the other customers as they notice one of the Flower Girls sitting down with her back to them, her collar turned up high.

'Let's order cake,' Max says. 'We're celebrating.'

'Are we? What for?' Jonny answers, glancing around.

'For fame, glory and all of its spoils. Harris Associates are desperate to take you on. Take us on. The whole shebang. They've got producers interested. Netflix, Amazon. They want to do a documentary. Hollywood beckons! We'll get Reese Witherspoon buying the film rights before you can say *Gone Girl*.'

Hazel is quiet, a look of concern on her face.

'What is it?'

She glances across at Jonny, who puts his arm round her shoulders. 'I don't know. It's all going so fast. I feel a little bit out of my depth, I suppose.'

'You mustn't worry,' Max says firmly. 'I'm here, aren't I? And Jonny? It's what I've always said, it's all about perception. People don't know what they believe until they're told what to believe. If the accepted line is that you're totally innocent, people will get it.'

'I am totally innocent.' Hazel's tone is sharp.

The memory of the cassette tape burns like a hot poker across Max's skull. With an effort he pushes it away. This is his chance. His chance to make something of his life.

'Yes, yes, I know.' He swallows, lowering his voice a little. He has had too much champagne at lunch and his gullet feels as though it's on fire. He needs to focus. 'But I'm talking about what's represented in the media. Look, if you had every paper globally telling you that the world was flat – every article, every expert, every TV show – eventually you'd start to believe it, wouldn't you? If all the photos of the world as round were removed so you had nothing to counter the arguments? People can't hold onto an idea if there's no foundation to it.

'What we're going to do with the book is start sowing the seeds of you as a charming, beautiful, *vulnerable* woman. Then we bolster that with more and more information, until all the search engines, all the available information, is about *that*, not you being associated with your sister.' Max shrugs, looks down at the empty table in front of them. 'It's just how things work.'

Jonny nods and squeezes Hazel's shoulder and she visibly relaxes, takes a look over Max's head to the counter full of cakes and muffins. 'I'm going to visit Laurel on Wednesday by the way.'

'What?' Max exclaims too loudly. An elderly woman at the table next to them stares over crossly. 'Why on earth would you do that?'

'I need to end things once and for all. I need to say goodbye.'

'I think it's a terrible idea,' Max forces himself to speak in a quieter tone. 'Before, I would have been all for it, positively encouraged it. But now . . . since the court case . . . she hates you for what you said about her in court. She must do. She won't get out now. I'm surprised she's even agreed to see you, if I'm honest.'

Hazel's lips tighten a fraction. 'Oh, she'll see me.' She puts her head on one side. 'Do you really think I shouldn't go?'

'I'm just looking out for you, Hazel.' Max lifts his head to meet her eyes. 'Look, shall we get some water? I'm feeling a tad warm.'

'Well, let's see,' Hazel says, and puts her elbows on the table and gives a little smile. She forms her hands into tight fists, the knuckles white.

'What are you doing?' Max stares at her, his head beginning to throb.

'It's a game Hazel used to play,' Jonny says. 'Back when she was younger.'

'Yes?' Max says, watching her, his mouth dry.

'I used to play it with my mum and my sister,' Hazel says. 'When one of us didn't want to do something that Mummy had asked us to do, we'd play it. Scissors, paper, stone. You know it? You bounce your hand down three times like this,' she says, moving her fist through the air above the table. 'Scissors beat paper, paper beats rock and rock beats scissors. Shall we do it?'

Max's laugh is nervous. 'What for, for God's sake?'

'No, you're right.' Hazel frowns in a strange way. 'It's a stupid idea. Sorry.' She looks up at him, her eyes big and round. 'I always used to lose the game anyway.'

Jonny laughs softly. 'How about that cake then?'

'Wait,' Hazel says, placing her hand on his. 'We need to tell him.'

'Tell him what?' Max says, his eyes flitting from Hazel to Jonny.

He is beginning to feel sick. The bookshop is too hot, too quiet. He watches her smiling at him, watches the way she takes him in, as if she knows him absolutely, is drinking in his deepest fears, his deepest insecurities. There is something so nauseating about it that, for the first time in her company, Max feels a delicate shiver move slowly down his spine.

'Romilly Harris,' Hazel says. 'Harris Associates.'

He knows what she is going to say before she says it. He sees then with a terrible clarity how he has been played and how he has let his greed and ambition lead him here, to become a person he doesn't recognise.

'I just spoke to her. Well . . .' she smiles at him and Jonny leans back, crossing his knee over his thigh '. . . we saw her actually, at her office.'

'You signed the contract.' Max's voice is practically a whisper. There is something wrong with his throat, he cannot seem to get enough air.

'We do want to thank you, Max. For everything you've done for us. But, well, I need an agent myself, really. What with everything that's happening for me right now. You're just a writer, aren't you? Romilly . . . she's the person who holds the key to everything. I'm sorry, I know you thought we'd do this together . . .' Hazel's voice trails off, her eyes dipping low.

'Romilly says you'll definitely still be paid for the proposal you did. And that you might be chosen,' Jonny says brightly. 'You know, to be the ghostwriter.'

Hazel nods. 'I'm sure they'll give you an acknowledgement inside the book,' she says. 'But I know that's not important to you. I know that you did all of this in my best interests. That's what you've always said, isn't it? That's why we're so grateful to you. Honestly, we are.'

Max has turned pale. He can feel a tightness in his chest, it's hard for him to breathe.

'Are you OK, Max?'

Hazel's voice is very far away all of a sudden.

'The tape . . .' he says. 'I heard the tape. Someone sent it to me.'

'What's that, Max? I can't hear you. What tape?'

And then the bookshop disappears, and the last thing Max sees is Hazel's face above him before everything turns dark.

CHAPTER SIXTY-FIVE

Dear Laurel,

I have wanted to write to you for a long time. I have actually wanted to come and see you. But the powers that be, probably quite rightly, judged it ill-advised. Nevertheless, for many years I have composed letters to you in my head. I have thought and thought about the words that I would choose. The words that would hurt you the most, cause you maximum distress.

I find myself today finally writing the letter I have imagined for all of these years. But, in the end, it's not quite the letter I thought I'd write.

Since your first parole hearing, I have been outside the walls of the prison where you are held. I have been the person most insistent on your guilt. And I have campaigned and fought to keep you where you are.

I have succeeded in helping with this.

I don't claim that it's solely down to me. But the actions of my family and myself have ensured that the country, the politicians, the press, have all been constantly reminded of the crime you committed in 1997 when you took the life of my niece, Kirstie Swann.

Kirstie was born on 1 September 1994. Did you know that? It was a Thursday, ironically. Forgive my sarcasm, but in this case Thursday's child didn't have far to go in the end, did she?

My sister Deborah is a better person than I am. She always has been. When we were kids, she was always the one with all the friends. I would hang behind her, wanting to join in, being a little pain. Was that what it was like for you and Rosie? Although – actually – I don't think I want to know. Debbie is a good woman and she proves it to me even now, when she suffers more grief than most people will ever know.

So why am I writing to you after all this time? I saw last week that you've had your big day in court. We don't know the outcome yet. I suspect you do. Will you be free, Laurel? Will you be able to drink in the air that is denied my niece? Or will you be locked up in your box for another stretch of time before we have to argue it all over again?

I think what I want is impossible. What I want cannot be achieved and that's what leaves me hanging here, caught between anger and resentment, never able to break out of the cycle.

Because what I want is for you never to have done what you did.

All the arguments we've had about it over the years, between your lawyers and my family's: all we argue about is whether you've been properly punished or not.

But, really, is that the point?

Even during the trial, we argued about *why* you did it. Did you mean it? Was it an accident? Had you watched something that changed the way your brain worked? Or were you just evil? Everyone had an opinion. Everyone had a view. We went back and forth and back and forth again. And we still don't know the truth.

That gave me solace for a long time. The thought that you *did* know the truth and that, one day, you would tell us. You'd let us know why you'd done it and things would change for the better because of it. Kirstie's death would be explained.

But you never said.

And so, for years, I've kept all of this down inside me, just like my sister has. Buried it deep so I could function in life. I've directed my anger towards you and it's propelled me on, let me survive.

But a while ago, Debbie told me she can't hate you any more and I couldn't understand it. She said she just wants to remember her daughter as she was. Not as a crusade but as a beautiful little girl we all loved.

And that must be right because she feels it. Kirstie's mother.

But where does it leave me?

We can't engineer time so that you never murdered Kirstie. And you won't tell us why you did it. And everyone else is deciding to save themselves by opening up to forgiveness. Even your sister is opening her heart to the press and the judiciary. Even she is trying to make it better.

I feel stymied, Laurel, in all honesty.

Sometimes I feel like I'm recovering. And then other times, I want to come and hurt you so badly, for how you've hurt me and my family.

But I won't.

But I can't forgive either.

All I can do, Laurel Bowman, is tell you as close as I can to face to face, that I will never forgive you for what you've done.

But that I let you go.

If I carry on hating you as much as I have done over the years, I'll end up destroying myself and I have a lot to give. More than you will ever be capable of doing, I'm sure.

So good luck to you, Laurel Bowman. I'm stepping back, I'll let the courts decide from hereon in. Let them see if you are worthy to feel the fresh air on your face.

I suspect you're not. But I've been wrong before.

Yours,

Joanna Denton

CHAPTER SIXTY-SIX

15 JULY 1997

The gate banged to a regular rhythm in the breeze. Amy watched it from the kitchen window where she stood immobile, unflinching from the heat of the sun which burnt her face through the glass.

The girls had run in from the canal. Flying over the grass as if a wolf were chasing them. They had pushed in through the back door, past her standing at the sink. Amy turned her head to the sounds of their voices upstairs. Laurel was crying, she thought. She should go up there and see what was wrong. Somehow, though, it was as if the heat of the afternoon was like molasses, fixing her to the floor, dripping through her and congealing at her feet. Even breathing was difficult, the air hot in her lungs as if she were on fire inside.

'I'm sorry!' she heard one of the girls yell. Perhaps Rosie. Her voice was higher, it still had the timbre of a baby's. Amy's forehead creased. She really needed to go and see what was wrong.

She turned and moved one foot, sliding it across the linoleum, her bare toes sticking to the dirt that covered the floor. Out of the corner of her eye, she could see something dark by the door, a puddle of rust. She dragged her other foot to meet the first and bent slowly to the stain. She straightened, frowning, and pulled the back door open. Another patch of colour spread across the stoop. She mustered the remaining energy she had and stepped outside into the garden. Across the grass, wide gaps between them, were more dots of brownish-red.

Before she knew it, Amy was at the gate, bringing her hand with surprising speed to grab it, stopping it mid-swing. She held it open and moved slowly outside the garden's boundary. A solitary chirp above in the trees accompanied her as she moved softly underneath the branches beside the canal, her feet gliding over the mulch and shingle.

As she walked, Amy felt her heart thumping inside her. It was an unfamiliar sensation. For months, she had been dead, banked down by cotton wool soaked in unhappiness. Now, though, as she watched the splashes of colour continue, leading her on, she could actually feel the blood swimming in her veins, bringing life to her arteries, her limbs.

When Amy reached the end of the trail of spots, she looked down at the dead girl for a long time. The girl's eyes were black, unseeing and cold. Blood had crusted along her hairline, the skin around her earlobe pulpy like coagulated porridge. Her limbs were extended in a star shape, hands thrown up next to her face. Amy's gaze travelled over her, taking it all in.

A rustle back down the path caused her to glance up. Outside the gate, balancing on her toes, was Rosie.

She stood there, her fingertips resting on the wood to steady herself, her dark hair reflecting the light of the sunbeams picking their way through the trees.

Amy looked at her daughter, drinking in her beauty, drinking in her obedience, warm and peaceful like something you could always, always depend upon.

308

She smiled at her, a genuine smile that lifted her face, caused her eyes to crinkle, in a motherly way, she thought. And Rosie smiled back, nodded quickly and then darted back through the gate.

The bird above Amy took flight, its wings ripping through the branches, startling her, making her blink. She felt the air kissing her skin, goosebumps flowing down her arms as she wondered again about the baby on the ground. Wondering what it had taken to make her little body so damaged and broken.

Amy turned and began to make her way back to her garden, thinking of her daughters, and particularly of her little Rose-Red. Such a precious girl.

And always so very eager to please.

CHAPTER SIXTY-SEVEN

Detective Sergeant Mike Gordon is at his desk when he is told that Lorna Hillier is downstairs waiting to see him. A few minutes later she enters his office, wet through from the latest downpour outside.

'I swear to God,' she says as she hauls herself into a chair opposite Gordon, 'I'm going to go and live by the Mediterranean one of these days. This weather . . .' She shakes her head like a dog emerging from water.

'Hillier,' he says. 'To what do I owe this honour?'

'Not going to offer me a cup of tea?'

Gordon gives her a look bordering on contempt. He inclines his head and waits.

'Clearly not. No problem. Anyway, I wanted to pop in and see you, to tidy up a few things on the Greenstreet case.'

'What Greenstreet case?' Gordon's tone is weary. 'As far as I'm aware, the matter is closed.'

'Well, yes. I suppose, strictly, you could say that. But the thing is,' says Hillier, bright-eyed, 'I have new evidence. Evidence that proves Hazel Archer was involved in the abduction of Georgie.'

Gordon leans forward. 'What evidence?'

'The clock in the kitchen was running slow. Karen Page the waitress says she saw Georgie come into the kitchen at three p.m. As did Marek Kaczka the sous-chef. By the way, they've both quit Balcombe Court now, which at first I thought was suspicious but I heard them talking the other night and I don't think they had anything to do with it.' Hillier speaks quickly, her thoughts tripping over themselves, but then she halts as if the conclusion is obvious.

'The clock?' Gordon prompts her.

'Ah, yes. The clock. So, Karen and Marek are convinced that Georgie was in the kitchen at three but actually it was about three-thirty-five because the clock was running slow.' Hillier spreads her hands. *Fait accompli.*

Gordon stares at her.

'Sunset was just before four that day. So it was nearly dark. Georgie said it was dark when she got lost coming out of the kitchen. Which it wouldn't have been at three.'

Hillier nods at Gordon, prompting him to catch up. When he doesn't speak, she sighs loudly.

'Georgie was let go, right? Whoever took her, let her go. That's what always bothered me. Given that most abuse happens between family members, at first I thought it meant Jane or Declan had taken her. And then they couldn't go through with it as she's their daughter. So I went to see Jane.'

'You went and talked to Georgie's mother?' A bead of sweat appears on Gordon's forehead.

'Yes. Remember we thought it was odd that she was so evasive? Well, turns out it's because she admits they can't remember when Georgie left them in the bar because they were drunk and arguing. She felt so guilty about it – and worried that we'd call in Children's Services – she wanted to forget the whole thing once Georgie was safe.'

'And you believe her?'

'Yes. Even though she lied about the timings. Or rather, she didn't tell the truth about not remembering. So, then I thought – well, who else would dump her? Dump a child after they'd taken the risk of snatching her? It wouldn't be Marek. Whatever he says, he's got an eye for a young 'un. He's the type who, if he geared himself up for something, would follow through, I reckon. I can't see him just letting Georgie go.'

'So because you can't see him letting her go, it means he must be innocent of her snatching?' Gordon sounds dumbfounded.

'Yep,' Hillier answers firmly.

'Right. So – just to get this straight – you went to see Jane Greenstreet off your own bat?'

'On my day off, yes.'

'Anyone else you've called on?' His voice has dipped dangerously low.

'Just Hazel Archer . . .'

Gordon covers his face with his hands. 'This is *madness*, Hillier!' he exclaims.

She halts, breathing hard. 'What?'

'For Pete's sake, Lorna! Georgie Greenstreet was found safe. She'd got lost and had sheltered in a cave. Why does it have to be any more complicated than that?'

Hillier narrows her eyes and folds her arms. 'The only person with the necessary psychology to have let Georgie go – once she had been taken – is Hazel Archer.'

Gordon takes a minute to compose himself although, when he speaks, his voice rings with steel. 'All right, Hillier. I'll humour you. Explain to me why that is.'

'Because,' Hillier explains slowly, 'she's got form.' She looks at him. 'Kirstie Swann.'

'That was down to her sister,' Gordon points out.

'Was it? Archer was never tried.'

Gordon tightens his lips.

'So she's got form,' Hillier insists. 'Proven or not. She was around, wasn't she? She's never denied being present when the Swann girl was murdered.'

'So why now? Why draw attention to herself, after all these years?' Gordon asks.

Hillier hesitates for a moment, looking to the ceiling as if she is searching for the right words. 'Look,' she says, 'admittedly, I don't know. Maybe she had some kind of mental breakdown. Maybe she'd read stuff about Laurel Bowman in the press, because of her court appeals, whatever. Maybe she's never really faced what happened in 1997. So she has a sort of crisis. She takes Georgie – for what purpose, I don't know, I'm not a psycho – and then, just as she's going to harm the child, it's like she wakes up, sees what she's doing. *And she sees that if something happens to the kid, she'll be the obvious suspect.* She can't go through with it. She panics and so she lets Georgie go.' Hillier sits back, triumphant.

Gordon is silent, his nostrils flaring.

'I saw a painting her mother did in Archer's flat,' Hillier continues. 'It looks like some kind of emotional explosion. What was their relationship exactly? Why did the parents never see Laurel Bowman again? It doesn't make sense. How could you abandon your own child?' Hillier stares at him. After a lengthy few seconds, the ticking clock the only sound in the room, she drops her eyes.

'I get it, Hillier,' Gordon says at last. 'I understand. 'I know that you want to be recognised, acknowledged for the very important work that you do . . .'

'That's not it, Sarge.'

'Oh, it is, Hillier. It is. You're haring around the countryside, determined to find some – any – kind of evidence to prove your theory about Hazel Archer. But, as you admit yourself, it doesn't stack up. It doesn't make sense. Why would she deliberately bring this attention to herself? She's led a private life for near-on twenty years. Why would she want this fuss? Why would she want the police crawling all over the place, looking into her and her life? And . . . no, let me finish.' He waves his hand at Hillier, who is spluttering at him, trying to interrupt. 'Let's say you're right, and she *did* take the child. Isn't it convenient that she wakes up from her fugue or whatever just in time so that she doesn't kill her? Everything you're saying is based on theory, there's no proof.

'And the *main* point you haven't answered is why Georgie didn't say anything. Why wouldn't she say it was Archer? Eh?' Gordon steeples his fingers and draws breath. 'It's all conjecture, Lorna. All of it. Listen to me. Take my advice. Go back to Brixham. Get back to your not inconsiderable paperwork. Please – for the sake of your career – please, just forget this now.'

'Georgie never said anything because she was never given the chance! We barely spoke to her. Her mother shut us down and we couldn't even interview the girl properly, never mind putting her in a position to identify anyone.' Hillier grips the arms of her chair, her face filled with conviction. 'Hazel Archer *is* a danger to children. She needs to be locked up. I'm not obsessed, whatever you think. I just want what's right. She's outside, preying on kids while her sister's in prison. It's the wrong way round. It's not right.'

Gordon glances at his door, wondering how long he'll have to listen to this. 'OK then. Where's your evidence?'

Hillier swallows hard.

'Where is it?'

Her shoulders droop. 'I've had fifteen years on the force. If that doesn't give you an instinct for what's true, I don't know what does.'

'It doesn't work like that, Lorna, and you know it. We need more. You got to the scene first, sure. But things move on from that. It's not always about first impressions.'

'I disagree, sir. First impressions are everything in this job,' she says, persisting, trying to make him understand. 'That's where life is. It doesn't just happen when you come in with your reports and forecasts and projections. It's there!' She jabs her finger. 'It's in the pub, it's in the school playground, it's in the hotel. And I get there first. I see it when it's raw and I've been doing it for a long time. And I know that Hazel Archer is guilty. I know that she is dangerous. I've looked her in the eye. I've seen where she lives. The woman isn't right. I know it.' She stops talking, breathing heavily, her lips pressed tightly together as if to stop more tumbling out.

Gordon sighs again and angles his chair to look out of the window. His voice turns persuasive, as if honey coats his tongue. 'Look, I can see you're very passionate, Hillier. And that's something I'm grateful for. Your work, when you arrive at a scene, is crucial to the rest of us who come along

315

afterwards. We rely on you, we really do.' He spins back to face her, his eyes kind. 'You're a good copper. I know you are. But . . .'

'But?' she says bitterly.

'But you have no evidence. What's the CPS going to do with what you've told me today? They'd have nothing to show in court apart from your instinct.'

'I *know* it, sir.'

He shakes his head, thinking. 'She hasn't said anything more? The little girl.'

'Because Jane Greenstreet *told* her not to say anything. Once Georgie was found, Jane got scared. She thought Declan would lose his job and then they wouldn't be able to meet their mortgage payments. They'd been drinking. Fighting. She thought Children's Services would get involved. I've said this . . .'

Hillier gets up and stands with her hands behind her back, her feet apart. She brings one alongside the other one in a manoeuvre reminiscent of a salute. 'Never mind, Sarge. I see I'm wasting my time here.'

She turns to leave and has her hand on the door when Gordon says, 'I'm sorry, Hillier. I really am.'

She looks back at him, sitting behind his desk in shirt-sleeves. Outside rain continues to lash against the windows and she will be back in it soon.

'I get there first,' she says quietly as she shuts the door behind her.

CHAPTER SIXTY-EIGHT

They are opposite each other again, in the small room with the low ceiling and wrap-around window. This time, there is no weather to interrupt them. The prison seems doused in silence, a loud drone of nothing that pushes in on them through the walls and up through the floors. Laurel takes in the sight of her sister on the other side of the table and, whatever she said previously to Fritz, has to force herself to quell the anxiety she feels scratching at the back of her throat.

It seems to her deliberately provocative that Hazel is so composed. She wears a blue-and-white striped top, and jeans Laurel can tell are expensive from the way they make her sister walk, as if she is proud of them, is showing them off. Her face is bare of make-up and her dark hair is neat as always, brushed to one side, her brown eyes fixed on Laurel.

'Thank you for seeing me,' she says, and at the sound of her voice, Laurel feels rage surge up like bile and has to cough, her hand over her mouth, reaching for the glass of stale water in front of her that she has never once drunk from, in all the visits she's had from Toby over the years.

She can't speak. She can't say anything without betraying her anger, or collapsing in grief. So, as usual, she stays silent, watching her sister and waiting.

Hazel puts her head on one side. 'You're very angry, aren't you?' she says. 'Oh, Laurel. I can see. I can see how angry you are. You're my sister, after all.'

Laurel feels her hands shake and she stills them by joining them together in her lap. She focuses on Hazel's neck, on the little silver cross that sits in her clavicle, on the paleness of her skin, the thin veins threading like waterways beneath.

She breathes. She waits.

'It was you, wasn't it?' Hazel says. 'You who sent me the anonymous emails, the dead flowers, the cards. Back before anything happened in Devon. You sorted it from in here, didn't you? Got one of your cronies to send it via addresses I wouldn't recognise. To frighten me. Punish me.'

Laurel is motionless, her chin dipped low.

'You even sent that writer, Max, one of our tapes, didn't you? He mentioned he'd heard it, right before he died, poor bloke. One of those tapes we made together, playing the game.' Hazel jerks her head forward. 'I always wondered why the police never used them in your trial. Never took them away with all the rest of your stuff.' She shrugs. 'Guess they weren't too bothered about an old bunch of cassettes with Spice Girls labels. You must have brought them with you when you went to Oakingham. Clever Laurel. Very clever. All the while, sitting in here, plotting your revenge. Working out ways to get your own back.'

Hazel raises one eyebrow at her sister.

'And do you know how I know? That that's what you did, that you're the one who sent all those vile things to me? Kept the tapes deliberately? Hmm? I know, because I would feel exactly the same way if I were you. I would want to hurt you very badly. It's funny, isn't it, how Mummy played us off against each other? With the game.'

Laurel's eyes flick briefly to Hazel's before resting back again on the silver cross.

'She did, didn't she? Scissors, paper, stone. Whoever loses has to do the job. I always lost, didn't I? It was always me who had to do it. Whatever she wanted. You were older – you knew. You just had an *instinct* for it. You knew what I would choose and you would always, always win.' Hazel gives a short laugh. 'But I grew up. Maybe that's why I see it clearly now. Because my instincts got better as I got older. Didn't they?'

Out of the corner of her eye, Laurel can see Hazel put her hand on her chest as if she is in pain. She wants to slap it away. Dig her fingernails into that skin like Hazel had told her Jane Greenstreet had done. Laurel has seen the faint scars from that attack on Hazel's cheeks. She wants to open them up again for her sister.

She wants to watch her bleed.

'But now it's over,' Hazel says softly, her fingertips lightly resting on the table in front of her. In her eyeline, Laurel catches sight of a diamond ring on her sister's left hand and stiffens involuntarily.

'Oh, did you notice?' Hazel asks. 'Jonny proposed.' She holds her hand up to the fluorescent light. 'It's nice, isn't it?' she says casually, moving her gaze to Laurel's hand where tattoos flower up two of her fingers like emerald snakes. 'Really pretty.'

She stops talking. Laurel has to swallow down the scream she feels clawing its way up inside of her. The desire to turn and run into the concrete wall, pound her head against the bricks until her skull is smashed to smithereens, is so strong, she can hardly focus. A tiny noise escapes from her, the smallest of moans, a gasp.

Hazel's head twitches at it, like a cat watching a mouse emerge from under a skirting board. A smile flares from her.

Laurel brings her mind back to her breathing. She thinks of Fritz sitting upstairs in her room. Of the gym where she will go after this, to pound the treadmill, lift weights, and sweat out all the poison that is back inside her once again. A vision of Toby's face swims into her head. Soon the cancer will claim him and he will have left her like everyone else in her life has always done. A painful sob bucks in her chest and she swallows roughly, packing it down.

Oh, Toby, she thinks. She should never have agreed to this visit. To any of them. But she had to know whether her sister had changed. Whether she had been redeemed in any way because of her life, her beautiful, lucky, wonderful life. The life that had been taken away from Laurel, that she had never, ever had. Not one day of it.

She can see though that Rosie is exactly the same as she was. That she is identical in spirit and breath to the little girl who marched alongside her sister, who always did their mother's bidding. Little Rose-Red. Always chasing after her sister. Always wanting more.

She has been silent all this time. But now Laurel raises her head – now she must speak.

'What you said. In court,' she says. 'Do you really remember what happened, Rosie?'

Hazel says nothing at first, her mouth pinched tight. But then she can't resist. 'I've always wondered why it was that you never talked about it. Why you never defended yourself ... Why was that?' Her voice is like cream. 'Why have you never told the truth? About what happened to Kirstie.'

'You were immune from prosecution,' Laurel says. 'What was the point?'

Hazel frowns. 'Maybe. But what about you? What about getting yourself off?'

Laurel looks up at the ceiling and Toby's face pops into her mind. 'You know the reason,' she says.

'No. I. Don't.' Hazel's voice is suddenly shrill.

'You don't get it, do you? You never have.'

'What?' Hazel stiffens and her voice is sharp as a needle. 'What is it I don't get?'

'What about Mummy?' Laurel says. 'Did you ever think about Mummy?'

A brief smile crosses Hazel's face and she moves her tongue around inside her cheek.

'I looked after you,' Laurel continues. 'Both of you. And when this thing happened, I knew. I knew what I had to do. What I had to sacrifice. For her. For Mummy.'

'You never looked after me!' Hazel snaps. 'Don't make me laugh! Making me lose the game all those times?'

'I *did*,' Laurel insists, leaning forward. 'I did everything Mummy wanted. All the jobs she gave us. All the things she made us do. Don't you remember? You *must*, Rosie. She would sit in the house in a daze, in a kind of coma. And we would tiptoe around, not wanting to make any noise. And when she got angry, I would send you away, outside, anywhere. I was the one who got the beatings, I was the one she used to lock in our room . . .' She breaks off, breathing hard. 'But then . . .'

321

'What?' Hazel asks. 'Then, what?'

Laurel rubs at her eyes angrily and her hand is wet when she pulls it away. 'I saw you change, Rosie. I saw you watching her, studying her. It was like . . . you were . . .'

Hazel's lips are white. She says nothing.

'Learning how to . . . *copy* her or something.' Laurel breathes in sharply. 'I didn't know what it was. But suddenly you were different. Harder somehow. Like with the cat . . .'

'That was the *game*,' Hazel cuts in, her voice low and harsh.

'Yes.' Laurel nods. 'But Mummy didn't tell us to do it that time. That was your idea. Remember?'

Hazel's chest moves up and down rapidly as she rubs the diamond on her finger. Her eyes roll upwards as if she is seeing something above her, her head cocked to one side as if she is listening for instructions, some kind of sign.

'Rosie – remember?'

Hazel lowers her eyes to meet Laurel's. The joint rhythm of their breathing pulses through the room.

'You killed that baby,' Laurel says carefully. 'You did it. You took it too far. You hit her and she went down on the ground. Her head was bleeding and she stopped crying. I was frightened by the quiet and the blood and I ran and waited for you by our garden gate. A bit later, you came back with bloodstains on your fingers and skin underneath your nails.

'That is what happened, Rosie. That is exactly what happened. Just like Toby told me you said in court last week. Except you switched around who did what. And fate, or the law, or whatever fucked-up system we live by, meant you got away with it. And I took it. I said nothing. I said nothing because I loved Mummy. I knew she couldn't lose you. Not her Rose-Red.' Her laugh is like ice and she doesn't bother hiding the tears any more. 'And the most fucked-up thing is that I loved you too. I loved our world, our games and the things we would imagine, conjure up from nothing. It was so special. All of it. Rosie? Look at me,' Laurel whispers. 'It was the best time of my life.'

Hazel takes in her sister, battered and tear-streaked. She says nothing.

'I've sat here for years thinking about you. Waiting for you to contact me. For us to talk about it. For you to say you're sorry. But nothing happened. Nobody came. All of you left me here to rot. I thought, well, whatever you did, you couldn't have meant it. It was a mistake. Mummy was a mess and she fucked us up. But we loved her, didn't we? She played us off against each other. I see that now. But, when they took me away, I saw the look on her face at the police station. I saw how her heart was breaking. I couldn't take you away from her too. She would have died. And I didn't want her to die. Because I did love her. And I know she loved me too. I *know* she did. I have that at least.'

Laurel rubs at her nose and scrapes at her wet cheeks as if she wants to bleach them clean. 'But then you all left me and went away. She had to leave me, didn't she? Because she knew I understood what you were. Both of you. So I had to be dropped. Abandoned. God knows what Daddy knows or believes. Sometimes, I think I hate him more than anyone else in the world . . .' Laurel's voice trails off, her face cold. 'You knew exactly what you were doing. And you still do.' Hazel's blank stare is remorseless. 'But you were my sister. And you still are.'

'Then why,' Hazel says bitterly, 'did you just up and leave me last time I visited? You walked out. Do you know how much that hurt me?'

Laurel gives a contorted smile. 'Ah, yes, dear sister. You hate to be left alone, don't you? You need to be begged. That was a mistake on my part, I realise now. But I got my punishment, didn't I, later on in court?'

'You *walked out* on me. Just left me sitting here by myself like some kind of *pariah*.' Hazel's eyes blaze and she closes them briefly, breathing in through her nose. 'Anyway,' she says, folding her hands in her lap, eyes flicking up towards the corner where a camera stealthily patrols the room, 'everything you've said, everything you *are* saying, is all lies. And everyone knows it. That's why you're still in this place. Not because you're protecting me. But because this is rightful punishment for what you did.'

Hazel slowly gets to her feet.

'I have *nothing*, Rosie,' Laurel pleads. 'Nothing. All of you left me here. My *family*. You let me go and you never even tried to get me out. Almost twenty years, Rosie. Inside these walls with *no one*. I kept loyal to you.' She passes a hand across her face. 'Please, God, now. Give me my truth if nothing else. Here in this room between us. I won't tell anyone, I swear. But admit it to me!' She bangs her chest. 'Give me that. Please, God, *please*.' Her fists are clenched, her face contorted with despair.

Hazel glances at her watch. 'It's probably time for me to go,' she says. 'I'll bet you have something on now anyway. Toby says you're doing a GCSE. That's really good, Laurel. Maybe you've got a class now? You certainly look like you work out. Do you go to the gym in here?'

Laurel stares at her. She bites at the inside of her mouth, tasting blood, causing the pain to stop more tears from falling. She swallows a hard, rough swallow and stares unaccountably at Hazel's ear where a little diamond earring sits in the lobe next to the freckle Laurel remembers stroking one night to get her sister to sleep in a storm.

She opens her mouth to speak but nothing comes out and, after a moment, Hazel turns and leaves the room.

CHAPTER SIXTY-NINE

Hazel is lying on the brass king-sized bed she shares with Jonny in his flat.

Their flat now.

She can hear him frying onions down the hall in the kitchen. The clatter of saucepans and the smell of roast meat, caramelised vegetables and garlic, floats around the flat. Now it is a comforting aroma. She lies on the bed and drinks in the warmth of their space, the feeling of her partner just feet away from her, the anticipation of a meal together, a glass of wine, everything ahead of them. Their future together.

'It's ready,' Jonny calls as he passes the doorway carrying a large serving dish. 'Are you coming through?'

Hazel gets off the bed and follows him to the dining table, which has been laid with silver cutlery, table mats, and a single white candle. Hazel turns on some music before she sits down, glancing out of the windows at the wet streets below, the shimmer of car bonnets, the cold night mixing with the convivial light of the flat in the window's reflection.

'Thank you, my love,' she says as she sits down.

Jonny pours her a glass of white wine and they touch glasses, smiling at each other, content.

'Here's to us,' he says. 'What a time it's been.'

'To us.'

'Did you see the flowers that Romilly sent?' Jonny drinks his wine, looking over at the sideboard where a huge vase of pink roses bloom in the corner. 'To congratulate you for that TV show and all the press you've done this week.'

'She's sweet.'

'By the way, I forgot to mention, sorry,' Jonny says as he picks up his knife and fork. 'Evie's coming to stay at the weekend. Now you're all moved in, I called her. Said I'd like her to spend some time with us. Get to know you better. She put up the usual fuss, blaming her mother . . . but then finally she agreed.' He points his fork at Hazel. 'I think she's impressed with all this media you're doing. Seems all the kids at school are fawning over her about it. Said if you could get on *The One Show*, she'd *love you forever*. Her words.' He smiles at her as he cuts a piece of chicken. 'So thank you for that.'

'I'm so pleased, Jonny. She's really a lovely girl.'

They eat in silence for a moment.

'So much has happened in the last few days. I feel like I haven't seen you for ages.' Jonny clears his throat. 'I was just thinking the other day . . . Did you ever hear anything again from the police down in Devon? That woman officer?'

'Why are you asking that now?' Hazel asks neutrally.

'No reason,' he replies lightly. 'I just wondered, with all the publicity you've had, whether she'd got in touch about anything. Asked any more questions about that girl going missing.'

Hazel picks up her fork and spears a carrot. 'She did come to see me actually. I didn't mention it because it was so stupid. It was the day before we signed the contract. The

327

day Max died from the heart attack.' She bites into the carrot and chews as she speaks. 'She was asking questions about the timings at the hotel when we were having tea that day. You know, after we came back from the beach?'

'Yep,' Jonny says, after swallowing his wine. 'We came back and had tea together in the lounge. And then we went to get changed for dinner.'

'Right. She was going on about it, like it mattered. So I just told her that we were together the whole time.'

'Which we were.'

'Yes. Well, apart from when you went to take that call, remember?' Hazel says, glancing up at him. 'You were gone for a while. That business call you took. You went outside because when you came back in, you didn't have your jacket and your shirt was soaked with the snow.'

'Did I?' he says. 'Was it?' He reaches across the table for the salt. 'I can't say I remember.'

'Yes,' Hazel says. 'I remember.' She smiles at him and sips again from her glass. 'We never did find your jacket, did we?'

Jonny's lips turn down and he jerks his head imperceptibly.

'I didn't say anything, though,' Hazel continues as she bites into a piece of chicken breast. 'What's the point? The girl just wandered off, right?'

'Right,' Jonny says, his eyes on his glass.

'Just one thing, though, darling,' Hazel says softly.

He says nothing, but stares at his glass.

'If it happens again, make sure you see it through.'

He whips his head up, looks at her.

'You were lucky this time, my love,' Hazel says. 'You won't be again.'

She leans over and turns up the music, the strains of 'Dido's Lament' filling the room.

'So everything's OK now, isn't it?' she says, stroking his arm. 'We're the same, you and me. I knew it from the moment we met. You, me and Evie. The three of us. All together. And also . . .'

Jonny lifts his eyes.

'. . . I found out today,' Hazel says, 'we're going to have a baby.' Her eyes are shining.

Jonny makes a sound like a cry and a laugh rolled into one. He finally meets her gaze. 'A baby?' he asks, his voice trembling. 'We're going to have a baby?'

Hazel nods, smiling at him. 'Yes, darling. A baby all of our own.' She reaches over and strokes the back of his hand. 'So there's no need to worry about anything. Is there, my love?'

'No,' he replies, wiping a tear from his cheek. 'There's no need to worry at all.'

Hazel exhales as the music swells, moving her hand over her stomach, feeling the burgeoning life within it.

Her own child, her own daughter.

Her own little precious girl.

ACKNOWLEDGEMENTS

The term 'Acknowledgements' seems to signify a nod of the head whereas, in this case, what I'd like to do is give every person a big thank you hug.

The writing of *The Flower Girls* has been a marathon rather than a sprint, and the main person passing me the water and jelly babies has been my amazing agent, Ariella Feiner. At the last few miles, when I'd lost all hope that the book would ever make it, she convinced me to have faith that the time was right and that the perfect publisher was out there.

Which is just what Raven Books have been. The enthusiasm, *joie de vivre*, and general awesomeness of everyone I've dealt with there has meant the editing process has been less a grind than actually (amazingly) fun. Thank you so much to Alison Hennessey for believing in the book, and me, and for welcoming me so fully into the Raven family. Also thanks to Marigold Atkey for being so superbly efficient and delightful with it. And to Ros Ellis, Rachel Wilkie, Lilidh Kendrick, Lisa Finch, Sarah Knight and Fabia Ma for being the comprehensive dream team. Thanks also to Molly Jamieson and Georgie Le Grice at United Agents and Eleanor Jackson at Dunow, Carlson and Lerner for their suggestions and help with everything over the last year.

Special thanks to Renee Jarvis who has been a writing stalwart and true champion of the book since its first imaginings. Her ideas and notes and support have kept me going and helped me cross more than one gaping plot ravine.

Thanks to the people who gave me brilliant advice on prisons and police procedure. Not least, Elizabeth Watts, Lisa Kinchin and Karen Veitch.

To my writing friends from The Singapore Writers' Group and from around the world who are always full of ideas, suggestions and general positivity. Thanks to Lisa Beazley, Jo Furniss, Grace Coleman, Elin Daniels, Heidi Perks, Dawn Goodwin, Moyette Gibbons, Alex Clare, Julietta Henderson and Catherine Bennetto. And to Alex, George, Antonia, Susie and Cate for all the coffees, chats and the odd glass of wine.

To Laura Bell for the amazing photographs.

To Fran Rittman and Lynda Woolf for keeping me sane.

To Mum and Dad for always listening and for the reading of hundreds of drafts... We may be far away, but it never feels like it really. I love you both very much.

Finally, to Tom, Connie and India for making me laugh, suggesting awesome book titles, for spurring me on and for being the best family I could possibly have.

A NOTE ON THE AUTHOR

ALICE CLARK-PLATTS is a former human rights lawyer who worked at the UN International Criminal Tribunal in connection with the Rwandan genocide and on cases involving Winnie Mandela and Snoop Dogg. She is the author of the police procedurals *Bitter Fruits* and *The Taken*. The latter was shortlisted for the Best Police Procedural in the Dead Good Reader Awards 2017. Her work was included in *Deadlier:100 of the Best Crime Stories Written by Women*, selected by Sophie Hannah.

A NOTE ON THE TYPE

The text of this book is set in Linotype Sabon, a typeface named after the type founder, Jacques Sabon. It was designed by Jan Tschichold and jointly developed by Linotype, Monotype and Stempel in response to a need for a typeface to be available in identical form for mechanical hot metal composition and hand composition using foundry type.

Tschichold based his design for Sabon roman on a font engraved by Garamond, and Sabon italic on a font by Granjon. It was first used in 1966 and has proved an enduring modern classic.